LIMESTONE MAN

for Decima and Ffion

LIMESTONE MAN

by
Robert Minhinnick

SEREN

Seren is the book imprint of
Poetry Wales Press Ltd
57 Nolton Street, Bridgend, Wales, CF31 3AE
www.serenbooks.com
Facebook: facebook.com/SerenBooks
Twitter: @SerenBooks

ISBNs:
978-1-78172-249-7 paperback
978-1-78172-250-3 kindle
978-1-78172-251-0 ebook

Typesetting by Elaine Sharples
Printed by Bell and Bain, Glasgow

The publisher works with the financial assistance of
The Welsh Books Council

1

I

I'm trying to remember. The last time I saw Lulu.

I know her back was showing its white scar. That part of her back above her three black moles. Orion's belt she called those moles. I used to wet my finger and trace her three black stars.

And then the scar. I always thought that scar resembled the shape of The Caib.

We used to joke about that. At least I thought it was funny. But yes, I did say something. Something like *The Caib, remember. The Caib! You always ask where I come from. That's where!*

And maybe I slapped her. Like anyone would. No harm in that. A slap.

Back of beyond, she had said.

Not really, I said.

But then she repeated it. Like she always did. Which was irritating. Yes, Lulu could have that effect.

Backofbeyonbackofbeyonfbackofbe...

I must have been tired. Yes, tired. So I said something. And regretted it instantly.

Better than... I said.

She turned then.

Better than what? she asked.

Better than the Outback of beyond.

1

Yes, I remember that scar. Above the cleft of her arse. A seam of quartz in red sandstone, that scar. Look, it's natural to slap. Someone there.

And we were tired. Not ourselves. The drought was over and we'd been celebrating. But we weren't ourselves.

I remember the gold dust on her shoulders. On her vest. In her hair. Whenever someone went in the dunny, they came out golden. From the paint dust. *We know where you've been!* we used to say.

Next, I heard the screen slamming. And then her wail.

Oh, for goodness sake… I'd said. I think I said.

Can't you..?

Take a joke?

Can't you…

II

I returned to old haunts. For the first time since my … *incident*, I drove to Adelaide. Walked into The Sebel and booked a room. Winter rates.

No, I'd never stayed there before. But I felt I owed it to myself. First of all I listed the places I needed to try. It's always lists with me, isn't it? Names of records I should be playing. Records to avoid.

2

PARRY'S DIARY
MONDAY

I felt excited. Any minute now, I thought. Any minute now I'll see that curly hair. That honey-coloured skin. Any minute now. How could she not be here?

I looked around the lounge, the marble pillars. Who'd left that drink at a corner table? It must have been Lulu. I even checked the Ladies.

But I avoided school and the chances of meeting staff. Didn't want to see Libby or anyone else in the department. And I was determined to be gone by Friday afternoon. That was when a group of teachers went out drinking.

Old haunts, past times. I ordered malbec but it was bravado. The wine tasted sour. I had the bottle decanted and left in my room to breathe.

Yes, it was early. The barman gave me a knowing smile. Seen it all, hadn't he? By 11am on a Monday I was already in the market at our favourite booth, a pot of lotus tea in front of me.

We'd drunk that sometimes on our city expeditions. The Chinese girl who worked there would put a lotus flower in a saucer of water on the table. But not this time. One cup only this time. And no flower.

I sat down and convinced myself again that Lulu had to be there. Nearby. The market was busy enough, full of the smells of cinnamon, cardamom, coffee. Everybody seemed to be doing something vital. Even if it was only sitting and waiting. There was a pattern to life. Everyone had a place and so did Lulu. Her place was in the seat opposite me. Her cup should have been the cup next to mine.

Lulu and I had this special way of saying goodbye. I'd say *So Long, Arcturus* and she'd say *Farewell, Arcturus.* Or something like that. After the star, naturally. Okay, sounds corny. But there you are.

Arcturus is a red star, moving away from us. In a couple of million years, Lulu had said, we won't be able to see Arcturus. The sky will be different. Imagine it, she said. Our sky without Arcturus.

How do you know that? I always asked her.

Because I read it, Mr Teacher, she always said.

And I know where you read it, I always said.

In marvellous books! we said together.

So, so long, Arcturus.

I sat in the market. Everything seemed right with the world. There they were, the mums with pushchairs, the kids in their school uniforms, mitching off. The lonely, the lovesick, the lost. Particularly the lost, you learn how to spot them.

Yes, that barman in The Sebel gave me a smile. But he was sharing that smile, if you know what I mean. It said, we're in this together. I know it and you know it. *Sport.*

Then a little Chinese girl came past, pushing a portable griddle of roasted ducks. Then a florist with a blue spike in a pot. Hyacinth, probably. Then two Chinese blokes arguing. And all walking past my table in that corner of the market. The Adelaide street, brimful, bountiful. This world as it came to me.

An hour later I was across the road in another café Lulu and I sometimes visited. This was a smaller place, almost under the Lion Gate at the market entrance.

It was lunchtime and I tried their wonton soup. I shared a table with an excitable couple, just married I think. But I was always looking round. Still searching for Lulu.

Two o clock, three. I'm still looking. The couple long gone. Only me in the café at 3.30, and there I am with green tea and more green tea. And a cake. I'd never tried Chinese cakes before but this was acceptable. No, maybe a little dry, even though it was green cake, soaked in green tea.

I remembered The Caib when Jack and Dora were together in the last year. Breakfast was what they called *sop*. Bread soaked in black tea. They would sit in the kitchen with bowls of sop and look out at the garden. Like two refugees, I often thought. Sucking up that horrible food, stale currant bun, cold tea. But they loved it.

At that time in the garden there were usually as many sunflowers as Dora could coax into life. I used to think about those sunflowers. How like people they were. In their slow decline. Yellow and splendid, those sunflower faces. And crawling with bees. But soon bowed, even the sturdiest.

Mum would stake them with bits of bamboo, tied with rags. And every sunflower different. Yes, like people.

Then a break. Then more tea. Then a different cake. Then a walk down Gouger Street, then another tour of the market, both directions. Then five minutes back in the first café.

Five o'clock, I was in the Botanic Gardens and the tropical house. Surely, I thought. Surely. Who was that girl? Whose was that voice?

But there were too many people. Lots of university students, lots of lovers, the lonely, the lost. Everyone mooching about. Moochers, yeah, moochers. That's what we do, isn't it? That's all we are. Well *moochers gracias* to us lost souls.

Long walk past The Sebel. Six o'clock, seven, and a decent crowd in the marble bar. It's close to the theatre and there was a performance due. I went up to my room and tried the malbec. Better, I thought. At least drinkable. So I took the bottle downstairs and finished it off. A different barman.

I checked the grand staircase, then took the walk back to Gouger Street. In the market everyone was packing up. Back out to the Lion Gate café. But they were getting ready for the next day. Tomorrow.

Christ, I thought. Christ. What happened to today?

It was dark. I looked in the smart Indian restaurant. Don't know why. Then the cheap Lebanese. Tried every bar with their attached gambling parlours. Tried the kebab queues, the places where Lulu had loved the wedges served with garlic mayo. But everything now was not right with the world.

Went back to The Sebel and sat where we'd always sat. And this time I tried the wedges myself, under a marble pillar at a tiny marble table. That marble cold as the quartz on The Caib.

Then maybe another red wine. Yeah, a crude and bloody Aussie shiraz. After that I sat in my room looking out at the city lights.

Always exciting, aren't they, cities at night? On The Caib you hear the sea like a record crackling over its final grooves. But sometimes I miss the neon, those orange and violet shadows of Adelaide. And I stayed at my table thinking I should be out there. Out there…

TUESDAY

From six, I tried the bus and tram stops. Up and down Rundle and Hindley Streets. Why not five? The buses start at 5am. Cleaners gong to work, the people who make your coffee. All the nameless people? They start at five. They're out there in the dark. At 5am.

Then the immigrants, the drifters? They're out there at five. Before five. But I began at six.

And yes, I had a photo and asked around. Have you seen this girl? Please, have you seen this girl?

Went over to the YMCA. That's a possible place, I thought. A likely place. Showed the photo at the desk and they said, yes, try the lounge. Special permission.

So I waited there from 9am. Watched those kids laboriously cooking breakfast. Getting ready. And I heard about all those places they'd been, remote outback, Papua, New Britain…

I thought surely someone was sleeping late, recovering from a sesh… Christ, I thought, Christ…

Not everyone was young. There were a few older couples. But everybody was interested and a few thought they'd seen her. One bloke was certain.

But then he started to doubt himself. He came back to tell me. No, he wasn't sure after all. Could he see the photo again? Yes, no, he wasn't sure. Any more. Could have been. Might have been. But possibly not. Maybe he was thinking of someone else… So hard to be… How old was the…?

Gradually everyone drifted away. Even those with books who seemed set for the day. By twelve I was on my own. Someone came to turn the telly off.

Then I walked over to the state gallery on North Terrace. I'd always loved that gallery. The paintings have room to breathe, and I'd taken Lulu there three, four times. Again, it was wonderful.

Maybe it was there I had the idea for my big canvas, *Mother of Pearl*. You know, 'Morning on The Caib'. That's my great idea. Told you. Told everyone about it. When I paint. When I paint my masterpiece.

Yes, all that space. Means the colours can breathe. Colours need to breathe, you see. Got to make room for colours. But there was hardly anyone in. Hardly anyone...

We'd seen a film there. But there had been better crowds for The Cockatoos I thought. Yeah, The Black Cockatoos. Again, I showed the photograph. Excuse me, have you seen, excuse me, have you... Please, could you look again, could you...

Over to the Mall and all those shops that Lulu pretended not to like. But of course, why not? Anyone her age. Anyone...

I'd have waited while she tried them on. New clothes, you see. That's what she needed. Better than those... Yeah, show herself off. And changing rooms in the corner, a seat while you wait. Be the first to see her. I could have been... I could have been...

Look. Someone's left that coat on the floor. No, it's not, it's not... But who chooses the music in those places? Who...

See, you have to think about your in-shop playlist. Says a lot. About you. About who you are. About who you think you are.

No, Miss. I'm just waiting. I'm just waiting for... Someone... She's coming back. Any...

Minute now. Slice of pizza from a stall outside. Black olives saltier than green. Mushrooms sliced. Not enough mozz, not enough I'd say. Masses of mozz, that's what Lulu liked. Real mozzquito was Lulu, those stones rolling, ungathering... The stones that filled my mouth...

Passed the Lebanese. Down the stairs. A brick cellar with nobody in. Make a great little jazz club, the Lebanese. Ornette,

I thought. *Miles Ahead.*

Ordered a bottle of their own. Oily, black. The coming place, it said. Restaurant review photocopied and pinned with a stiletto to a beam. Yeah, a knife. Still quivering. As I live and...

Lebanon's time is here, it said and why not? it asked. There are so many Aussies now with Lebanese blood. And we all have a time, don't we?

I tasted the wine. Oh, I thought. Oh...

The Lebanese breads arrived, the hummus. Garlic, I thought. The white garlic bulbs, the purple skins of the garlic cloves.

I planted garlic once. Watched the shoots curl in winter. Out of the old fruits those little fingers.

Here's the *mezze,* I said to myself. In tiny bowls, as if they held paints.

And then, *arak.* The clean *arak* to wash away the dark, the feculent...

Ah *arak.* Its white fire. In the bottle with the milled glass stopper.

You eat alone? the man asked.

No, I said. Any minute now. Any...

But he commanded:

You.

Eat.

Alone.

WEDNESDAY

5am, the tram stops, the buses. Women hunched, men vacant. Who's slept? I wondered. Who's dreamed.

A group of native people were sitting in a corner of that park by the market. Tinnies not even crushed.

One of the men was lugging a fifteen-litre box of Henley's

Estate red. I showed them all the photograph. And, fair play, a few might have looked.

Yeah, one said. I know her. I know her.

How d'you know her? I asked.

I know her, he said again.

From where? I asked.

One of the women, seamed and haggard but maybe only twenty, in a ruined overcoat with gold braid on the shoulders, spat at my feet. Her gums were bleeding.

Lulu, I said. She's called Lulu.

Yeah, Lulu, the man said.

Don't you know? the woman hissed, bloody drool on her chin. Don't you know? We're all of us called Lulu. Look, I'm Lulu. She's Lulu. He's Lulu. Hey, mister, say hello to Lulu.

That earned her a laugh. Maybe I laughed too.

They'd made their camp under acacia bushes. Spread out on sheets of Panasonic cardboard. There was a loaf, a milk carton and a roll of toilet paper one of their kids had been playing with. All unrolled, that pink paper. Yeah, pink. All unrolled.

You know Kath? I asked. Kath?

Hey mister, the woman said. What happened to Lulu?

That broke them up. I know I laughed too.

Listen, mister, the woman said. Don't you know? Did no one ever tell you? We're all of us Kath. We're all of us Lulu.

Kath's older than Lulu, I said. But in my mind I was walking away.

Please, I said. Look at the picture again.

Yeah, said the woman, looking once more. You know who that is? You know who that is?

That's... the man said.

That's Lulu, the woman spat.

No, the man laughed. No, that's...

Kath.

Then everyone was saying it. That's Lulu, that's Lulu. That's Kath.

Have you seen her this week? I asked. Can you think? Please? This week.

Hey, tell me what day it is, boss, said the man. And I'll tell you if I've seen her.

Half an hour later I was in the university library on North Terrace. My card dated from teaching days and I remembered clearly where I had to go.

The reading room was full of yellow light. I wondered, as I had been first in line, how the other readers had entered. There were already three men standing behind the desks. Men my age, I suppose. But older looking, surely. Older than me. Everyone else was stereotypically a student.

Students seemed younger than I recalled. I thought of hairy, bearded men. With something to say. These kids seemed pallid, even bloodless.

I found the latest *Astronomy Today* where I knew it belonged. Magazines weren't date-stamped but this edition, brand new, didn't look as if it had been consulted, even opened. I raised it to my nose. New glue of a fresh edition.

On the cover was a galaxy inside the darkness of space. So many lights. Each light a star or another galaxy. So many lights…

I think of the quartz in the caves at The Caib. That quartz with the sun on it. Like stars, I've thought at times recently. That orange-red of Arcturus, the blue and orange of Albireo. As if the quartz had fallen to earth. To shine a moment in cave gloom. Stars trapped in stone. Fossils of starlight.

So here I am, I said to myself. What do I do now? I was trying Facebook. I was trying Bebo. But I thought what I've always thought in the library. That I have lived my life without studying physics. Without understanding mathematics. That I've spent too long with pictures. Too long with poems and plays. With other men's art.

In school, in fact, I'd hated physics. If only…

But it was the same with the guitar, the piano. The failure to persevere. Nicky Hopkins played on thirteen albums by the Stones. He was waiting for the call and Keith always called. Nicky was ready. But I…

My right hand still felt cold. Ice at the fingertips. As if I had cupped water from a rock pool. Yes, the hand was still traumatised.

When I looked round again, there was Sophia, crossing the reading room. Sophia, who helped sometimes in *Hey Bulldog*.

Well… I said. Well…

Fancy meeting you, she continued. Here.

Here, I said. Yes, here.

Oh, she said. You've stopped shaving. Maybe…

And I stood. Looking at Sophia's hair. She must have done something to her hair. There was a blonde kink in her hair. Now. Surely that kink was new. The colour was different.

Sophia seemed older, more confident somehow. At least more adult. But people change. Only the dead stay the same.

How's the writing? I asked.

Great, she said. Sometimes it seems like it's not me doing it. The writing, I mean. It feels that I'm being written. Does that make sense?

Yeah, I said. I suppose that's how everyone feels. Eventually. Listen…

Yes, she said. I expect…

Listen. Have you seen Lu?

Sophia looked at me then. I felt I was being appraised.

No, she said finally. Not since before the rains. But I've been away. Lucky you caught me. Why?

No reason, I said. Just thought Lu might be up here. She loved this library.

She's been getting tired of Goolwa, nodded Sophia.

You think?

Oh yes. Everybody gets tired of that place. Like, who wouldn't?

Yeah. I know what you mean.

Yes, she said.

But no reason, I said. I was just… I was just…

Wondering? she asked.

I looked round the main refectory while I was waiting for our coffees. We'd both decided on chocolate bars. I also had a plate of biscuits.

So, the lyrics are…

The songs, she corrected. The songs are going pretty well. I feel playing those sets in the shop brought me on. You know. Confidence wise…

And I played the records you mentioned. Thought about song structure, like you said. Because it's structure that counts. Isn't it?

Oh yes. Always. Can't be left to chance. Can it?

No, she said. You've got to interpose.

Yeah, show your intelligence.

Always. That's right. Always show your intelligence.

A girl with long blonde hair pushed past. She wasn't Lulu. Then a plump, moon-faced Korean. He wasn't Lulu.

Look, breathed Sophia. I have a friend up here. Maybe we could go to her room.

I'd been looking around, I think. There seemed to be hundreds of people who weren't Lulu. In a hubbub of voices. There was a coat draped over a chair. A bag encrusted with badges. Maybe students still wore badges.

And yes, I recalled the badges we had worn. Badges about the miners' strike. Badges to save the rainforests.

But maybe I hadn't been listening.

Pardon? I said.

Room 48. Second floor, Flinders. We could go there.

Three chocolate biscuits, I thought. And a pink wafer. No one ever liked the pink wafer. No, no one liked the pink wafer. Did they? Did anyone like the pink wafer? But the chocolate was melting.

We could go there? I repeated.

If you want. If you'd like.

If I'd like? Room…

Forty-eight. Second floor on Flinders. I could try out my new song. That's where my guitar is. Been working for ages on it. You heard a version that time in the shop. I'd called it 'Southern Rain'. Well, excuse me, but it's really changed since then… It's unrecognisable. Different key. And the tempo's much slower. The words mean so much more now. I just feel more experienced. A different person.

Yeah. You look…

Older, you said. I take that as a compliment.

Different key?

C. That's C major. But I don't want it to be too mournful. It's got to… *move*. You know?

Move?

All music moves. Doesn't it?

But, to room 48?

Yes. We could go. There.

Great, I said. I'd like that. I'd love that. Flinders?

Forty-eight. Second floor. Up the stairs. Look, I'll see you there.

Course, I said. I'm coming. Now. But what did you say that

song is…

Is called now? 'Southern Rain'. Oh yeah, it's still 'Southern Rain'. I won't change that for anything.

And was it called 'Southern Rain' when I heard it first? I asked.

Yes. It's always been 'Southern Rain'. Always will be 'Southern Rain'.

And she hummed it. Hummed a song called 'Southern Rain'.

I tried to remember where I'd heard the song before. I was sure I'd heard it. But there are so many songs these days. Thousands of downloads, millions if you thought. Who needs? I wondered, who needs…?

The Spotify songs. All the box sets. Like cutlery, I thought. The spoons you've never used. Polishing the spoons you'll never need. Your reflection in every spoon. Your face stretched in a silver spoon. All the medicine you've taken. The medicine…

See you, she said. In a bit.

See you, I said. Her hair was different now. Fairer, almost blonde… It was…

She turned and was about to leave.

Hey, I said, as she was disappearing. Let's have a drink. Is it? At the bar? It's crowded in here. Don't you think? The Central's bound to be quieter.

Sophia seemed surprised.

Scores of new people were now coming past. The lovers, the lonely. All with songs in their heads.

Then Sophia smiled.

Yes, it's the lunchtime rush. Getting worse. You know, she whispered. I hardly know any of these people.

Nor me, I said. Maybe I taught some of them. Last year. Or the year before that.

There was a corner of the Central Bar where I put down

our drinks. We'd both decided on glasses of sauvignon blanc.

Must be strange, said Sophia. To be a teacher, I mean. Every year, your classes the same age. The girls, the boys. But you, another year older. Must be strange.

Oh yes, I agreed. It's ... peculiar. If you think about it. So maybe a teacher shouldn't think about it. But then, you reach a particular age and perhaps it's better...

Yeah?

Not to think about anything at all.

Because? Oh, well. Obviously...

Yeah. Obviously.

But how long? asked Sophia. Have you been a teacher?

Thirty years. Started late. But thirty's enough.

I suppose so. But then, I'm a writer. I'll be a writer forever.

Maybe I looked at her then. Maybe at our yellow wine.

Will you? Really?

Oh yes. Look at Leonard Cohen. Still doing it. A cousin of mine saw him in Sydney.

Yeah, great, I said. Maybe I should try the miserable old bastard again. Give him another chance.

You're not a writer? Are you?

No.

Well then...

Well what?

Maybe you don't understand...

Maybe I took a long pull.

Christ, Soph. I understand all right. When I was your age my friends couldn't imagine a group still playing gigs at thirty. *Thirty?* we thought. Thirty's ridiculous. But what if you're fifty, sixty. Seventy-bloody-five? Do you stop?

Leonard's seventy-bloody-eight, breathed Sophia triumph-

16

antly.

But do you stop?

No. Like, what for? Because…

Soon enough you're dead?

Well … yeah.

Then good on Leonard Cohen. I'm having another.

Not for me, please.

Go on.

I hardly ever drink.

Got to start. If you're a writer you do.

That's a myth. Don't typecast me. Look, just because I'm a writer you can't turn me into a cliché.

Hey, relax. White wine's nothing terrible. I'm sure I'm always better with a drink inside me. Most people are.

Well … okay, she smiled. But I know I'll always want to write. Now I've … discovered writing. Now I've felt how good it is. How real it is.

It's like you can't remember what you used to do before?

That's it. Spot on.

See. I get it.

It's like, there was all this time and I just wasted it. But now I understand what I was born for. Born to do.

And no one's going to argue with that.

But I bet you do, she said, turning up her face. Write that is. I bet you do.

Perhaps I allowed the question to float. I came back with the sauvignon in an ice bucket. Then two new glasses and a bowl of pistachios.

Cheers.

Cheers, she said. Sipping her first glass for the first time.

Course I do, I said. Of course I write.

Then I corrected myself. Or maybe what I write down are

ideas. Ideas for writing. No, not the words themselves. Not the actual words.

We both looked round, then.

I suppose I make lists, I said. That's writing. Isn't it?

Oh … yes. I suppose.

Yeah, I compile. I'm a brilliant compiler, me.

And what do you compile?

The soundtrack.

Sophia raised an eyebrow.

Yes, I compile the soundtrack to our lives. Okay, my life. Not yours. But mine. And a pretty good soundtrack it is too.

Essential task, she smiled.

So, should I say, of course I want to write. But first of all, I read. Which is an art. An occupation we're in danger of losing.

Why don't you paint? You teach art. After all.

I was always … about to start. Always on the brink. Waiting for the moment it felt right.

It always feels right for me. Now.

Hold on to that feeling. And practise that guitar!

Every day.

You could play here, I told her. At the Central. There's a stage at the far end. But it might be possible down in this corner…

Don't worry. I've checked it out already. We were here last night. It seems Thursdays are unplugged nights. You put your name down and wait for the call. So Thursday it's going to be. And that's tomorrow. Oh, Richard!

Thursday? Wonderful. Soon you'll be quite the troubadour.

Trobawhat?

Don't tell me…? You know … a travelling minstrel type. There's a club in London. Called The Troubadour.

But … I'm not … very good.

Was Leonard bloody Cohen very good? He had to start

somewhere.

I just strum in C.

One chord? If I knew one chord you couldn't keep me off that stage. One chord's all you need.

Actually … I'll be over there. Sophia gestured to the corner where she'd perform.

But one chord? That's all it takes. Confidence is your only ingredient. Promise me you'll do it.

Another guitarist would help. Maybe bass. Fill out the terrible silence. But yes, I'll do it. Of course I will.

So do it.

Yes, she said. I have to. You've just got to … push yourself forward. Haven't you?

Tomorrow evening? I said. I'm staying at The Sebel. Maybe I'll come over. Hear how you fill that terrible silence. Hey, I've thought of your first album title. What about Troubles of a Troubadour? What about…?

THURSDAY

5am.

Darkness.

A raindrop on the tip of my tongue.

I thought of the Caib Caves. The cold of the walls. The roofs of rock. Where even the quartz is grey. Where it's always raining. That limestone rain.

Out at the bus and tram stops. That group of natives was being moved away. One of their children was crying. It's police policy, someone said. Two, three days, then move 'em on. Standard practice. Don't let them get comfortable. Don't let…

It's not easy to see the photograph in first light. Still, people seemed to think about it. I might have appeared desperate. Or needy. So they looked.

Maybe that's how I must be to everybody. Because I haven't shaved all week. Haven't thought about it. There are more important things to do than shave.

You see, I don't want to pretend anything now. Yes, I've finished pretending. Maybe that's the last part of growing up. When you realise you can stop pretending. The relief of not pretending. The terror of it.

Because you realise that's what life can be. Pretending. If you allow it. You realise that's how you're spending every minute. Maybe even your last minute. Pretending.

But pretending what? Pretending you haven't pissed yourself. Pretending you care. Pretending you don't care. Pretending you know what you're talking about. Pretending you know what everybody else is talking about.

Pretending you don't care that the barman hasn't cleaned this table. I care about that. Does that make me alive? Because, look, there's wine spilled in the middle of the table. Or icewater. My glass is leaving rings in last night's spills.

When I showed the photograph to a man at the bar he shook his head. Shook his head. But was he pretending not to know? Or pretending not to care?

Yes, the barman's coming round now. Excuse me, boss, he says, excuse me. I lift my glass and allow him to do his job and I can still see the wet rings my glass leaves and maybe I should be doing this in my room, this thinking, this searching my thoughts, but I don't want to be alone, don't want to drink that way, because The Brecknock is where I brought Lulu once and she seemed to like it.

When he wipes the table I show the photo again. He says already seen it, sport. And the answer's the same.

But no, I think. It's a different world now. So the answer

cannot be the same. In a different world the answer can never be the same.

I think Lulu and I sat in the same seats that afternoon. Under the mirror. Lulu ordered wedges. Yes with spicy mayo. There are so many places we sat together. Toasting our lives. *So long, Arcturus. So long.*

A notice on the wall tells me there have been only three landlords at The Brecknock in one hundred and fifty years.

The man who wiped my table might be twenty-five. He's a strong-looking kid but tiredness has entered his eyes. His eyelids are mauve. He has a small-hours pallor.

Take it easy, I want to say to that boy. Son, rest your head. Upon the bar. Try and remember your dreams. Because this is the country of the Dreaming.

When he cleans my table he uses an old tee shirt with a yellow smiley face design. And look, here he comes again. He's here again.

Instead of sleeping he's working. Instead of placing his cheek against the cold metal of the counter, he comes back.

I think he asks can I get you another. And I am surprised. Yes, I am disconcerted.

Yes, thank you, I say. Another would be good.

And I think I mean what I say. I think that's what he said.

And no, I wasn't pretending. About that. Because that's another challenge, isn't it? To understand you're pretending you're not pretending. Or is it the other way around?

And what? I say. What's that?

Yes it would be better for you, he says. Better for you. If you did. Yes better for you…

If I what?

Better for you. Better all round.

Better for…

If I?

If you
Better all round.
If I…?
Shove off.

But it's a girl now. A girl behind the aluminium rail of the counter. This new girl at the bar I haven't seen before. She lights a candle and the glow runs through the room. Like a fuse.

No, she says, no, I haven't seen her. You've asked everyone, sir. No one has seen the girl in the photograph. And sir, sir.

Someone is pointing out there's blood on my cheek. That blood is dripping from my nose. It's happening again, I don't know why. It happened this week. Or maybe last month.

Maybe that man hit me. Maybe that man on the high stool at the bar. He was there a moment ago. I didn't like the look of him. No, not at all. But I showed him the photograph, asked him to remember.

But it's a woman on the stool now. A woman with long legs. With black, with black. Stockings. Yes her legs so long. Stretched out before her. A woman taller than me. Yes she's taller. But how tall is she really? I wonder, how tall is the woman at the bar?

Now someone is wiping my cheek. There's blood on the cloth. Blood on that tee shirt with the yellow smiley face. Yes maybe he hit me. And maybe he didn't. Or maybe the woman with long…

But the blood's running over my fingers and I think, in that one hundred and fifty years in all that time you'd suppose you'd suppose on the streets of Adelaide for one hundred and fifty years I've been searching the violet light creeping up the glass the southern rain starting to speckle the glass and the signs in a language no one understands.

Everyone is pretending. Everyone today, tonight in The

Brecknock. So here we are.

Pretending I haven't pissed myself.

Pretending they've not seen Lulu.

And salty, I think. My blood warm. And so salty.

Like rain on The Caib. That rain's cold, but it's colder in the caves.

Yes, I've stood listening. To that dripping. That dripping that goes on forever. I've waited for it to stop and realised that it's music that will last for. Ever.

Stood there shivering. Felt my whole body. Shiver. Yes looked around and seen the ages of starlight grow dim in the stone. Seen the corals white and dead locked into the stone. And I've run away. Over the pebbles and through the pools. Run away as quickly as I could.

FRIDAY

Woke and slept. Woke and realised something was wrong.

Bleeding again. The bright noseblood everywhere. When I found the light I was afraid.

There was so much. A red pond in the dint my head had left. A wet stain on the cream Sebel Hotel pillowcase. The Sebel monogram in the corner.

My first reaction was to hide it. Yes, hide the evidence. Of bleeding. Of whatever's wrong. But Thursday was my last night here. When I go down to reception this morning I will pay the bill and walk out and then and then…

I put on all the lights and fill the bath with everything the hotel's provided. The soap, the shampoos, the conditioners, the body lotions in their plastic sachets.

And I don't even look. Simply pour it all into the water. Roaring into my 5am bath.

And I soak. Up to my eyebrows. Then immerse myself until I splutter up from the hot water. Then down again. Then up. Then down. Again.

I think of The Chasm. My face between Lizzy's legs. My blood on her thighs and Lizzy's seawater taste mixing with the taste of my blood.

That afternoon, all of us ready. The sun shining into the caves. No trace of a shadow on the neolithic blue of The Caib. All of us ready. For the rest of our … the rest of…

At reception I look at how my bill has been calculated.

No, I say. You're confusing me with…

The girl tries to specify each item. Then has to wait for an older woman to come. Then wait for the man who had smiled at me on Monday. Ages ago. Eons…

I paid for the malbec at the bar, I say. On Monday. Paid with cash.

But the Tuesday malbec, sir?

Tuesday?

Also on Tuesday sir, the peanuts? The crisps? Please look at the details, sir. Then the malbec on the Wednesday, sir? Both miniatures of the scotch on Wednesday, sir. Wednesday supper brought to your room. Both miniatures again, sir. You ordered the minibar replenished every day. I spoke to you myself on Thursday, sir. That was yesterday.

Replenished? I asked. What a word that is. A terrible word. A word from a different world.

I was trying to make a joke of it, I said.

A joke, sir. Yes, I understand, sir. And the telephone account is such as it is because you regularly called the same number.

Goolwa, I say. I rang a shop. Goolwa's sixty miles away. Sweet sixty.

I know, sir. You often called at night, sir. Or very early in the morning.

Just checking, I said. I had to check up. But it was always answerphone. Except the day that...

Some of these calls were made at unusual hours, sir. And you must have left long messages on the answerphone, sir. Do you remember, sir? One of these calls lasted ninety-three minutes.

Ninety-three...?

Ninety-three minutes and fifty-seven seconds. A call made at 2.30 in the morning.

It's a big responsibility, I tell him. When I'm away.

And this call? It's longer. One hundred and twenty-seven minutes.

One hundred...?

Of course, sir, I can itemise the charges for you once again. If it will help. Of course, we already have your credit card details.

And the man smiles at me. For the last time, I am sure. There he stands, dark shoulders, no dandruff. Perfect Windsor knot. Today he is wearing a name badge. Perhaps he had worn it on Monday.

Stephen Wright, it says.

Woah! I say. Woah!

Pardon, sir?

Hold up, Stevie! I say. Hold up, Little Stevie Wright. Woah, boy.

Pardon, sir?

Stephen Wright, I repeat. Wow, it's Stevie Wright.

And the man does smile again. A face I expected to be full of loathing lights with long-suffering good humour.

My parents were fans, sir. I live with it.

And do you sing, Stephen? I ask.

Regrettably not, sir. My mother was the driving force. More

25

so than my father. In fact she attended Stevie Wright's, what shall we say, his comeback concert. The Legends of Rock, sir. Held up in Byron Bay? Oh yes, sir, I know all about Little Stevie Wright.

Hard to credit, I say. That he's still alive. After everything he's been through. And, did you, did you ever…

Sing, sir? Lots of people have asked me, though less often now of course. But no, never, I never sang. I used to be asked all the time, sir, but I never wanted it. My career took a different direction.

And I look at Stephen Wright behind The Sebel Hotel's polished counter. Stephen Wright with his fat silver tie. His brushed shoulders.

Well, Stephen, I say, '*It's gonna happen… It's gonna happen…*

…*In the city,* sir? Where *I'll be with my girl, sir? She's so pretty,* sir.

Yes, perhaps it's going to happen, sir, You see, I used to listen to that song, when I was much younger. In fact, I bought a copy. The first record I ever bought.

She looks fine tonight, I say.

And she is out of sight, returns Stephen Wright. *To me.*

It's gonna happen, I say. *It's gonna happen, it's gonna happen…*

In the city, sir? Oh yes, sir. Where everything happens. After all. Please sign here and thank you for staying at The Sebel.

I collect my car and drive through the Adelaide traffic down the peninsula. I wait above some of the beaches we'd visited. Everything is a dream.

In Victor Harbour it is easy to park. Then I hop on to the horse tram setting out for Granite Island. There are only two other passengers.

Yes, I ask them whether they'd seen Lulu. And they quiz one another. Taking it seriously.

Have we, Daddy? Have we?

I think so, says the man.

I think so, says the woman.

Oh boy. They are doing their best.

Such a sweet-looking child, the woman says. Is she your… I mean, is she your…?

No. No, she's not.

Eventually, they decided. No, they hadn't. No, they were sure.

The woman put the photograph back into my hand. Her mouth tight.

Thank you, I say. And wander off uphill.

But how might anyone be sure? Even I who had looked one hundred times at that photograph, could now remember none of the details. Could recall nothing.

Lulu is vanishing. A mirage above the Murray. A wisp from the ashen hills.

There are penguins on the island. They make the island famous. Everything is done to preserve those penguins.

You know, I say to a man on the granite track. They don't deserve it, do they? They bloody don't deserve it.

Who doesn't deserve what? he asks.

All this, I gestured. The whole island. Those stupid bloody…

But he shrugs and pushes on. So I am able to have the bald rock of the granite headland to myself.

Penguins.

At the lookout, I am alone. I think a few people pass. Then I head down to the restaurant at the bottom. Where I sit and stare. Contemplating the ocean.

That sea is like old silver paper. Crushed and crinkled. Like the silver paper I used day after day at The Works. Its silver darkening, getting dirtier…

I remember my mother with tins of Silvo. That filthy stuff. Just a gritty paste. But she'd rub it in and gradually all the tarnishing of anything silver, her best cutlery, a few vases, would vanish.

A miracle, for a while. I used to watch her polishing. And wondered why she bothered. Why she would make that effort. Now I understand.

It was the same silver as the beach when the tide was going out. The same silver as the smoke that poured out of The Works. I used to walk west and see that silver beach spread out. The mosques and minarets of industry. All silvered in the dawn.

And I thought, up on the Granite Island lookout, there's nothing now. No, nothing between me and the icefields. Nothing between me and Mount Erebus, that volcano at the start, at the end of the world. Nothing between me and Wilkes Land, that desert at the start, at the end of the world.

No, there's nothing. And I asked myself, how did I get here? To Granite Island? With all these, all these … *penguins*.

Yeah. How did I…? How…

And I thought, no, not how? Why? Why is the question.

I looked at the sea. There were cloud shadows on the waves. As if the water was deeper there. As if the sea was tarnishing. That water was a different colour, like ice I'd see in rain barrels on the allotment. Silver skins around black embryos, that ice.

Yes, that ice was like drowned babies. It's what I always thought. Cycling down Amazon Street, going past The Lily, then The Cat, going through The Ghetto and under The Ziggurat, that's what I thought.

Because I saw one once. Or thought I saw. A drowned baby in our rain barrel.

Can't remember if it was a joke Dad made. Or something my mother said. Or maybe a dead cat, or a bat.

Yes, I found a drowned bat once in the rain butt. And that's when the idea came to me. From then on I always looked specially.

And I came to expect it. But then, when there was no drowned baby, I'd be, I'd be … *disappointed*. How strange is that?

So, I used to push the ice down. Into the barrel. Or sometimes I broke that ice, sometimes smashed it to splinters, scarring it white. And I scratched my name on that ice a few times. Yes, RIP, scratched it with a pen or an old fork we kept in the toolbox. The only writing I've ever managed.

Then I would look into the water of the rain barrel. Water too cold to touch. Too cold to bear. Water as cold as the seawater around Granite Island.

There were hundreds of miles of water until the next land. And the next land was the dead land where no one had ever lived. Only marooned sailors, or fur trappers who might have survived mutiny or shipwreck.

Because there are more islands than you'd think off that coast. Islands all the way to Antarctica. I used to know their names. Islands like splinters of ice.

You see, that's how I passed my interview for Adelaide. By my diligence. I prepared for days. No, for weeks. Yes, I even researched those barren islands. Where no one has ever existed and never will live.

Imagine that, no history, no culture. Nothing to inherit. Only thousands of years of birdshit whitening the cliffs. And bird song. That insane racket no one will ever hear.

But I fooled them, didn't I? Those worthies on the interview panel. Yes, they told me they would be taking a risk. Told me on the video link. Told me it was a very long way, a very long way from…Where is it you come from, Mr Parry? How close is that to…? How far from…?

I tell you, that interview is the most coherent I've ever been. I knew when it was over I had the job. I couldn't imagine not getting that job. No snuffling, no coughing. No bloody stammering.

All those speech therapy lessons worked out. Didn't they? Richard Ieuan Parry, stone cold cert.

Yes, all that speaking with a limestone pebble in my mouth. Thank you, limestone. I remember how you tasted. Yes, the salt of you. The dangerous limestone taste of the sea.

I could swallow this, I always thought. Break my teeth on this pebble. And ruin my smile, ha ha.

But don't tell me they didn't get their money's worth. I slaved for that school. Early mornings, late evenings, weekends. And then *Hey Bulldog*, as if school wasn't enough. On top of it all I ran the Bulldog.

When I put my hands in the water in the barrel I would hold them there. As long as it was bearable. Then I'd examine my skin. The white, the mottled, the purple skin.

And I'd think, this must be what it's like when you're dead.

I sat on that lookout rock until I realised I was aching. The lights were on in Vincent Harbour by then. The horse ferry long gone. I had to walk back along the causeway.

Before that I returned to the restaurant. It was deserted. But I stepped over the chain and sat at the table Lulu and I had first chosen.

That afternoon I had ordered a bottle of sauvignon. Yes, like they say, it reminded me of gooseberries.

That's the cliché, isn't it? And that's what I told my best kids. Between twelve and twenty, it didn't matter.

Don't use clichés, I'd say. Try and discover what no one else has ever said.

You know, all my classes ended with 'P'. Started out with 12P. Moved on to older kids. By the end it was 17P. Bigger than me, the boys in 17P. And in 16P they were bigger too. And 15P.

And don't mention the girls. Just don't…

But every year, they'd call me the same name. Ripper. Sometimes Jack, but generally Ripper. Or Mr Parry to be formal.

Talking of 16P, who became 17Z by the way, under the care of Mrs Zacharias, I once told them about the corals of The Caib.

You what, sir? they all asked. Show us on the map where you come from. Show us again.

So I'd point out The Caib and they'd laugh and ask if I'd ever been to the Great Barrier Reef. That's where the coral is, Ripper, they said. The GBR.

Caib coral is fossilised, I'd say. It's the ghosts of corals that lived millions of years ago. Some of it's white or bleached. Generally, it's no colour at all.

Ghost coral sounds dead, sir, the clever ones would say.

But there are real corals, still corals around where…

And I'd lose them in the reaction. As I was howled down.

Seems I wasn't allowed to trespass on Aussie territory. All I was doing was telling them about what I'd dig up in the sand at home. Coral the colour of pearls of arsenic. Coral like droplets of fog.

So much we used to uncover. In the limestone earth. Thousands of pieces of china, most with a pattern of blue flowers. Unrecognisable bits of iron. Old iron.

I never said to those kids they might find nothing in Adelaide. Course I didn't. But so little of the land had been settled. Not that it would have been an insult. Not at all. But you know what I mean.

You see, I was going to make an installation of everything I'd dug up. I thought of it years before I met Libby.

I kept all those bits in glass jars. The corals, the pottery. Kept them ready. I wanted to exhibit my own archaeology.

Then, one night, I threw them away. Went over to the allotment and dug them back in. Where they belonged.

But gooseberries were my favourite fruit at the allotment. My mother learned not to pick those gooseberries too soon. She allowed the fruits to darken. Until the skins were the colour of iron, she always said. The flesh softening.

Listen to me, she'd say. Wait a day. And a day would become a week and then she'd say again, wait a day. Listen to me. Wait a day. Are the skins bursting?

But no, they could never be sweet. Even then, after a day and another day, after weeks, they set my teeth on edge. Those iron-coloured goosegogs.

So on Granite Island I sat in the darkness and looked at the harbour lights. The penguins were snuffling and coughing in their burrows.

I imagine it was penguins making those sounds. I never saw any penguins on that visit to the island. I simply accepted what I was told. That this was where the penguins lived. But, when I think about it, perhaps there were no penguins.

Yes I waited at that table behind the chain in the dark. And I thought about my mother's plans to make an astronomical garden.

It was going to be in the back at our house. Under the apple tree. Well after we'd given up the allotment.

She had decided to plant red sunflowers that would be the

same colour as Arcturus. Next she would grow a bed of blue flowers like forget-me-nots beside a bed of orange flowers. Maybe marigolds, in honour of Albireo. This was supposed to be the most spectacular double star in the sky.

I'd looked at that star with Lulu during the drought. I can remember the night we searched for it, the Murray slummocking past, snuffling and coughing like those bloody penguins, the reek of mud and wet sand, Jupiter so fat it was reflected off the sea. The riverbanks were silvered the same as that solder they'd spilled at The Works.

I thought about that a long time. That memory of home. Then, slowly, slowly, I started to laugh.

You what? I asked myself. You what?

Because I had never talked to my mother about Arcturus. And certainly not Albireo. Everything I knew about stars I had learned from Lulu. I'd never discussed the subject with Mum.

No, I had dreamed about the astronomical garden. It was all in my head.

It was all in my head.

The restaurant was full that afternoon when I was there with Lulu. There was a crowd on Granite Island, too many to be comfortable, too many on the horse ferry. And too many jumping off the jetty as we used to do on The Caib, jumping off the breakwater or a boulder at The Horns.

Jumping like that was dangerous at home. I recall a boy breaking his back and killing himself. His friend brought the body to shore. Limp as a rag doll. I watched him carry it in, the dead boy's head thrown back, his throat blue, his hair like seaweed. And his neck so white, so white...

David, the dead boy was called. Older than us. For years his parents used to leave bouquets on the nearest bench. They still do.

I'd think, I still think, when I look at those flowers, his mother's not even taken the cellophane off.

But I know I bought the sauvignon. I can remember the taste and the green colour of the wine. And the price. That bottle was ridiculously expensive.

I remember thinking maybe I shouldn't pay that much. But then Lulu called me stingy after I hesitated.

Yes, it was the best. Then I recall Lulu ordering wedges and me telling her, hey, I think you're putting on weight. And her answering, that's all right then boss, I'm allowed aren't I? I'm allowed.

I think I remember that. I think it happened. But look, if it didn't, if it didn't actually … happen like that, or if it happened like something else, does it … Does it even matter?

As far as I'm concerned, the astronomy garden is real. Yes, it was a dream. Of course it was a dream. But if I say it's real, then…

3

I

At the top of Amazon Street a pale sun, a sun greyly glittering. A sun of deadwhite coral. Around that sun a smoky aurora.

II

A man passed Parry in the fog, a man with a backpack. He was walking slowly and seemed to be searching for something.

These days, there were many such. Some with suitcases, some with black bags. Men usually. But Parry noted there were now women.

These people looked bewildered, almost lost. They stood on street corners, sometimes outside *Badfinger,* unsure of themselves. Some turned towards the sea. Some walked away from the sea.

These were people who had never visited The Caib before. All eventually disappeared into the fog.

III

Ghosts? asked Parry of Serene. Maybe. But every town is full of ghosts.

There was a man, he remembered, who collected cuttlefish bones. Sometimes they would find his stooks on the sand. Those cuttle pyramids yellow-white as bonfire smoke.

It was said he sold the cuttle in the local pet shop. Parry doubted it, no matter how abundant the harvest. Sometimes he had seen the man sitting on the stones of The Horns, whittling cuttlebone.

A sculptor, Parry had thought. An artist whose shavings lay like foam.

It took him years to realise the man had disappeared. He never heard what happened to him.

IV

Possibly the pink, suggested Serene. But you look good in pink, too. Well, sort of. And all the others are … black? Or grey.

I dress for the fog, said Parry. So I can blend in. But aren't we all creatures of the fog these days?

But why all the black?

I'm in mourning, he said. For my life.

No, why?

Got rid of my clothes in Oz, and my wardrobe hasn't recovered. But maybe there are things here Glan might like?

Okay, give him the pink.

Deal. It's his. If I can wear it just once more.

I'll hold you to that. But where did that blood come from? On the hanky?

Nose bleed. I walked into the door.

V

What we used to do, said Parry, was find a pebble. A round pebble, as heavy as possible. Or lots of smaller pebbles. From the heaps of pebbles near the slipway.

Grey or mauve or stonewashed blue, those pebbles. All the same, you'd think, but no. Every pebble was different.

Sometimes I'd have to go for pebbles like that for the garden or the allotment. My mother always had a use for them, even if it was only as part of the rockery.

Then I'd find one of our big pans and boil the water, making sure the pebble was fully immersed. Then added salt and a little pepper to taste. I'd boil that pebble for an hour, add more salt, and there it was.

Where was what? asked Serene.

Our soup.

Soup?

Limestone soup.

Serene looked around as though she was lost.

What did it taste like? she asked.

Limestone soup tasted like you would, straight after a swim off The Horns. Or like you if you'd dared to touch bottom at The Chasm.

Serene made a face.

Limestone soup tasted like the sea. It tasted like the sky. The air in Caib Caves.

Never been there.

Yeah, it tasted like Glan would taste. Straight after an afternoon swim. Or better, a midnight swim. Because at midnight, or any time in the dark, a swimmer tastes different from a swimmer in the day.

What colour was this limestone soup?

Grey, if I boiled a grey pebble. Pink, if it was a pink pebble.

But… said Serene. Stone soup? Why should I believe you?

Why shouldn't you believe me?

Serene held the pink shirt to her face.

Oh, what were you wearing? When you last wore this? It's a perfume I recognise. I've smelled it before.

And she breathed Parry in.

He smiled at her, that long-breasted girl in her gaudy. In her mauves and purples. Then he looked away.

4

I

Something was coming down the street. A vehicle gaining colour and speed. But it maintained a stately pace, as if the mist was reluctant to set it free. Parry took another box of DVDs from the back of the car.

The vehicle was pink, Parry decided. And long. Yes, here it came. One of those limousines you saw nowadays. A stretchlimo that groups booked for evenings out. Chauffeurs in peaked caps, champagne flutes. You could hire it all.

Yes, here it came. Despite the hour, despite the weather, the limousine roof was open. A young woman, brandishing a wineglass, was standing up in the back seat, toasting it seemed, anyone who might be passing. But Caib Street was empty. All of The Caib was deserted.

It was about noon, Parry decided, and he had never known the town quieter. This morning he had passed the surgery. A man was lying on the gravel forecourt, maybe dead or simply unconscious.

Parry had considered his discovery. And asked himself why he should feel no surprise. He looked at the man's face. Aged forty, bruised cheek, hair matted. The sleep of oblivion. Inside, Parry hadn't had time to explain.

Yes, doctor's coming, said the receptionist. Thank you for telling us. The doctor is aware.

Outside once more, Parry had given the man a last look. How tenderly he had been sleeping, the mist around him like dry ice from some cabaret act, rising out of the ground in shreds, in industrial rags. The doctor was aware. Then everything was fine.

The pink limo drew level. The young woman, who was obviously drunk, and on her way to or from a party, toasted the street. He looked around. There was nobody else in view. So Parry waved his hand in brief salute.

Stop, the girl shouted. Stop.

And the car had come to a halt outside *Badfinger*. The front door was open, boxes piled around its entrance. Thirty-three, Caib Street, the only shop that boasted signs of life. Parry's shop.

No, the woman shrilled. No, no, no. I wasn't talking to you. I wasn't fucking talking to you. Or to any other dirty old men.

Another woman in the back seat stood up. Another blonde with a wineglass.

No. Not you, she hissed through a bridal veil. Never you.

The limousine gradually took off again, a pink blur soon lost in the fret. On the pavement, Parry stood looking after it. Then he started to manhandle another cardboard box.

Time to wake Glan. He shouldn't be allowed to sleep late. And it was late. Parry looked up at the window as if he expected the young man to appear. Glan, ghost-pale, his hands clenched in his armpits. Shoulders and hairless chest shivering. Yes, it was time Glan revealed himself to the world.

Parry decided he'd make porridge for breakfast. He smiled to himself. Yes, porridge with a drop of Drambuie. To sweeten things up. Stop the anaesthetic wearing off.

II

Outside, the mist rubbed itself like a cat against the glass. Oh yes, Parry thought, he'd seen this mist before. This was familiar weather, ancient in the bones of anyone brought up on The Caib. Colder yet in the bloodstream of anyone fool enough to return.

What had he been? Possibly seventeen. Acne-eaten, unprepossessingly thin. Exams were coming up and Parry's regime was to work for three hours every night, then stop for supper. Strong tea, roasted cheese.

Then start again. Today, he could hardly credit such diligence. Such pointless resolve.

He remembered the television droning on downstairs, his hands over his ears. What was the time? Easter, but light nights at least. A blue evening sun intruded into the room. He screwed up his eyes and stared again at the notes. He had read the pages twenty times. But they made no sense. So he'd go out for an hour. To clear his head. He'd go out to see the whale.

The idea scared him. But at once he was putting on his coat, calling down he'd be back soon. Slamming the front door.

Yes, he was going to see the whale. While the tide and the light allowed he was going to see the whale.

He even made up a song as he walked.

Dare not fail
To see the whale.

The whale that had been in the evening paper. It was a small whale, yet weighed an estimated ten tons. There it waited on the rocks at Caib Caves. Piebald, wedged in a crevice.

From the photograph Parry imagined a heap of melting ice, such as fishmongers tipped out in the evenings. To smoke in the gutters of The Caib, soon yellow with dogpiss.

Yes, he was going to see the whale. He must not fail. His very own whale. The certainty of it pumped out his chest and filled his belly. And Parry ran over the common. Beyond the district known as the West End.

Parry had expected throngs of people such as himself. Everyone would be eager and amazed, all come to gaze at the whale. The ten tons of whale calf, grey as ice, that now fumed in the gulches of The Caib.

But it was strange. There was no one. No one to tell him he had arrived at the right place.

Later, Parry had not been able to explain himself. When his parents asked, the coastguard and even the police enquired, he had shaken his head. Shaken his head and wept and kept silent. Why had he done it?

He couldn't answer why. There was the whale, as long as a bus. Or a rowing boat. A rotting hulk, a carcass. Of interest only to the gulls screaming overhead.

It was the gulls that showed the way. The gulls that pursued the whale-lice through the runnels on the whale corpse.

And the police told him it must have been you. Yes, you, son. Come on, boy. Parry must have done it because no one else was present. It had to have been him. No question.

But Parry hadn't answered. Merely sat before the inspector, the coastguard and his parents. And cried.

No, the boy couldn't remember. But it must have been him. Oh yes, it was him all right. The seventeen-year-old Parry who everyone said was old enough to know better. Who had taken his penknife out of his pocket. And carved his initials into the body of the whale.

Cut his own incredible initials into the velvet hull of the whale. The body of the leviathan, as one of the coastguards insisted on calling it.

Who else, the inspector asked, would have carved those letters in the whale flesh? RIP?

Bit of a giveaway, that, one of the policemen had smiled. Which had made Parry feel worse. Made Parry cry harder until his father had told him to shut up, he had cried enough.

Stop your sobbing, was the phrase.

III

Yeah, good song, thought Richard Ieuan Parry now, finishing his toast. Nothing had happened. No charges been brought.

Parry had not killed the creature. So he had submitted to the lecture. No one had even asked where the penknife had come from. Parry said he didn't own a knife.

The next week there was another story in the newspaper. The body of the Sowerby's beaked whale that had been washed up near Caib Caves had been towed off the rocks. And disposed of.

His mad period, as he might have described it. First of many. Yes, that had been a difficult year all round. And coming back to The Caib put everything into new perspective. Coming back was not easy.

But yes, maybe Parry had gone mad. For a while. Until it dawned on him that madness was allowable. That madness was part of the process. That going mad was necessary. Fail in that, fail in madness, he had considered, and there is the true failure of nerve.

Not that he'd been especially mad. Not a bit of it. But the incident on the water chute, coming so quickly after the whale business, had perplexed his parents.

It was early summer and the fairground had recently reopened. Parry had undergone two hours of maths tuition with Rosser, a young graduate.

Yes, maths tuition on top of the history, the geography, the bloody Chaucer. Parry had failed mathematics twice so far. This was his last chance.

Or so people said. Needed a grade six, just a six, everyone told him. All his friends had passed. Everyone else in the year had managed it.

Even the yobs and slobs with their mohicans, their mohawks, the teds in their drainpipes, the hippies, the mods and all the legions of the damned in their immaculate ties and blazers. They had all scraped at least a six. And so were embarked on the next stage of their lives. Were off and running.

All except Parry. All except Parry and the losers, the weirdos. And here he was with Roz Rosser, with his pebble lenses and lingering aftershock of TCP.

Normally, tuition took place at Rosser's. But that evening, it was inconvenient. So the lesson was held in Parry's front room. On the dinner table that smelled of lavender furniture polish. Or sea lavender, as his mother once insisted. It grows in the rocks, you know.

I'm starving, announced Rosser, after what felt like hours. Fancy some chips?

And they had somehow found themselves in the fairground. Sharing one of the measly portions from the Farmhouse Fry.

How about a ride? Rosser had then asked. Out of the blue. Yes, Rosser had suggested the idea. It must have been Rosser's idea. Because Parry never had any money of his own. So it was obviously Rosser's suggestion to try the water chute. But nothing at all had happened. Nothing at all.

Only that Rosser touched Parry's leg. Yes, Rosser had put out his hand and touched Parry's left leg. The inside of his leg. Rosser had put out his hand and left it on the inside of Parry's left leg.

Had left his hand there while there was screaming and laughter and the echoes of laughter. Laughter from the ghost train. Screaming from the waxworks. Screaming and laughter from everywhere else in the fairground, that mid May evening with the petrolblue sunset. And the swifts had come back. Returning that moment.

Because Rosser had been the older boy. Had been twenty-five at least. And that was what everyone was expecting anyway. Wasn't it all somehow falling into place?

Because when the water chute ride was over, why was Parry's headmaster waiting where the carriages pulled in?

Yes, why was the headmaster waiting for Rosser? Immediately the carriage door was opened? Like police on a tip-off, Parry thought now. Nothing happened, Rosser had protested immediately. As if he was waiting to make his protest. As if he understood such a denial would be expected of him.

Nothing happened, added Parry, as if he sensed such a rejection was his due. His right.

But poor Rosser, thought Parry now. Whatever he had hoped or planned to do. Rosser who had touched his left leg. And allowed his hand to rest there. For a moment. An instant, a shaming eternity. But hardly a moment.

To be greeted by his headmaster in hat and mackintosh. Under that May sunset. With the head of English also there. In Nescafé-coloured trousers.

5

I

The town had been quiet but not silent. There was a sound Parry recognised from the past. Some old muezzin of the back streets, voice cracked and plaintive.

Parry hadn't heard such a voice for years. He thought the tribe extinct. But here was the voice once again, the voice that called for iron. Old iron. And once again it called. A voice in the acid mist that rolled over the coast. Eerie in the saturating fog.

Iron. Old iron. Out of season that voice. And out of time. But there it was again. Rasping like a jay.

Yet, there was music in that voice. A rusty desperation. And maybe, not so desperate. The voice of a back-street singer, restoring the world to order. A singer who sang of what he knew and understood. Grief in that melody. Ancient resignation.

Parry had listened, head cocked, but the voice never came again. It had vanished utterly.

II

Who is the patron saint of lost causes? asked Parry.

Search me, said Mina.

Saint Jude, said Parry. Lost causes and grievous situations.

Please don't say it, said Mina.

Say what?

'Hey Jude', that's what, said Mina.

Am I so predictable?

Collars up, the couple walked seawards through the mist. They turned in at the entrance of Clwb y Môr.

Haven't been in here for ages, said Mina. Thought it was all shut up. Talking of lost causes.

Parry smiled at the young woman behind the bar.

I know you, he said. You're John Vine's daughter. I've known you since you were kneehigh to a great green cricket.

And you're Parry, replied Nia Vine. Always Parry. Never your first name. Which is Richard. So I know about you too. You've just opened that new shop in Caib Street. What's it called now?

Tesco, said Parry.

Something … *peculiar*.

I'll say, said Mina.

Oh yes, *Badfinger*, said Nia Vine. Terrible name for a shop. I'll give it three months.

As long as that?

I was being kind, said Nia. You're in a dead spot.

Called The Caib, said Parry. The only way for a new business to work here is giving away free drinks.

It was 9pm. Parry had come to Clwb y Môr because of the poster he had been asked to display in *Badfinger*. This proclaimed that if you could ask for your first drink in 'the language' then that drink was free.

Now Parry tested himself. He found Nia Vine as good as her word. There was a crowd at the counter who might not have been renowned for their linguistic abilities.

Admire the spirit, said Parry. You remind me of myself.

Australia lost its allure has it?

Everyone comes home, said Parry. Eventually. It's one of the golden rules of business. Of life. But yes, I know what you're taking on.

Which is? asked Nia.

Apathy. Alienation. Despair. Dandruff. Put them together and it's quite a challenge.

Sounds tough.

Missionary work usually is.

Found yourself in missionary positions before now? asked Nia.

Had my moments, said Parry. He looked around. But my problem has never been too much space. Now at *Badfinger,* we could do with some of the room here. Anyone helping you out?

Nia shrugged. The committee are good people. But they're getting on.

Parry gestured to the woman at his side. This is Mina, he explained. She keeps the off-licence next to *Badfinger.*

Basement Booze, added Mina as an explanation. Parry had shown Mina the poster about free drinks and she had laughed and said if they were that desperate for custom, then fine. As long as the Queen's English was still allowed.

And Mina's named after a poet, said Parry.

So you keep telling me, said Mina.

A pretty peculiar poet, too, he said.

Oh yes?

But quite a role model.

III

While they were waiting for the drinks, Parry said he'd go off exploring.

48

The corridor to the toilets was a municipal cream. There were three different rooms, all with smashed locks. These held nothing but broken tables and chairs and two ancient fruit machines. At the far end of the corridor was a larger space with a stage, and a sign that said 'to the dressing rooms'. On stage were papier-mâché segments of a model whale, painted grey and blue.

Next, Parry climbed the stairs. In an empty bar, he found a crate of Schweppes' mixers, a medical skeleton, a book titled *Hymnau Calfinaidd*, and an album by Showaddywaddy, *The Arista Singles Volume One*.

The damp was worse up here. The paint on two walls behind the counter had disintegrated into dust. Above a chapel harmonium a tendril of ivy lay under a broken pane. There was another flight of stairs, leading up.

The noise from the bar below was filtering upstairs, but Parry thought he heard someone else in the room he had left. He paused and walked back, looking around. But saw no one.

Exactly as I thought, he announced returning to the front bar.

Any hope for us? smiled Nia. And looked expectant. As if Parry might know what he was talking about.

Of course, Parry said. Turn it all into apartments. Perfect sea view. In fact, so perfect that the sea's coming through your excuse for a roof. Who owns this place?

Not sure, said Nia. The committee administers everything. There's a chair, and a treasurer. But the vultures are massing.

Stick in there, kid, said Mina, taking an interest. Who opens up for you?

I do, said Nia.

Who closes up?

Me too.

Hey, maybe you could help, encouraged Parry, looking at Mina. After all, you're always telling me about your insomnia.

Bore you, do I?

No, said Parry. But you say it's tough. And I know what it's like. Sometimes I can't sleep.

Maybe you should all come down here, smiled Nia. Doesn't anyone sleep round here?

It gets better, said Mina. After a few years. You know, I used to think I wasn't tired enough, that I shouldn't have gone to bed. But it's not that. Some nights, dead of night, it's just me and the World Service. On quiet in case the flat next door can hear.

That's... said Nia

Life, said Mina. Had problems with sleep on and off for twenty years. Maybe it started when my daughter was about ten. But it's not always so bad. Have my little rituals of course, with candles and drapes over the lamps. So everything's red and pink. But subdued. Like a Paris brothel.

I'll bring some CDs round, said Parry. Got these gentle Indian ragas that last forever. You play them so low you hardly know they're on. They help you switch off.

And I love the radio, added Mina. That's my greatest friend. Radio and halogen heater, with that orange glow.

Soothing, said Nia.

Making life bearable, laughed Mina. Yes anything as long as it's not pills. A friend gave me some of those.

Okay, she added, it's own up time. I've tried the lot, and yes, some worked. But I took this different tablet once. Was told it would really do the trick. Woke up fifteen hours later with a head like a bucket. My tongue had turned green. Not healthy, those sleeping pills. Take my word.

Yes, said Parry. Stay off the medication. Music's the answer. Try 'Riverman' by Nick Drake. Or I'll record the sea for you. You know, that slap and tickle of the tide on Caib Slipway.

Hey, maybe I'll market a CD in the shop. Call it 'Soothing Sounds'. Then we'd expand the idea. Record the wind in the dunes, then real Caib seagulls. Call one record 'All the Moods of the Sea'. We could create Caib Records...What sound does the fog make?

Is there no stopping the man? asked Nia.

We know people who'd join in, said Parry, warming to his subject. Think of Gil and his website and all that recording equipment...

Nia raised her eyes in mock horror.

No, we need younger people, added Parry. Like Glan and Serene, so we can spot trends...

Was it to do with children that you stopped sleeping? Nia asked Mina.

No, Alys was only ten. Perfect age. Before the terrible twelve.

She looked round the bar. There were fewer people in now the excitement generated by free drinks was wearing off.

There was a man in the corner, the moisture on his sleeves pearls in the striplight. He hadn't pulled down his hood. Yet Mina thought she had seen him somewhere before.

IV

Once, Parry recalled, he had fallen into stinging nettles. The rash had lasted three weeks. Or so it had seemed.

Parry could still see those nettles. Tall and violet, the flowers bearded. How his fingertips had tingled, smothered in white freckles. Sea foam on limestone.

His father's fault, of course. Jack Parry wanted to cut nettles for his 'luxurious nettle soup'.

Ideally the nettles should have been fresh and green. But the whole expedition proved a disaster. Parry had tumbled into the nettle bed and the soup turned into gruel. Even his father refused his own cooking. Parry sat blowing on his fingers, tormented by the nettles' needles.

But now the discomfort was elsewhere. He tested his tongue again, pushing it between his teeth. Yes, the dentist had been a careless fool. He had nipped his tongue and weeks later, Parry still felt tender.

As a child he remembered visiting the speech therapist. Being told to keep a pebble in his mouth. A stone that rolled around, an impossible word in his cheek.

But it had worked. There was barely a trace of the stammer he had suffered as a boy. The hesitancy was gone. The unhappiness it brought hardly a memory.

V

Like a hamster, he thought. Or more likely a chicken. A stone in its gizzard. A grindstone of the throat.

Yet it had worked for him. A forgotten miracle of childhood had restored language. Stones in the mouth, breathing through straws.

Whatever the treatment, it had helped. He had been able to quit the classes, leaving the stutterers behind with their smashed words.

Yet Parry imagined he knew what was causing the hold up ahead. Words, he guessed. Unsayable words.

All Parry wanted was a morning paper. He had waited outside the supermarket until 7am.

He liked the idea of a routine that a newspaper created. Also, the unbroken bundles of newsprint that could be glimpsed at such an hour. Newspapers he never otherwise saw, Irish and Polish titles, racing papers, red-topped bales. All possessed a seductive urgency.

But the man ahead who was guilty of the delay was no

stammerer. Rather, he was counting out change from a succession of moneybags.

None of the aisles was yet open, only the kiosk working. The man had asked for a bottle of the supermarket's own-label vodka, *Krazy Kremlin*, £3.53 for 500mms. Now he was telling the assistant to count it again.

You're over 50 pence short, the girl explained. Do you want a miniature instead?

Can't be, the man explained. Added it up this morning. Spot on.

But conscious of the queue for newspapers and lottery tickets behind, he decided to abandon the purchase.

Back in the street, Parry caught him up. The mist was raw, the morning black. And as Parry was pocketing his own change, a figure pushed past, a man who loomed suddenly out of the junction with Cato Street. Out of and into the fog.

Look, have that, said Parry. He proffered a pound coin. It's only a quid.

It was all there if that idiot kid had been able to count, the man said. I added it up this morning. It was perfect. Counted it twice.

Don't teach them anything these days, do they? laughed Parry. Look, go back and get it.

And he pressed the coin into the man's hand and walked past. A cold coin on a cold morning, the man with no jacket or hood but jewels already in his hair. A man dealing with the day's first shame, a first ignominious encounter and dawn not broken. Something not even *Krazy Kremlin* would put right.

Not made for this, were we? the man said. I said we're not made for this.

You're not wrong about that, said Parry, turning for home. He had bought milk, in case anyone called round. And both Glan and Serene needed it in their tea. Their coffee. Parry had also bought three bottles of red wine, on special offer.

Not such a giveaway as *Krazy Kremlin,* he considered. Nor had the girl in the kiosk blinked at his purchase. She was too young to serve him but experienced enough not to worry.

In the kitchenette at 33, Caib Street he made himself black coffee. Then set to thrashing the porridge.

VI

Eventually Richard Parry had found employment in The Works. The job was offered for the August holidays, with the chance of more hours any time he wanted.

More hours, he soon discovered, might last for weeks. Maybe months. There were workers on the payroll still considered temporary or casual after serving years. Some of them preferred it like that.

Indeed, it occurred to Parry, that whole working lifetimes spent at The Works might be passed that way. His father outlined certain practices he would encounter.

You'll see, said Jack Parry. And laughed. And shrugged.

No matter how weird you think it's going to be, it will always be much stranger still.

Listen, to understand The Works, you need to learn to think like everybody else. But by the time you've learned to think like everybody else, it'll be too late to get out. Too late to save your skin, my son. You'll be paralysed. All part of the great myth.

What great myth?

The myth of work. By the time you understand that, they've got you.

But it's good money, said Richard Parry.

Oh yes. Good money. That's the trap.

What trap?

The trap of life.

Myth of work? Trap of life? There's no trap.

Beware, laughed Jack Parry. There were pastry flakes on his tie.

But it is good money. Everybody says so.

See. It's started already.

What has?

Indoctrination. Mind control. Hallucination. I'm not joking.

I'll be earning almost as much as you, Dad.

Probably more, the way my sales are going.

Well then?

What if it was twice as much money? asked Jack Parry. Or, or … what about ten times as much? You'll see. You'll see.

You're a really poor role model, Dad. In fact, I believe you're a bad influence all round.

Thanks. So now it's only me. Only me who's holding out.

Holding out?

Only me not working. In that place.

You're pathetic, Dad, said the younger Parry, laughing too. You know that?

VII

Severin also told Parry about The Works.

My brother surfs up there. Round the outfall.

Why up there?

He surfs everywhere. But some good sets, he says. Like today. I'm going in now.

Sets?

Series of waves.

Dangerous, isn't it?

Nah. Well, depends. He's got conjunctivitis.

What's that?

Going blind, isn't he?

What?

Says he doesn't care. Says he'll be the only blind surfer.

Blind?

Kind of. All the surfers get it.

Dirty water?

Yeah. You don't surf but you swim. You could get the rash.

What rash?

What the surfers get.

Dai as well?

Dai and Fflinty. All the boys. Maybe Branwen. She surfs. She's good. Rashes and runs. My brother's got it on his legs.

He goes round the outfall?

Yeah. Says it's incredible, what comes out of the pipe. After dark, mostly. But my father tells him. When to go. When not.

Your father works there?

Yeah. Says when the best times are. The times to avoid.

Blind?

Fucking crazy, my brother. I'm going with him.

Parry paused.

I've seen you with that thing on your leg, he said.

You what?

That rope.

You mean the leash?

Suppose.

You attach the leash to the board.

Why?

So the board doesn't drift off. You are thick. Look, got to go.

Yes, hot, isn't it?

High pressure. Forecast all week.

56

And Severin continued down Cato Street in his American shorts. Parry remembered seeing surfers like him on TV. Sev's freckles were prominent and there were darker blotches on his shoulders. His hair was blonder than Parry had ever seen it. On his feet ruined canvas shoes. The boy was already deeply tanned. Even his toes.

Parry was left gazing at Sev's slender back. He realised it tapered like a candleflame. The image came to him like a thunderflash.

SIX

I

Six in the morning, Richard Parry caught a bus in Cato Street. He felt ill. Maybe that was how everyone felt at The Works.

But the swifts were screaming through the town, twenty, fifty, two hundred swifts. Black boomerangs over the terraces and gwlis of The Caib.

Here ragwort already stood in braziers. Bindweed hung its mattresses over walls and hedges.

After thirty minutes, the bus dropped its passengers at one of the canteens.

Hundred and Seventeen duty?

Think so, said Parry. But...

Fucking know so, said an older man in blue overalls.

Ignore him, said a young voice. You're with me, butt. Stick close.

Parry attached himself to this young man in ragged jeans. Whose enormous boots were bleached the colour of driftwood.

With others, they piled into a minibus. Familiar as he thought The Works was, this would be the first time he had travelled into its remoter fastnesses.

He already knew the plant was seven miles in extent. That was part of its legend. Also legendary was that it constituted a bigger town than The Caib.

The minibus sped off, crossing loco tracks. Somehow it missed what Parry thought certain collision with a small train, hauling fiery slag.

II

When his mother asked him that night what he had done to get so dirty, Parry said simply, 'carbon paper'.

This he discovered, was what constituted duty One Hundred and Seventeen. But he never again heard his job referred to like that.

One Hundred and Seventeen, he gradually learned, was part of The Works' mythology. One Hundred and Seventeen might have been One Million and Seventeen for all it mattered.

But work itself was divided into thousands of specialised separate activities. All were protected by demarcation.

You must have done something, his mother smiled.

What Richard Parry had done was to pull miles of carbon paper from green-lined computer print-outs used by The Works accounts department.

This paper was to be salvaged as a waste product. The carbon paper had to be incinerated.

There's miles of it, he told his mother. We're as black as this. Like coalminers, because of it. Miles and miles of carbon paper that we have to squash into something called the incinerator.

And no water for washing. Or drinking when you're parched. There's no tap anywhere. My throat's raw.

The carbon paper gang worked in a breezeblock garage. Maintenance might have once been done on Works vehicles there. Yet no one in the gang of six labourers remembered the premises ever being used.

Two of Parry's colleagues were, like him, starting their

careers that day. The first was the same age. Parry recognised him from primary school. The second, he learned, was called Bran, a mute young giant.

Blocks of print-outs were delivered from the computer department, located next door to accounts, three miles distant.

This occurred at ten every morning and at one in the afternoon. Otherwise, there were no visitors for the team. The carbon paper shift was supposed to commence at 7am.

Parry gradually realised they were in a part of The Works best described as abandoned.

Welcome to Hell, said Daf who had spoken to him first. Smoke?

There were three cavernous sheds. Each was divided into a honeycomb of workshops. Once devoted to vehicle repair, these were constructed on an area of subsiding tarmacadam, bigger than a football pitch.

Each shed was fifty yards long. They held vats of waste oil, carboys of acid in straw paliasses, and inspection pits. Some of these were flooded with filthy rainwater.

The work benches bristled with frozen vices, seized lathes and grease guns, oxy acetylene lances and spraypaint cartridges and nozzles. All were sheathed in rust.

Watch out for them, mumbled Daf. He had nodded towards a corner where glass bottles were stored.

The vitriols, he explained. Watch them vitriols.

Parry had never heard the word used before.

Daf saw he was looking puzzled, and explained.

Watch this, then, he said. If it teaches you something.

He wrapped a rag around his hand and took one of the vials. Then he unscrewed its milled glass stopper. It held an oily brown liquid. On to a heap of swarf in the corner Daf poured a thin stream. The mixture started to smoulder.

See! he said triumphantly. No one told me about this stuff. No one. Had to work it out for myself.

Yeah, myself. He looked toward Parry but his gaze was wide.

But I say, Daf continued, I say, that could burn straight through you. Could burn right through a man. If he didn't know, like. If he didn't know.

He cleared his throat, as if the liquid was releasing fumes.

Aqua Fortis, they call it. *Aqua*'s water. Just water. But water of death, I call it.

Parry looked at the smoke. Why? he asked. Why are they here? These … *vitriols*?

Daf shrugged. It was as if years ago, a full shift had departed for lunch and not returned. Some of their sodden magazines still lay on the benches. Hung on a wall, Parry noted a cap, an overcoat felted in green mould.

In another of the workshops, there were the torn remnants of glossy photographs. Parry stared, but could make no sense. Who were those people?

Girls? Possibly. But hardly men. Rather, monstrous, inarticulate shapes. He doubted they could be human.

Parry thought of an angling journal he had once seen. These had displayed conger eels, fanged, muscular. Immense torsos, wrenched from ancient wrecks. Now, when he touched one of the pages, it crumbled to dust.

There was no glass in the windows. Some were blocked with ivy trunks and purple buddleia.

Entrance to the sheds was permitted by sliding doors. Each of these had been deliberately run off its castors. A van had been driven into one of the entrances and set alight. Its four tyres were quivers of wreathwire.

The whole tarmac expanse was covered in tyres, engine parts, and pools of scummy petrol. There were gear wheels and flywheels on every surface, like iron-gilled fungi. Flanges and brackets. Unnameable parts.

On that first day, it seemed to Parry that he spent most of

his time coughing. It was scorching weather but a breeze blew in from the sea, disturbing dust from the sinter heaps. These had been spread over the beach and dunes.

The sinter had been flattened by the enormous tyres of the vehicles. When he looked around, Parry saw only a basalt-coloured desert.

In the weeks to come he found there were people who lived amongst the waste. Yet he never came close enough to learn about them. Parry was convinced some of the desert's inhabitants were foreigners. He had no idea from where.

What is this place? he asked Daf, the only person who had spoken to him on his first day.

This place? asked the boy in driftwood boots. He looked around with genuine surprise. As if he had never noticed it before. As if he was slowly realising where he was.

The Works, I suppose, he said, squinting. Then he said it again, as if for reassurance.

The Works.

After this, the boy closed his eyes against the sun's assault, its dazzle leaping off the oil-stained macadam.

He and Parry lay on the tarmac under a buddleia bush that had smashed through the tarry crust. Parry had never met anyone more at ease with himself than Daf. At least, as undemanding.

Now it was morning break. The two had come back from a visit to the incinerator, one hundred yards distant. They had carried panniers of crushed grey carbon paper on their backs. The salvaged paper he was told would be picked up when a lorryload was ready.

The incinerator was simply a metal cage. All Parry had to do was stuff the carbon paper inside and fire it with a match, or Daf's Rizla lighter. It burned to grey shreds, leaving a filthy ash.

Parry decided to try another tack.

What else will we have to do today? he asked.

This is it.

Burning carbon paper?

Mm.

These miles of carbon paper?

That's it.

Pulling rolls of carbon paper out of the print-outs and taking it for burning?

That is it.

Bit boring isn't it?

Daf opened his eyes.

No, he said. It's not boring. It's just work. But last week, last week was great. There was no carbon at all. No burning. No nothing.

What did you do?

I said. Nothing.

Nothing?

Yeah. Nothing. Played football. Went down the beach on Thursday and Friday. Wednesday, we just lay around. Remember that hot day? That was Wednesday. Hottest day of the summer it was.

Parry considered this. There was a tarn of melted polythene, ten yards by ten, in a dint of the fractured tarmac before him. It gleamed a noxious yellow in the sun. A seagull had disintegrated on the surface.

But today we got work?

Yeah. Plenty of work today. But quiet tomorrow. Guaranteed.

How do you know?

You can always tell.

But how can you tell?

You just can.

How long you had a job here?

Two years.

Parry considered this.

Fuck, he gradually heard himself saying. Daring himself. Allowing the word into his mouth.

Yeah, said the boy with driftwood boots.

Fuck.

SEVEN

I

When Parry woke his watch said 15:19. So much of his life was now dreamlike. Anything was possible. Everything impossible.

Parry realised he had been dreaming about a workshop he and his father had sometimes visited. It was owned by a man called Yonderley.

He didn't know how he came to be there. Or for how long he had sat against the sofa. But there was a watchmaker's lathe he needed to reassemble, gravers and collets, chucks and bits to clean. Each had its special place. Nothing else, nowhere else, could suffice...

The light in the room had been on. Someone had switched it off. The fog breathed against the glass. Nitric acid, he thought. In its oily cloud. *Aqua fortis* in the glass bottle. In his right hand was a bloody handkerchief. The blood was new.

II

Glan looked at Parry as he came out of the bathroom.

Just cleaning myself up, said the older man. I feel better now. Nothing like a swill in the bosh.

What's a bosh?

Oh, a sink, I suppose. But yes, restored.

Glan regarded him and looked away.

I better find Serene, he said.

Yes, restored, smiled Parry. Like a painting. And he gently cuffed Glan.

You know, I was talking to my best class in Adelaide not long before I came back. About restoration.

Oh yeah?

There was a painting I'd always remembered. Leonardo da Vinci's 'St Jerome'. Do you know it?

No.

Dates to about 1480. I think Leonardo was just under thirty. Not far off your age.

I'm twenty-three.

And he'd already done extraordinary things. By your age. Learned to think. Developed enormous curiosity.

Serene says you've got a shirt for me.

Oh, I do. Follow me, young man.

Parry led the way into his bedroom. Every surface was piled with clothes.

She said it was dusky pink.

Oh it's pink, all right. I can tell it suits you. But that painting had always fascinated me. Wonderful draughtsmanship, unusual angles, like most of Leonardo's work. What we have of it. But don't think I'm an expert. Because really I'm not…

You taught art, didn't you?

Sort of. But maybe a teacher doesn't know as much as people believe.

Oh, that's true, laughed Glan. My teachers knew nothing. Always down the pub, my teachers. Or getting things wrong, my teachers. Giving the wrong grades.

But I loved this painting, said Parry. Because it was

unfinished. Leonardo simply hadn't got round to finishing what he'd started. Maybe he was hoping one of his pupils would complete it. After instruction. That's the way they did things. In those days.

Lazy type, was he?

The very opposite, man. He'd gone on to other projects. Other disciplines. A thousand different all-consuming tasks.

Oh yes?

But St Jerome attracted me for that very reason.

That it was incomplete. The saint's right arm, and the lion in the picture, are unpainted. You see, he seems to be taking a thorn out of the lion's paw. Jerome's arm and all of the lion are drawn in. But not coloured.

Maybe he was on a break?

Leonardo didn't have breaks. Or dinner hours. But I've a print of that painting, that cartoon, as it's called. And I've studied that lion. Ah yes, what a lion. No lion in art had ever been so carefully proportioned. Maybe since the cave painters thousands of years ago.

You can see every aspect of that lion, and Jerome's arm too. But to me, it's as though it's a ghost lion. That lion is disappearing in front of our eyes. It's been disappearing since the painting was first discovered. Like Jerome is disappearing too.

Yeah, that shirt.

First his right arm. But the implication is, the rest of the saint will also vanish. A man becoming a ghost. Beside a ghostly lion. Cell by cell. Atom by atom, the man is disappearing. Like the lion has disappeared. And that's what happens, isn't it?

What happens?

To people. To all of us. It's what happens to everybody and everything. Atom by atom. Cell by cell. Till all that's left are our outlines. Which are made up of memories. And eventually, those memories disappear as well.

Glan scratched his stomach.

Pity old…

So most of the people you meet on Amazon Street are like that, said Parry. They're slowly vanishing. Right in front of your eyes.

Then it's a pity old Leonardo didn't invent the camera, isn't it? said Glan. Pity he didn't have a camera phone.

Have you one of those?

You bet.

Pricey, aren't they? Where d'you find the money?

Glan smiled at Parry. Saving up, see. Better try that shirt on, hadn't I? Dusky pink, Serene said. Well, why not?

III

The Clwb seemed surprisingly full. Dai Pretty was in, and Fflint, his hair slicked back, black beads on his shoulders. He must have walked from the brimming gutters of Senhora Street.

Parry ordered a bottle of red.

Don't tell me, he laughed. No decent malbec. So I hope the shiraz is okay.

Anything for you, said Nia. My best customer tonight.

Never tell any customer that, warned Mina.

In Goolwa we always suspected customers arrived by mistake, said Parry. Or by destiny.

So what did you sell out there in the Land of Oz? asked Fflint.

An experience, said Parry. What we described as a … *scene*. Anybody who had the guts to walk through our door was considered someone of immense discernment. Of cutting-edge taste. They acquired immediate respect.

Parry looked around. He had an audience.

That's right, he claimed. Sometimes we used to give away our stock. Free. Dylan bootleg of 'Precious Angel', taped in Sydney. Free. Battered translation of Rimbaud's *Illuminations*. No cover. Free. Anything like that. It had probably arrived in job lots, in garage sale surpluses. So was free to start with. We were simply redistributing culture that already belonged to people.

Christ, once a hippy ... laughed Fflint. And that's what you're hoping for? With Dirtfinger? Or Badbreath? Or whatever it's called?

Well, these are unpropitious times, Parry admitted. The new austerity take its toll. And that's why we're having this gig. This celebration. New Year's Eve. You're all invited. Been planning it for months. Haven't we, Nia?

Er ... no. You've mentioned it a few times. But nothing's definitely fixed... Is it?

Surprise party, said Parry. Kind of launch event. Giving the flyers out tomorrow. Just a few. Only a modest proposal. No, of course we don't expect many to turn up. But we'll be in the bar here, like old times. The stage is fine. What can go wrong?

Not been used for years, warned Nia doubtfully.

No big deal, said Parry. And you'll play? he asked Fflint. Gil's already agreed. Seemed keen. Was delighted someone's showing an interest. When was the last time you saw the old bastard? Drag him away from that bloody website of his.

I haven't played in public for years, spat Fflint. Are you mental?

Relax. It's spontaneous. Life should be spontaneous, my friends.

Spontaneous doesn't mean suicidal.

Just a couple of numbers.

No way.

I said relax. We're alive, said Parry. Remember what it used to be like?

Absolutely no chance.

IV

Parry was still talking.

Over in Oz, the shop was at one end of a long street. The busy end, if you can believe it. Okay, neither end was busy. But rents were rock bottom and we fitted in. For a while. For eighteen months we were famous.

The shop was called *Hey Bulldog*. That gave us irony, a British, imperial quality. An intriguing English tone. A crucial cachet. Unmistakeable as Gibson feedback through a Leslie speaker. For those who understood. For those who enjoyed the cool joke.

A girl called Lulu helped, first on weekends if I wasn't able to turn up. Then she was permanent. It just happened. I inherited her with the premises.

Quite a kid. Lulu was clever and talkative. I gave her some money I couldn't afford. She was interested in everything, poetry, where she came from. And me. With my peculiar accent.

Listen, I would tell her. We could be twins. Sand brother and sand sister.

I got two brothers already, she'd say.

Okay, I'd say. But The Caib, where I come from, is like this place. Sand hills and salt lagoons. Red sun in a black bayou.

What's a bayou?

Oh, that's a word I heard once in a song. I get lots of my words from songs.

My grandmother tells me songs, said Lulu. How about your

grandmother?

She died, Parry said. But she told me about cuckoospit and snakeberries. And rhubarb and itching powder.

You're crazy.

Getting there, Parry said.

My grandmother once told me about kingfisher nests, Lulu said. How they were made of bleached bones. You reached your arm in and there were the eggs. Hot white stones in a chamber at the very end. Sometimes snakes crept in too and stole the eggs.

Where's your grandmother now? Parry asked.

Adelaide. I'm going there soon. She lives near Gouger Street, walking up and down. Used to work on a stall in the market. Oh, I love that market. The fish wriggling around on the ice.

I love that market too, Parry said. See, I have this dream about Gouger Street market. To go there on Saturday morning for coffee.

And cinnamon doughnuts?

Or potato wedges and a bowl of soured cream. And then a bowl of chillied mayo. They make the best wedges in the world on Gouger Street.

But yes, I'd go there for coffee first thing, and work on my novel. Because I should be working on a novel. Writing about whatever comes to mind. Anything at all.

On Gouger Street! she laughed.

Yeah, great street. See the dusty lorries arriving with their apples in cardboard boxes. And all those Chinese vegetables, and those crispy ducks, and those lobsters with elastic bands around their claws. I love the smell of apples in cardboard boxes.

And me.

And I'd get on with my writing and not have to worry about *Hey Bulldog*. Just live in the market on Gouger Street.

71

Letting the city come to me. Then have another coffee.

On Gouger Street!

Wouldn't it be great?

But you live in Goolwa and Adelaide. Two places at once!

So no coffee allowed. And no wedges with sour cream. Because I have to teach the naughty children who don't do their homework. And then mark their exams and talk to their parents and keep the Art department happy. And drive on the expressway over the flattened snakes.

But if I had been a real writer, I know that Gouger Street market would have been the place for me. I'd just sit in a corner, at one of those old stained tables. Hiding away.

Some old Chinese man would be there too, the only other customer. And they'd keep the coffee coming.

V

They all sell out, said Fflint. Who hasn't? Who wouldn't?

Not everyone, said Parry.

Nia at the counter came closer.

Everyone who has the chance, hissed Fflint. And by now, that's everybody. Everybody's implicated. Everybody's doing it.

Not everyone, said Parry again.

Yeah, everyone sells out, said Fflint. So, don't drone on to me about the sainted sixties. They're all at it.

And if the bands are defunct or the singers are dead, then it's their wives or lovers. Or their children. Or their friends who were never part of it to start with.

Yeah, any tune they ripped off in the first place. Any photograph they can exploit. Anything that makes money. Anything that helps keep the putrid ghosts of their reputations alive.

No, not everyone, said Parry again. And he realised it sounded like an appeal.

And you, spat Fflint. *You*. Starting a shop called *Badfinger*. Of all the names you could have chosen, *Badfinger* stands out.

Why's that? asked Nia.

Why? said Fflint, Because of betrayed bands, *Badfinger* was the worst treated.

Two of the members hanged themselves, they were in such despair. Supposedly. That group sums it all up… The whole rotten world of rock and roll. A world of agents and managers and soul-dead middlemen.

And worse than that were the bands themselves. Jealousy at its most loathsome. Envy at its most blatant. A life made up of deadly resentments. Christ…I'm going for a piss.

What's eating him? asked Nia. All of a sudden.

Our friend Fflint knows what he's talking about, smirked Mina. Or likes to pretend he does.

Course. Fflint was in a band, wasn't he? asked Nia.

Yip. So know our history, girlie. And that's ancient history. They used to play in here, once upon a time. When it was called *The Paradise Club*.

Heard the name, said Nia. But that's before my era.

You got an era have you? laughed Mina.

You know what I mean.

Oh yes. We all have an era. Hard to believe, isn't it? For some of us? Enjoy it while it lasts, chicken.

In fact, there's a sign upstairs for The Paradise, said Nia slowly. And ledgers and dockets and rolls of posters and a little book with carbon paper. All gone mouldy damp.

They were quite a gang, smiled Mina. Your dad was one of them. With his friend, Gil. And who was their girl singer? Long red hair. Pre-Raphaelite bottle red, if you know what I mean. Quite striking. Nice personality. Couldn't sing of course. But

73

she looked the part in those miniskirts she used to wear. But they must have done a few things together before the band broke up.

Lizzy, said Parry. Her name was Lizzy.

And Fflint? asked Nia.

Guitarist, said Mina. Nothing flash, but steady. Held it all together. Chugga chugga man. Every band needed a chugga chugga man just to keep it rolling.

You talk as if…

Hey chicken, I haven't always worked in Basement Booze, said Mina. Don't think that. It used to be Paradise in here, remember. Just down the corridor. I feel the curls in my perm tighten at the very thought of it. Or maybe it's the ghost of the lacquer in my beehive.

Beehive? said Parry. Now that's before my day.

Used to call me the burning bush, laughed Mina. Yeah, I suppose it was a fire hazard. Gold it was. Tall and gold and stiff as candyfloss. I was fifteen and my friend Vanno would come over and we'd play records and…

Don't tell me, said Parry. Bit of Dusty…

Bit of Cilla, said Mina. We worshipped our Cilla then. 'Love of the Loved', God help us.

'Shy of Love' on the B side, said Parry.

Didn't play B sides, chicken. Beneath me. Anyway, we couldn't get the American groups round here for love or money. But as to that hairspray, we'd have to open the window. Otherwise we'd be choking. Gassing ourselves. Yes, The Paradise used to be a little bit special. Here and that place in Cato Street were the scenes…

What you come back for, anyway? asked Fflint, restored. He was staring at Parry.

You want to know?

We all want to know.

74

VI

Parry looked around. There was Nia, Mina, Fflint. Someone else stood at the end of the bar. A black dew shone on the shoulders of his anorak.

He sighed and poured himself another glass of red wine, proffering the bottle.

Parry smiled. People always wanted answers. To problems. To riddles. But above all, people wished for explanations. To the everyday mysteries. Explanations that would make sense of themselves.

I woke up one morning, he said.

In Australia, you mean? asked Nia.

Sssh, said Mina.

I woke up early. In the town of Goolwa, South Australia. Call it sixty miles outside the city of Adelaide. That city was where I worked in a high school, teaching art history. But it was Sunday. So…

So no sodding school, said Fflint. Hooray.

And no student courses. No student assignments. No plays or exhibitions to visit. No one to meet. No football, cricket, swimming, netball. No Aussie Rules, no athletics that I was supposed to oversee. No need even to open the strange little shop I ran, in Goolwa.

My bedroom was the back of the shop. Like a junkroom, really. Full of books and tapes and DVDs through an old green curtain.

And as the green sunlight poured through that morning, I remember thinking about nothing at all. Because everything was sorted out. There was no need to drive anywhere.

So, yeah, I remember lying in bed with that green light streaming through the window. Over my hairy legs. My hairy belly. All dark green.

Fateful day, looking back. It was seven o'clock, late for me.

I was usually gone by six. Would be in school at 7.15. And OK, as you've asked, I'll bloody tell you.

We're waiting, said Fflint.

There was a woman in my bed. She had never slept in that bed before. She never slept there again. Her name was Libby and she was a teacher at the same school in Adelaide.

Teachers, laughed Mina, looking serious.

I know teachers, said Nia.

Don't tell me, said Fflint. From the art department. It's all women's libby there.

Spot on, said Parry. Now, are you listening? Because I'm not saying this twice.

Listening, said Mina. Honestly. The man further down the bar had ordered another drink. The black mist on his sleeves was dull now. His coat was sodden.

Then I got up. Slowly. Bit of a heavy night, if I'm honest. I think Libby put on one of my sports shirts and went to the kitchen.

I could hear her in the next room. Said she'd make the tea and asked where the breakfast was. Fat chance. Usually I had porridge but there wasn't a crust in the house.

So, I dressed. Just tee shirt and shorts. It wasn't summer any more, but that's all it took. Warm enough compared with The Caib. I went into the kitchen and found a mug.

No comment, said Fflint.

And I must have said something to Libby. Something that took a few words. And she looked at me strangely. Asked why I was speaking as I did.

Speaking like what? I asked. But I noticed it too. Speaking with a slurred, drunken accent. When I wasn't drunk. Heavy night or not, I swear I wasn't drunk.

Yeah. Sunday morning coming down, said Fflint.

It turns out, children, said Parry, that I'd had a stroke.

Iesu, said Mina.

My God, said Nia.

Cut a long story short, I was in hospital for a week. Brain scan, heart scan, carotid investigation. The works. Had some time off and yes, could have returned to teaching. It was a real option. But thought better of it. So the school asked me to stay for three months. To find a replacement. Couldn't have been nicer. But that was it.

And Libby? asked Nia.

She had a shock. That's all. It's not as if I died on top of her.

Tut, said Mina.

But I have to say…

What? asked Fflint.

That Libby was the headmaster's wife.

Better and better, said Fflint. Like I said, those art teachers…

Two children of her own, said Parry. She was thirty, I suppose. Much younger than me. Much younger than the Head. Can't say I even…

What? asked Nia.

Even liked her I suppose.

Just enough to get her into bed though, said Mina. Poor cow. If she wasn't Australian, I'd feel sympathy.

I'm sorry for Libby, said Nia. She was risking everything for you.

For me? Yes, said Parry. I understand that. Now.

VII

Slim, always dark. That was Libby. Yes, Libby in black bondage trousers and black lipstick. Or, possibly aubergine. With her hair dyed black. And cut short in black feathers.

Libby, who imagined she was an artist. Who thought Parry

77

was funny. Or original. Or at least, novel. Parry the pom who drove in from the sticks somewhere. Way out near Lake Alexandrina. The bloke who hated sport and took her to the Chinese cafés in Gouger Street market. Who once bought her a Chinese dragon amulet carved from water buffalo bone.

Yeah, Libby. He'd left her as he found her. Undamaged and possibly untouched. A long respectable life ahead of her, as the headmaster cruised towards his pension, then bought the *Rough Guide to Western Europe*. For the tour he'd always planned. As her sons went to university and into business. Two boys who never thought about art. Who never dreamed of asking their mother about that cobwebby canvas rolled up in the attic. The pieces of her installations scattered around the garden.

Yes, he remembered waking. And Libby waking at the same time. She must have turned over because she asked him something.

What's that? Libby had wondered.

Parry had pulled himself up to look. There was a greasy plate on the bedside table, piled with oyster shells. An empty sauvignon bottle. Beside them was a pebble he had brought from The Caib. He'd had it for years, found on one of his expeditions around Caib Caves. A grey pebble with a white ball of quartz in its centre. Within the white quartz was a core of red quartz.

Parry had discovered it and his friend Severin had wanted it.

Like a red eye, Sev had insisted. Can I have the eye? Go on, I'll be your friend forever.

Parry had considered the request. The pebble fitted his fist. It felt exactly right, the heft of it. He licked the stone and tasted its salt. Then looked into the quartz, the white, the red. It was smooth after aeons in prehistoric seas.

Libby had picked up the pebble and balanced it in her palm.

The evil eye, she laughed. My God, don't tell me this has been looking at us all this time? At us in bed? It gives me the creeps, this thing. And it's hot? Why's that?

Coming to, Parry had shrugged. But on the day he had discovered it he had kept the pebble all the way home, Sev whining about friendship. Which wasn't Sev's style.

On one occasion Sev had complained so loudly, Parry had made ready to fling the stone into the sea. But he had held on.

The white quartz, the red quartz were, yes, Sev was right, like an eye. And the pebble was perfect in his palm. He resolved to keep it.

EIGHT

I

Parry walked into the fog. The air was salty and saturated. It was foolish to persist but he felt determined. In Goolwa he had dreamed of a fret such as this. Even more so on his expeditions out of Adelaide. In that red dust country of iron meteorites, the days were dry as ash.

Now he remembered a nearby cove, no more than an inlet. It was impassable terrain, a scattering of enormous rocks. He had often wondered how many thousands of years those stones had lain there.

The rocks were at the bottom of The Caib's highest cliff, as if tipped from the summit. Each boulder was the size of a room, the largest as big as a house.

Parry had always thought the crags looked cut from carding by a tailor's scissors. Impossibly shaped boulders in relief against the cliff.

Like flowers, he had once said to himself. As extraordinary as flowers could be. Ice-grey lilies, beneath a rind of salt. But here the lily petals were pearls of limestone.

Parry moved on through the mist. It tickled his eyebrows. He remembered his friends used to camp in that inlet, sharing flagons. Sometimes they lit driftwood fires that burned with iodine's green flame.

A loose gang of girls and boys, maybe ten in all. Vine was sometimes there, always with Sian. They had married early, the fools. Weren't they called *the invincibles*?

And Gil? Gil who was going to do great things. As they all were.

But usually there were only four or five in the group. From sixteen, Parry was one of those who stayed all night, sand-rashed and tipsy. Before a final plunge into the surf and the crawl home.

II

Often it was the girls who led the way. The girls Parry recalled, who smelled of vinegar, tasted of salt. Their hair stiff and black as wrack.

There was Lizzy with her sunglasses hooked on her bikini strap. And Branwen, a local Aphrodite, cuttle-white skin, floating in foam.

Yes, those all-nighters, he thought now. Talking coal strikes and the iniquity of scab hauliers on the motorway. Or whatever were the best tracks from 'Exile on Main Street'. The riff from 'Tumbling Dice' was still in his head. Its underwater throb.

Despite that, he'd hated the Stones. There was something calculating in their communal sneers, the band's indestructibility.

But what was the inlet called? Immediately, it came. As few other things did these days.

The Horns, that was it.

Going over The Horns tonight? was the question everyone asked.

But 'The Gods' was Parry's private name. And the moment now returned.

Yes, The Gods. Grey polygons, those boulders. Streaming

even at low tide in summer, surrounded by rock pools. The Gods of the Caib. If there were ever gods in that godless place, there they were. And still were, under the cliff. Hulking stone toads. Strange melted megaliths.

Or that's what Parry could remember thinking. The maze at the cliff's base was never free of shadow. There was a continuous settling of the limestone lagoons.

He remembered one occasion. He had scrambled down the cliff alone. To find no one else from the gang had appeared. And yet he decided to stay.

Far out, the surf was a silver stave. But no other swimmer was to be seen. Gradually Parry had become afraid. That time in the dark he had listened as intently as he had ever listened. As a kestrel listened. Looked and listened, poised above the darkening thrift. The hawk electric in its last stoop.

III

Summer-cold and uneasy, Parry had waited for whatever was out there. His belly was shrunken, the hairs on his nape erect as the eyelashes of anemones.

He had listened until he overheard the sighing of his own blood. And, yes, he was sure he had heard the boulders. Heard the boulders breathe. An endless exhalation that was not the distant tide or the wind that riffled the surface of the rock pools. The boulders breathing. As alive as he.

Such was the beach at night. And the beach was always a different world in darkness, a salt forest of groans and whispers. To the south was the surf's drone. But there was something else. Inaudible yet always present. The murmur of great engines cooling. Liquids returning to equilibrium.

He imagined the rock roaches on the cliffs around him.

Those sea lice were almost fragments of the stone themselves. Some lice were three inches long, armoured, alien, as they crept over the stone tablets. The girls hated them.

Down at The Horns, Parry had crouched in the starlight, amongst the phosphorus and fizzing lime. This was where the fossils were found. For Parry the fossils resembled pocket watches. Frosted jewellery, ghostly in the rock.

And again he overheard the boulders sigh as they settled. As the stones gasped in their sockets. On their immemorial plinths.

He remembered even then there were satellites crossing the sky. All that starry traffic, for those who cared to look. Dared to look. But when had Parry ever looked?

Years later, Lulu had looked. Yet it had not saved her.

Yes, Lulu, yes, he now heard his own voice. A man in the mist on the coastal path, muttering to himself.

One day, girl, they will name a star after you.

And he saw the child again, Lulu raising her forefinger to her lips. And then to the bloody pinprick of Mars. As if that dry world could explain her own. So Parry had stared into himself. And found nothing.

IV

Maybe near here, he thought.

One Saturday afternoon, he recalled, it was cold, dry. He had been walking with Severin at low tide. Gulls had been attracted to something in the water. The boys had gone over to explore.

Yes, Parry supposed. Possibly near here.

A net, about thirty yards long, had been washed up. Sev took one end and pulled. He succeeded only in raising the closest edge. The net, of green nylon mesh, rose and fell with each slack wave. Parry examined what was caught in its stave.

Durex.

Okay.

'Nother Durex.

Yeah, well…

Dead fish.

Spiny dogfish, said Sev. Big fucker. See the barb? Through the roof of the mouth. Through the excuse for a brain.

It's speckled, said Parry. Brown and cream.

Camouflage. But dogfish can glow in the dark.

Christ, it stinks, said Parry.

I can see the backbone, said Sev.

Look, said Parry. A crab. Inside the fish. Eating it.

Shore crab.

A crab eating a fish from the inside?

That's what crabs do.

Fuck me.

Found a sheep once, said Sev. Just a sack of crabs it was. All wriggling. You could see the belly move.

Double fuck me.

Ever heard crab music?

You what?

They whistle, do crabs.

Oh yeah.

Believe it.

Don't think so.

Choose a hot night. Come down here in the dark.

What's that? asked Parry.

Soft-bodied crab, said Sev. Bait for bass.

Tampon, said Parry.

Jamrag, spat Sev. My mum hides her jamrags all over the house.

My mum...

Don't wear no jamrags, laughed Sev.

'Nother Durex.

Yip.

'Nother Durex.

Some fucker got lucky.

'Nother dead fish.

Yeah. 'Nother dogfish.

Seaweed?

Dead man's rope.

What's that there?

Sinker, said Sev. Line still attached. You see sinkers on The Horns. Look, spider crab. The French eat spider crabs.

Gives me the creeps, said Parry. They're like...

Massive fucking spiders, said Sev.

And what's that? asked Parry.

Some kind of fucking abortion come down the sewer, said Severin.

Both boys spat.

What's that, then?

Sun tan lotion. *Ambre Solaire*. What's written on that box?

It's a sea chest, said Parry. No, it's an icebox. Says 'Fulton Street Fish Market'. Where's Fulton Street?

New York, said Sev. Seen one before. Currents, see.

Oh yeah?

Might take years, nodded Sev.

Tin of paint, said Parry.

Tributyl chloride. They paint hulls with that. Goes on silver. Seen my dad.

Got a boat, has he?

Loves it. Your dad?

Nah, said Parry. Not his thing, boats. Can't even swim, my dad. Hopeless, my dad. 'Nother fish.

Yeah, sunfish, said Sev. Little one, considering. They're rare. Looks deformed, that fucker. Like that thalidomide kid. Fucking mong of a fish. *Mola mola* they call them.

And what's that?

'Nother Durex.

No. That?

Oh yeah. Dunno. It's weird.

Jellyfish, said Sev. Big bastard.

Biggest I ever saw, said Parry.

Know another word for jellyfish? asked Severin.

Parry considered. No, he said, finally.

Sea cunt.

No.

S'true.

Ya lying jellyfish.

God's honour. Sea cunt.

Why?

You'll find out. Maybe. And maybe not.

Aerosol, said Parry.

That could be Japanese writing on it, said Sev.

'Nother fish.

Mullet, said Sev.

Sure, are you?

Yeah, sure. Ever seen a goat?

Course.

Mullets are like goats. Eat anything. Eat thorns, goats will. Eat stones, do goats.

What's that then? Pollution?

Mullet shit, said Sev. When there's a big shoal of mullet you get mullet shit. Stands to reason.

Durex. And another. Christ, there's hundreds.

From the outfall, said Sev.

How d'you know all this stuff? asked Parry.

How don't you know all this stuff?

Sev spat again into the water. It might have been the very moment that the tide remained constant. And then began to turn.

I was up The Tramlines last week, he said. Had a fire going. Good driftwood.

On your own?

Yeah. On my own. Maybe it was eight by then. And this bloke appears. Really quiet, he was. Wearing green, like a uniform.

One of those wardens?

Yeah. Careful, he says. Gotta be careful with fires, he says.

I know, I say. Why?

Beetles, he says. There's a rare species of beetle around here. It lives in the driftwood.

Oh, I said.

Yeah, he says. And that's the beetle's habitat you're burning.

Habitat? asked Parry.

Habitat, yeah. Straight after that, he was gone. Sloped off up the sand.

What you do?

What I did was chuck another log on the fucking fire. Burnt every fucking piece of driftwood around there.

Yeah?

Yeah. But beetles. What can you do?

V

Long ago, Parry had dreamed a plan. Yes, he would photograph each boulder. Show each rock as separate. Not a mass of stone, no, he would picture every boulder distinctly. Because The Gods of The Horns were unique.

He remembered his excitement. But for all the planning he had lavished on the idea, he had not taken the photographs.

What he recalled was the confusion of shapes at that cliff base. Yes, it was dangerous there, especially with the tide racing in, the spume flying. Each boulder possessed, it seemed to him, its own personality. Parry had always remembered that. And smiled to think of it, forty years later. The souls of stones, he said to himself. And such grotesque creations.

Yes, he should go back, take a camera and agonise over the shots. And, why not, display them in *Badfinger?* Local art? He owed it to himself. Show the features of the landscape here. The power of limestone…

Yes, something like bones, he thought now, those boulders. Impossible vertebrae, crudely hexagonal. Peculiar as people, The Gods of The Horns. Barnacled gods, veined with paler zigzag minerals. Inset with shells.

Because everywhere ran quartz in its seams. Quartz and calcite in mauve veins, in white capillaries. Yes, quartz, as white as milk. Quartz milk. Those were the stones he had once supposed might make his name.

VI

Perhaps Serene had been in the front room with him. But when he awoke, Parry was alone.

What a night. He had slept and dreamed, dreamed and slept. This happened frequently now. It wasn't that he felt tired. But he certainly yawned more often. Yeah, yawned, farted, belched.

But it was better since he'd stopped taking his tablets. And his body was changing naturally, he reckoned. Getting tired. Getting on. Remember, sport, I've never been this old before. The blessings of middle age.

But of course it was the fucking drugs, he next reasoned. I'm surprised I didn't rattle. All that muck I had to pour into myself. Twice a day. Somehow, it felt shameful. As if he should apologise. For being ill.

He had also been losing weight. This had become noticeable in Goolwa, and the loss had continued. Until Parry had decided to stop the medication.

Whatever you're taking, Mina had told him, I want some of it.

They seem to have found the right pills for me, he said. Takes time. At the start it's hit and miss.

Yes, he had shed a stone, maybe more. Say twenty pounds since the first trauma. This weight had fallen away without Parry trying to lose it. Not that he had ever been heavy. Also, his skin felt smoother.

Maybe the drugs can work, he murmured to no one. Putting endless tablets into yourself must mean something. But look at the possible side effects. Heart failure, kidney failure, epilepsy, impotence, death. No joke, they were all written down.

Nine months, it had been, he calculated. Without his tablets. Maybe a year. The weight loss had stopped. There was no other sign he was missing the drugs.

Parry found himself on the rug in front of his electric fire. His shins were raw. Yes, he had dreamed. He remembered waves booming at the mouths of caves. As if boulders were moving over the seabed.

He realised the sound was thunder and recalled the storms when the Australian drought had finally broken.

In this dream he had looked into the west and seen the first lightning. A vein bright as solder against a darkening sky. When the rain fell the first drops were hot. Then, immediately, he was drenched.

There was a pool near The Horns that locals called The Chasm. Edged with weed, its mouth was a green gouge. Parry knew some of the gang had explored it, but he had never dared.

He wasn't the best swimmer and the idea of The Chasm gave him claustrophobia. His friends said all he had to do was duck under the limestone lintel. Then he'd sense the pool widen.

It's wonderful, they teased. You can look up to the surface. The pool's a jagged green star. Like the entry point of a missile that exploded there.

But once was enough for Parry. The only time he had attempted to enter The Chasm, he had panicked and cut his brow on the overhang.

He felt his blood mix with the brine. Then seen its drops in the water. A dirty citrine, their dark infusion. He had lain with his head in Lizzy's crotch, as his friends attempted to staunch the flow.

But when he dreamed again he found he could descend effortlessly into the pool. Either he was smaller in this dream or somehow the entry was enlarged.

Above his head was the roof of water with its same spangled light. And there was Mina, sorting postcards. Glan too, with a glass of red wine, Glan with a bloodied head, Glan naked and white, a pulse beating in his neck as he and Parry danced over the pool's sandy floor.

Yes, the sand was red. And the water filled with creatures that Parry had glimpsed in the swollen Murray: snakes that could not flee the flood, parakeets that could. And there was Mina, calling Parry across the sand, to look at this bloody postcard.

Yes, Parry had told her. That tells the whole story. We have to send it quickly. Post the card before the last collection.

He knew his mother had looked for the postman in those days when he lived in Adelaide. Jack Parry had described his wife listening for the rattle of the letter box, the slither of letters across polished linoleum. In those days, not so long ago, the postman always arrived at the same time.

That postman had walked their part of The Caib for years. Parry himself knew the different walks by heart. He had been a volunteer postman when not serving shifts at The Works.

The toughest delivery started in George Street, then Mary Street, moved to Amazon Street, on to Nuestra Senhora del Carmen Street, and finished at the Gouger Street market. But how good of that postman to collect letters from The Chasm, where Parry now danced with Glan, his hands cupping the boy's hips.

Above their heads he noticed again the cave's entrance. Too narrow to permit their return to that other world. But why should they try to go back? Everything they needed was here in this water, with its slow, rusty seepage of blood.

VII

Hey, said Mina.

Hey, said Parry.

Who catches a falling knife?

They both seemed to be speaking underwater.

The woman's voice disturbed Parry. But, awaking in front of the fire, he found he was alone.

Who catches…?

Who…?

He remembered standing on the cliff, looking down on The Horns.

But that had been years ago.

He had been eighteen years of age.

A lifetime past.

Parry's wine glass stood before him, its violet grains of malbec dried by the fire. It might have been there years.

The room was dark. The only light came from the two-bar electric fire.

Hey, look at this, Mina had called.

Hey, look at this.

There might have been someone else in the room with Parry. Whoever it was had left only seconds previously. That someone had surely been whispering to him.

Yes, someone had kissed him. Someone had pushed their tongue into his ear.

Who catches…? he heard again.

Who catches…?

He could smell wet sand. Or the sea mist that hung in the streetlight outside *Badfinger*. Yes, he could smell the fret. Smell The Caib's lagoons. But something else. Something familiar.

Yes, I know how Amazon Street smells tonight, he told himself. And the gutters of The Ghetto. All the way to the Senhora Street garages. Where that boy was found after he'd hung for six months. Gnawed white. A rat's nest under his heart.

Parry inhaled. Maybe he smelled the mist in his own clothes. The black saturation of the night.

Some things could never make sense, he said to himself. His legs were hot, his shoulders cold.

A falling knife, he whispered to the empty room.

VIII

Whenever Parry recalled Lulu speaking, he knew her words were his words. Lulu spoke as Parry spoke. As did everyone he remembered. Libby, even his father, spoke as Parry did.

Quite the ventriloquist, aren't you? he accused himself. Such a clever bastard.

He heard Lulu's voice again and saw the girl in the green gloom of *Hey Bulldog*, blinking under the sunscreen. She was sorting postcards, hundreds of them, that Parry had once liberated in a job lot from Gouger Street market.

Might be something rare, he had promised.

She grimaced, but while she worked, Lulu talked about what made life worthwhile. One of the things was walking.

Don't laugh, she said. Walking builds your soul. Breath by breath. Everybody should know that.

She also mentioned the Pistol Star. Parry had to ask her what she meant.

The Pistol Star was discovered only a few years ago, she said. It might be the biggest star in the universe. At least in the Milky Way. And it's the biggest star until they find an even bigger star.

Maybe, she said, it's two hundred times larger than our sun. Which means it's on the very edge of existence.

Again, Parry had to ask her what she meant. And how she knew such things.

I go to the library and read *Astronomy Today*, laughed Lulu. It's no secret. So many things they're discovering now. Really.

And if the Pistol Star was any bigger, she said, it would … offend the natural laws. If it was bigger, then its gravity wouldn't … *work*. That means it would simply explode. Size counts. As far as stars are concerned.

And yes, Lulu said, I think about the Pistol Star before I go to sleep. Does that sound strange? Who cares? Just imagine its fiery surface. You know, it releases millions of times more energy than our sun.

Astronomy Today? smiled Parry.

Don't mock. Pick it up, schoolteacher. And you know what

I think? The girl grinned at Parry. She was missing a tooth. And he loved her for it.

What's great about people is I'll never see the Pistol Star. Never travel to the Pistol Star. Never go close to the Pistol Star. But I can … *imagine it.* I can imagine the Pistol Star like a cool blue eye in the universe. An acid lake. A lakebed of cobalt ash and toxic lavender. The Pistol Star just some old tarp with meths-coloured rainwater in a corner. And it's … *comforting.* When I'm in my bed, or even outside under a gum, my mind catches fire.

Parry thought about Lulu's bed in *Hey Bulldog.* Once she'd moved in properly she had made do with a corner chair covered with one of his coats. Sometimes she even slept in a tea chest in the shop, the records piled on the floor. The child had a genius for sleeping. All she needed was to curl up and she'd be snoring, wet breaths and low animal grunts.

Often there would be other people kipping in the shop. Writers and musicians usually, sleeping off a session. Probably he preferred the musos. Less self-absorbed. He remembered a white-haired poet wandering through at dawn, brandishing the shop's enamel quart-sized tea mug. In the other hand she clutched a knitted volume of haiku. Otherwise she was naked.

The whole building was primitive. There was no shower, so everyone bathed in the sink. The dunny was out back, in traditional style.

Remember what astronomers say, Lulu had continued. When the lights go out then the lights come on. I close my eyes and I can see what nobody else has seen. And never will imagine.

Like the blues of icebergs and the blue of wolf eyes. Are wolf eyes blue? They should be. Speedwell blue, the blue of those flowers that trail from the eyelets of an old man's boots. As he crosses the garden for the last time. That's your story, teacher!

94

Remember telling me?

Parry hugged himself in the mist. Lulu might have been standing in front of him. The child was suddenly real again.

A blue variable, they call that type of star, he heard her say. The Pistol Star, in the Pistol Nebula. So big, some people think it might be the centre of all things. There are all sorts of websites they say, celebrating that star. But other people, other clever people, know it's only a raindrop in the monsoon.

So there I am, said Lulu, balancing on the edge of sleep. In another corner of the universe, a lonely corner too. And I'm comforted by the blue deserts of an impossible world.

See, I'm lying there, listening to the solar wind from the Pistol Star. And all the other stars in that part of the sky. The dark stars, the pulsars. And it's stranger than strange. But still comforting.

How do you know these … *words*? asked Parry.

Lulu picked out a postcard and held it up. It was an image of the River Murray at Goolwa, with one of the old-time paddle steamers.

That star created a real fuss, she laughed, when the telescope people first discovered it. Like, it was the biggest object in the universe. And located where it was, in the centre of our own galaxy, people started to wonder.

You know what, schoolteacher? she asked with her gap-toothed smile, examining another card. Then rejecting it.

One day they'll name a planet after me. Or surely a star. But as there are billions of stars, that might apply to all of us. There'll even be a Parry star one day. Certain to be. So, a star for everyone. It's my new campaign. It's what we deserve. You'll see.

NINE

I

Coughing? said Jack Parry. That's the sulphur. That's the sulphur penetrating your mask.

I don't wear a mask, said Richard Parry.

Hear that, Mam? said Jack Parry. Hear that? No masks. Typical.

No one wears a mask, Dad. The very idea seemed ridiculous to the boy.

No. They don't care who they murder. Want to know why? Because there's always somebody willing to take their place. To fill the dead man's shoes.

So Jack Parry had told his son everything he knew about sulphur. When Parry thought about it now, years later, it wasn't his father's words he heard. The words were his own. But it was Jack Parry's voice that pronounced them.

You'll come home, said Jack Parry, and straightaway you'll need a bath. Your mother will say supper's ready, yellow cheese roasted on the coal fire. But you'll lock the bathroom door and pull the bolt. In your teenage shame.

You'll put the hot tap on full and the cold tap on full. You do this because your skin smells of brimstone. Then you'll lie in your own yellow pondwater, a scummy ring around the enamel, rubbing yourself with a loaf of black pumice.

You'll lick your own armpits and suck your own crotch. If

96

you can reach that far. You'll taste your own belly fluff. And you'll realise you stink. You stink like fartgas. Because this is poison I'm talking about. Sulphur is yellow. Sulphur is green-yellow poison. It's a roman candle, yellow as a sandhills moon. Sulphur dioxide and hydrogen sulphide and all the other sulphurs are invisible gases. But for you they should be the yellowest, the greeny-yellowest gases you can imagine.

So listen to me. Listen to Jack Parry for once. Listen to your fat old father who likes his yellow piecrust a little bit too much and the yellow jelly in that piecrust a little bit more.

Now, I don't know everything but this I do know. Sulphur will paint a coat of yellow distemper over you. From the inside. Sulphur will anoint your liver and infiltrate your dirtbox. Sulphur will foam in your spleen and overwhelm your tubes. From today, sulphur's already yellowing your blood. Sulphur's yellowing the cells of your lungs.

Yes, that's sulphur. A green-yellow mist like a fenland vapour. The yellow heart of the rotten tree. That'll be your breath. That's why you're coughing. Coughing up the fool's gold. That's why you'll be coughing the rest of your life. Clearing your throat through a volcanic winter. Yes, that's sulphur. A fret off the marsh. A fume, a fug, a fog. A veil on the bog. Green flowerwater in a graveside vase. A London peasouper. Fried noodles with yellow beanskins. Chrysanthemums killed in the frost. It's roses require sulphur, my son, not children.

Yes, with time, sulphur will rot your hair. Shakespeare never said sulphur is jealousy's colour, but it might be. Like sulphur is the ambergris of envy. How d'you like that for poetry, kiddo? Sulphur will tie its chokechain tighter and the tighter it pulls the louder you will cough. Hacking like a silicotic miner. And surely it will strangle you.

So when you smell its addled eggs up your arse and between your toes and under your fingernails, get used to it.

Because sulphur will be there forever. Then you will smell sulphur in your sweat and realise it's already too late. The pollen of dead flowers. In the yellow rain. The yellow rain falling on the asbestos roof of a ruined shithouse. Yes, that's sulphur. Smelling of money. Of banknotes that have been used over and over again. Which is what happens to money. Eventually it stinks.

Ever really sniffed at money? Properly breathed in the money perfume? There will be blood on the money and vomit on the money and shit on the money.

So, my son, read your books. Read all your books because your life might depend on those books. But if you still insist on working in that shed, then wear your mask.

II

Sometimes Parry was delegated to help out with digging and weeding. He didn't mind. The allotment comprised sandy soil, close to the dunes. It was light and well-drained limestone. Not arduous work.

What he enjoyed most was gathering produce. Especially the raspberry-picking duties. These were autumn raspberries and fruited in September.

The best-ever season Parry recalled was when kidney beans, French beans, and a troupe of sunflowers that had been sown beside the raspberries, appeared together.

That year, crops proved prodigious. There were courgettes, striped like jesters, and purple cobs with pantomime wigs. Every morning they found a glut of raspberries. Their gouts clung to the canes.

No eating, said his mother, noting the raspberry juice on Parry's school shirt. We're freezing these.

But as Jack Parry also had his mouth full, warnings could be ignored.

Greedy, Dora Parry shouted. Greedy men.

Parry remembered the morning light, burnished and metallic. But an iron colour had entered the bean leaves, although there remained plenty of petals.

The beans the Parrys favoured were called 'Cherokee', after the 'trail of tears'. Legend claimed these had saved the Cherokee nation from starvation.

The trail of tears furnished his father with predictable jokes.

I suppose it's down to the trail of tears this morning, he'd say. Any chance of a day off?

Or: back on the tearful trail tonight, I suppose. No wonder those Cherokees died out.

They didn't die out, Richard Parry would correct him. They went to Oklahoma.

Wish I could go to Oklahoma then, said Jack Parry. It's a great musical.

This was the garden at its best. But Parry enjoyed the winter too. Not that he had visited often in the cold. But he could recall one morning with his mother, a screed of frost over the limestone soil. And he had peered into a water barrel as his father always did. No bees, no green crickets. But gradually, in the depth of the plastic, he had discovered the embryo of ice that pulsed there. Like something mechanical. An engine's oily alternator. A battery awaiting recharge.

The school term was a month old but still the weather didn't break. Dora Parry was filling a colander with raspberries, while Jack Parry held a bus conductor's cashbag to collect the cherokees. It proved too small.

Take a shopping bag, for goodness sake, his wife had urged.

But as ever his father seemed less interested in picking than in counting the bees that clung to sunflower faces. Or rescuing bees from the water butts. Or pricking out sunflower seeds from their honeycombs.

This grove had already been called 'Sunflower Street' by Jack Parry. The son marvelled at the size of the blooms. He recalled transplanting self-seeded sunflowers in May and not giving them a thought.

Those stems had promised little. Yet many of the heads were now monstrous. As cumbersome as nylon backpacks, Parry considered, pleased with the image. Other sunflowers had branched, so that twenty, even fifty faces jostled above a single stalk.

Parry liked the corner of the allotment best where the beans had climbed over the sunflowers and canes. Three crops, tangled together. Poor husbandry, he imagined. But the results were spectacular. He could stand in the same position and pick three different fruits.

Blame your father, who else? Dora Parry had complained. I wish he was a better salesman than a gardener. But he's hopeless at both.

Eccentric might be a fairer description, said Jack Parry, peering up at a sunflower face. Now, eccentric I could bear. In fact, eccentric might be considered a compliment. I wouldn't mind being known as eccentric. Jack Parry the celebrated eccentric. Implies depth, does eccentricity.

Implies a lot of things, said his wife.

Implies intelligence, does eccentricity.

A sunflower's more intelligent than some, said Dora Parry.

Freezer's full, said Parry. Next-door freezer's full too. And that's the only other freezer in the street.

Not cold enough, they say next door, muttered Dora. And who sold it to them do you think?

Can you make raspberry-ripple ice cream? Parry asked his mother to head her off.

No. Your father'd eat it.

Go on, Jack Parry had said. Who could resist raspberry rabble? I mean ripple? How about some raspberry ripple for the raspberry rebels?

III

Parry remembered going over the rocks. The outcrops were covered in lichen.

Yellow as eggyolk, Parry had thought. A good sign too. Clean air. Despite The Works and its sulphur, the breeze was refreshing.

It was near here that Parry had found a lark's nest. It was cupped in a hoofprint, a little mattress of straw and samphire leaves.

There were three skylark eggs, and he remembered trying out the words. *Storm-coloured.* Yes, that was it. The scribbling on a skylark's egg. Exactly the colour of the rainclouds that hung over The Caib.

As a boy, Parry had collected eggs. But his heart hadn't been in it. Someone in school, maybe Sev, had once brought in a whole collection. Hawfinch, black redstart, the green china lantern of a mute swan, muddy from the bullrushes. The scarcer the better.

Yes, the rules of diminishing returns. Seductive even then. He could recall blowing a wren's egg, the smallest egg he had ever found. Its orange bubble hung against his lower lip and chin, grown to a glassblower's ball.

Larks had been common in those days. They tumbled out of the wind. Because it always blew on The Caib. The wind was forever restless. Until the fog arrived.

Wind'll put the caibosh on The Caib, just watch.

That's what his father said. And almost before his phone had time to ring, Parry had taken it from his pocket and switched it on. Getting ready. For the summons.

But there was no breeze today. The mist welled around the scarps, hung on the gorse.

As to skylarks, now they were scarce. Victims of thieves such as Parry and his friends.

Where were those boys now? he wondered. Ransacking the City, perhaps. Still taking what didn't belong to them. What could never belong.

Parry's phone rang. The yolk must have been addled in that egg, he thought. That wren's egg, gone bad.

He listened but did not say anything. There was no voice, but a rustling. As if something was being unwrapped. Something slowly and laboriously revealed. Maybe something precious. As, yes, it was.

Parry listened for a minute longer while the rustling continued. There was a life there. A presence at the end of the telephone. Maybe something insubstantial. A skylark, perhaps. He thought of a skylark's heart beating in his hand. The maze of hot capillaries. Or a lark's egg warm against the kiss of the egg thief. The lips of the snake.

Dad? Parry said. Dad, is that you?

The rustling continued. As if words were being unwrapped. As if at last the caller would be revealed.

Hey, Dad. It's me.

Jack Parry had been a salesman. His son had once worked out that he had driven a million miles in the last thirty years of his career. Although, 'career' might be the wrong word. Selling things was what Parry did. Or found himself doing. But yes, one million miles. Four times to the moon.

Not that Jack Parry had been a good driver. He was usually in the wrong gear. Especially on hills.

Yes, his father the professional driver, the commercial

102

salesman. His father on those endless local roads, the fernbanked lanes and the motorway when at last it was opened.

He remembered Jack's tuneless whistle in the dark of dawn. And the summer afternoon when it was good to be driving. A man, out and about. A man like Jack Parry.

Parry still marvelled at his father. Jack, he thought now, was a rakish name yet. Jack the Lad. Good old Jack. You had to expect something from a Jack. Dependable Jack? Loyal Jack? Possibly untrustworthy Jack. The son smiled at the thought.

Yet when Parry considered his father, it was the dust he left behind him, the summer slipstream that the boy loved, the rush of that early car they had owned. In its British racing green.

Or his father's sweat on the steering wheel, the black polished arc before him, on the Hillman Hawk, the Humber Hawk. And then the cheaper Fords, the old green Austin, as business became difficult. As competition increased. As the roads filled with other salesmen. With men stronger than his father. With men more ruthless. With better drivers. With men who could sell anything.

And always the car radio playing. First days of Radio One, and before that 'Whistle While You Work'. How Jack Parry had despised the jaunty songs written specially for the proletariat. To keep them happy, he said. At their toil.

Once Jack Parry had pointed to a hayfield.

I used to ride on a gambo, he said. That was real haymaking. Over on Morfa Field, the whole village came out together.

Yes, working together. We drank lemonade flavoured with fennel. My mother made it. That, or stone ginger. Blades of grass prickling your neck. Sunburn and nettlerash everywhere. Rats in the grass. Hares too.

The radio stayed on, despite the dismal soundtrack. Window down, Jack Parry's right elbow rested on the rubber frame.

Sometimes it was coffee machines that Parry sold. Occasionally it had been portable Scheidigger typewriters. With cutprice typing courses for housewives.

Before that it had been slimming powders. Then paperback books.

Easy come, easy go was Jack Parry's attitude. Some things worked. Others were duds. Blow-up globes was another line. Once there had been encyclopaedias. Then ice boxes. Packets of mustard and cress.

What Parry remembered was his father's weight increasing. Chocolates, choc ices, ham sandwiches with pink ham, naked as a nestling's throat. It all became Jack's comfort food.

Yes, raw ham and buttery hanks of an uncut loaf, made up breakfast, lunch, tea.

It was all one intermittent mealtime. Washed down with Coca Cola. That's what the boy could never understand. His father's insatiable thirst for Coke.

It's horrible, he always said.

Yes, agreed Jack. Gripewater for grown-ups.

Then why drink it?

You're right, laughed the father. It only makes me piss.

Then why?

Piss like a panther.

What?

Or piss like a porcupine.

And Parry would collapse in laughter. Then wait in the car while Jack went behind a hedge.

IV

Slowly, in the driver's seat, the cushion collapsed. And Parry it was, along for the ride, who occupied the front passenger seat. At Whitsun, at August.

The boy rarely talked, allowing his father to drive. Glad to be with his old man. The pair together.

In summer, his father's window was rolled down. There was a smell of gorse in the air. A tang of petrol.

And how often were they together at night, passing The Works like some blitzed city? Both of them silent. As if in awe. Whilst the miles of fire went by on the plain.

This was The Works that had been built where the dunes once rose. Where the plover pools had stretched, green as battery acid. The Works that now employed everyone.

Everyone included the losers, the wasters, the no-hopers. Everyone who had given up. Everyone who wanted to collect a pension. Everyone except Jack Parry.

Why don't you work down there? Parry had once asked his father. He was afraid to use the giveaway words: The Works.

Down there? asked Parry. Also avoiding the word. With everybody else, you mean?

Yes.

Would you like me to?

The boy pondered.

Dunno.

Go on, say. Tell me.

Well...

Good money, said Jack Parry. Or better money than now.

Then why? Don't you?

Perhaps I will.

Parry had looked at the flares from the chimneys. Yellow and silver, the flames. Ninety-five chimneys he had once counted. Now the fires were reflected on his father's face. A ghostly brightness, blue-silver, yellow-silver. Like the foil wrapping of the chocolate biscuits Jack Parry had discarded and which lay at his son's feet.

Ninety-five flags of fire. Ninety-five separate blazes that called the workers across the mountains, the sandblown plain.

Yeah. Perhaps I will, said Jack Parry.

Really good money, said his son. And laughed.

Jack Parry laughed too.

Yes, perhaps I will.

And then Jack laughed louder.

And perhaps I won't. Yeah. Perhaps I bloody won't.

Parry loved it when his father swore.

That's it, Parry sniggered. Perhaps you bloody won't.

Because I don't want to be like all the other fuckers.

Parry choked.

Because you don't want to be like all the other fuckers?

No, I don't want to be like all the other fuckers.

And they had made up a song. On the spot. An industrial blues.

It's called, said Jack Parry, 'Why we don't want to be like all the other fuckers'. And they had sung it while The Works smouldered before them. Streetlamps revealed the sulphuric squall that lay over the town.

But the town itself was invisible. A spectral citadel. Yes, The Citadel. Which is what Parry had began to call The Works in his teenage years.

About this time, Richard Parry remembered asking his father why he didn't play the guitar. Or any musical instruments. The response was predictable.

Well I'm good at comb and paper, Jack had said.

No. A proper instrument.

Once tried the ukulele.

No. Proper.

Uke's proper.

You know.

Used to fancy the bassoon.

No, no.

Bassoon's a proper instrument.

Why not the guitar?

Bassoon's classical. There are bassoon concertos in the classical repertoire.

Why do you have to turn everything into a…

What? asked Jack.

Nothing.

No. Say.

A joke.

Do I?

Yes, said Parry. Always. Always

Oh, dear, said Jack. Sorry.

You always, always do.

Oh. Double dear.

And why, asked his son, warming to the subject, both laughing and crying now, why didn't you teach me the guitar?

Jack Parry looked abashed.

Or the piano. Or the, or the … the fucking ukulele?

And they had both broken into laughter then. Snorts and aching guffaws. The son louder than the father.

Yeah, sorry, spluttered Jack Parry. We failed you there good and proper. Bad parents, aren't we. You could have been the new George Formby.

Who? screamed Parry. Who the fuck's George Forty?

And they had collapsed again.

Who the…? Who the fuck is who? asked Jack Parry, wiping his tears away.

George somebody, you said, spluttered his son. George the fucking Third.

And obviously ruined your life?

But why?

Your miserable fucking life.

Why not?

Why not what?

Why not teach me. Why didn't you teach me to play?

Yeah, good question, said Jack Parry when he had recovered.

Because, everyone…

Because everyone plays nowadays. Is that what you mean?

Yes. Everyone. Plays nowadays.

I don't, said Jack Parry.

No. You don't.

I definitely don't.

But it's only you.

I'm the last one, said Jack Parry.

And me, said the son. I'm just like you.

Like me? You're like me?

Yeah. Like you.

God help you, then, said the father. Like me? There's nobody like me. Is there?

Only me, said Richard Parry.

Oh no. Not you.

Yes. Me.

Well, said Jack Parry, putting another ham sandwich into his mouth, taking a draught of the foaming Coke.

Could be worse.

No it couldn't.

Yes it could.

No it couldn't. Couldn't possibly be worse…

A guitar? You're sure.

Yes, said Parry. A guitar.

I could have sold guitar strings instead of typewriter lessons. Sold guitar lessons.

But you don't. Do you?

Look, I'll buy you a guitar. Like everybody else, I'll buy you a guitar. In fact, I'll buy everyone a guitar.

Don't want a guitar, said the son.

Now you don't want a guitar.

No.

First you want a guitar. Then you don't want a guitar. What do you fucking want then?

His son had choked again.

A fucking ukulele, he at last managed to say.

And they had dissolved for the last time.

V

But while Jack continued to sing their blues, his son grew quiet.

Parry looked about him at the other cars. He saw redbrick terraces, back-street foundries, tyre depots, Chinese chipshops. And everywhere the barbed wire that hung above the walls of The Works.

He wondered whether he would spend his life there. Or celebrate his escape from that future waiting for the children of the plain.

In fact, 'Citadel' was a word Parry loved. It was the title of a song by the Rolling Stones.

Parry had once enjoyed that song. But only because it featured his favourite musician, Nicky Hopkins, who had played on the recording.

Yes, that Nicky Hopkins, Parry would smile at anyone he thought was listening. A genius. Yes, a session genius. But always in the background, as the classic sessionman must be.

Parry would explain this in his sitting room above *Badfinger,* in the shop itself, or The Paradise when ordering a bottle of red.

Nicky Hopkins? Parry would announce. What a musician. Could play all day. All night. But someone who never received his dues.

Then, poor bastard, he has Crohn's Disease. I'd say he was dead by fifty. Surely no more. And by then, he was alienated. Had a bellyful, if you pardon the expression. So he hated the industry.

You know, Parry would say, if he had drunk enough, I was going to write Nicky's biography. Got the title, the only title possible. 'Sideman'. Like it? Yes, 'Sideman'. Says it all.

And, remember this, Nicky Hopkins even played with The Easybeats. We had a poster of him in *Hey Bulldog* back in Oz. People used to ask who it was, this young man with muttonchop whiskers. Just a kid. Spare as a sparrow. Always bent over a white piano.

That Dutch couple who ran the Goolwa Motel? They thought Nicky Hopkins was wonderful. Understood about good and bad luck, see. Classic yin and yang. Yes, they'd say. Nicky, Nicky, poor Nicky. He wasn't famous enough. Yet maybe he was too famous.

Remember, he was the pianist on 'She's a Rainbow'. And that's enough for some people. His role amongst the immortals is guaranteed by performing on that single track. Despite the harmonies.

Yeah, Little Nicky. With his dodgy guts. Being a genius and making it seem easy. Not everyone could forgive him that.

And Lulu? She loved Nicky as well. And if Lulu loved you, that was good enough for me.

Her eyes on the stars. Beautiful-looking boy, she thought he was. With great hair. Remember, he played the harpsichord on 'Citadel'. Brian Jones was on that track too. Another angelic bastard. Brian played the mellotron. One of the first rock musicians ever to try that instrument.

Yes, poor Brian. Brian and Nicky, carrying their own doom. That pair, cursed by their own black magic. Gave their best away too easily. Not ruthless enough. Or perhaps too ruthless. Who's to say after all these years?

They weren't the inheritors, you see. Not the true inheritors. But we know the ones who cleaned up, don't we? The ones who kept their ears open. And are doing it still. That doesn't take much guessing.

Listen. Nicky Hopkins played on 'Imagine'. And thirteen different albums by the Stones. Thirteen! That's more than Brian. The Stones thought he was the business.

Keith kept making the call. And Nicky kept answering. Got him playing on 'Citadel', adding all sorts of colour. That was Nicky, see. Colouring the tone. Enriching it. Adding crimson where there was only the idea of red. Experimenting with scarlet. With cadmium red. Black keys and the white keys reversed. Remember they used to do that to harpsichords.

And the sound like gemstones. Or a fringe of firelight. Think of making a sound like that. Creating music like that. And that was why people like Keith Richards wanted his number.

VI

When Parry's phone rang there was no one there.

Hey, Dad, I know it's you, said Parry. Look, I'm coming round soon. I promise, Dad. I'm coming. Soon.

TEN

I

All those brassy trumpets, said Parry. The flowers were insane. But it was the heat that ruined it for me. Or made it too difficult. I was used to a sky the colour of oyster shells. But Adelaide was blue, accusing. The mirages in suburbia trembled like cellophane.

And Goolwa grew heavier as the river dried up. Soon the town was hot as a foundry. Even the tropical flowers were unbearable. Yes, brassy trumpets. All that molten growth.

One evening I went with Lulu down to the river and she told me what I'd see.

Quiet a moment, she said. Be quiet just an itsy bitsy moment.

Good advice. I'd been telling her it was impossible to keep *Hey Bulldog* running. I thought of the dust on the window. The red dust on the counter.

It was all costing money, though not what the shop is setting me back here on The Caib. Yet it was a drain on my time. My precious time. But above all, it meant too many people were unhappy with me. That I was displeasing them.

And no, I didn't like that. Can't stand disappointing people. If you're an adult, you have to learn the dangers of upsetting others. How much you can get away with. How long you might dare.

Maybe I was tired. But I was asking questions that were unnecessary. Like, what was the point in it all? The point in keeping a junkshop open on a quiet street. In a one horse town. The point in building, no, creating a 'scene'.

When anyone who cared had left for Adelaide, and was wearing mad mascara. And drinking cappuchinos on Gouger Street. Or talking about bloody Blur. Or even 'Seventy One Fragments in a Chronology of Chance'. Imagine that on The Caib.

Yes, the real city. Not a back garden with tea candles and jacaranda blossom. Where 'Wonderful Land' was played till the vinyl was white. Yeah, a wonderful land under the baffling constellations. Wonderful even with the red ants, the black ants. Like something Lulu's dad might have done. If Lulu had a dad.

II

Parry continued talking.

Now, said Lulu. Here they come. Right on time. For you.

It was almost dark. Maybe it was midnight, I can't remember. The night was full of green music, the river whispering, the current sliding by, thicker than oil. Thicker than blood.

Those Goolwa nights, when we ventured out, were always filled with mysterious sounds. With dangerous aromas.

Once I'd seen two camels in the paddock behind the barrage. The field rubbed bald. Not a blade of grass remaining. Just two camels, snoring on the red rubber racetrack where the athletes trained. And I had to remind myself, yeah, this is Oz. Summer in Oz. Where else?

All evening I'd seen dragonflies on the splintered waters of the Murray. Green dragonflies circling the flood, crawling over the dried pools. Those pools with bleached punky crusts. Green dragonflies, maybe a foot long. Even longer. Yes, definitely longer. Dragonflies uglier than iguanas. Dragonflies whose wings crackled and droned like something electric left on overnight.

To look at them, it was as if their bodies were made of glass. Or beads, or emeralds. Amethyst engines, Indian ornaments. Yes, glass beads held together by green cotton pulleys. Greener than jewellery boxes pricked out in green lacquer.

Green was the devil's colour in medieval times. All art students are taught that. On The Caib, the green woodpecker is the devil's bird. Because of its mad laugh.

And those dragonflies looked devilish. Think of the television wars. Army uniforms with their green stars. Those flags sewn full of green stars.

Yes, the dragonfly bodies rustled in the green darkness under the willow leaves. Below the gum trees with their peeling bark.

And every tree was wilting in the stagnant air. Because the air itself felt as if it was vanishing. And the camels snoring. The camels whimpering in their dreams. Imagine camel dreams.

Then imagine the air trembling with all of the nameless creatures that crept down to drink in the shrinking pools. All those animals sharing the atrocity of thirst. Creatures whose names I was afraid to ask.

Lulu laughed and told me to watch for snakes. She hissed her warning. Hissed and that's all I could hear, Lulu hissing, hissing, where the black water joined the black earth. Those disappearing pools black as tarsand.

Then Lulu touched my arm. I'll never forget that touch. She stroked me as a mother might stroke her child. As a lover might. But natural and innocent.

And rising out of the dust we disturbed I could see moths. Bright as tournament flags, those moths. Yet moths as pale as the inside pockets of best clothes. Clothes never worn.

And the Murray waters were suddenly deep at our feet.

Green as baize, those waters. Green as shantung silk.

Then I saw the dragonfly hawks. Suddenly the hawks were there and out of nowhere they were feasting on the dragonflies. Sucking the dragonflies' green blood. Crunching the dragonflies' bodies like prawn crackers, the dragonflies' green bones splintering in the hawks' mechanical mouths. Until those bodies were like some Thai green curry paste.

Yes, when those hawks passed over us they were so close I could sense their wings beating. Sense the green gossamer of the hawk feathers.

I asked Lulu if there were any alligators and she laughed.

Other end of the country, she said. The rainy end. Good job you don't teach geography.

There was a full moon in Goolwa that midnight. And I could see the full moon's milk, its membrane on the Murray. That moonskin on the mirrors of the dying river pools.

Those pools were where the children always swam. That was where I watched Lulu shimmy out of her underwear and slip into the current, the riverwater warmer than bloodheat as she held her arms above her head. Such skinny arms.

Then Lulu was naked. Her breasts were unbroken buds. Buds never to burst. Boyish Lulu, red as Goolwa honey. Red as the hibiscus honey I once bought from that Dutch couple.

Yes, a rich river, the Murray. Delirious with drought. Dangerous with drought.

But the earth was dry. There was barely a skillet of dew to be boiled where the midnight dragons crawled in their cannibal carnival. And lay in ruin on the water.

III

Yeah, Lulu was quite a kid, said Parry.

Look, I didn't have time for the shop. Teaching had to come first. But for a while, for a wild eighteen months, it worked.

And *Hey Bulldog* built a reputation for having let's say, intriguing stock. Postcards, posters, paperbacks. And events, always events. Launches and little festivals.

Okay, there was nothing coherent in what we sold. But endless fascination. There'd be piled up magazines from Australian poets, old tapes, art books. Anything vaguely alternative. Or self-improving.

Yes, including yoga. Sorry, not my idea. Some religious stuff got mixed in with it all. With the environmentalism and the more metaphysical material. Again, not my plan, But a garage sale for the soul, all right. A carboot jamboree.

You see, said Parry, I still believe in self-improvement.

In that I might conceivably somehow get better.

That's the giveaway morality that explains everything I've done. The clue to *Hey Bulldog* that was, and the clue to *Badfinger* which is starting out. My last wager. No doubting how it will end.

How did it end at *Hey Bulldog?* asked Mina.

Badly. Like all premature endings. Frankly, I couldn't keep up the pace. There was the job, which was more than enough. On top of that was the deadly commute. It was sixty miles into Adelaide, and I'd hit the road at 6.30am.

You know what I recall on that journey? Fields of sunflowers the farmers planted.

Then one day I was driving through those sunflowers. And I realised they were dying. The landowner must have sprayed them with poison. Perhaps so the sunflowers died at the same time. Sunflowers with faces bigger than television satellite dishes.

I stopped my car in the middle of the sunflower field. And the sunflowers went on for miles. Tell the truth, I was surprised they planted sunflowers. Don't they take all the water from the soil? Their rootballs are like huge fists.

You know, sunflower leaves are sharp. Rough and sharp like an old man's skin. No, rougher than that. Because an old man has gentle skin. Tender skin, like old stained satin.

But these sunflowers were dying together. There must have been a million sunflowers. Every sunflower face was green and black and swollen with seed. And every seed sharp in its satchel. All I could do was stare at those sunflowers stretching as far as the surf.

It felt as if I was the only driver on the road. The single commuter. What a fool I was. The solitary driver on that brand new autobahn they'd carved through the bush. And the roadkill was black as the sun came up over the concrete. Watersnakes coiled like lilyroots, dying in agony. Maybe they'd poisoned the snakes as well.

And it dawned on me what I'd done. The enormity of it all. On a rise I pulled over in the middle of the black sunflowers. And I could see the ocean far away. Its line blue as surgical stitching.

But God help me, it was the Antarctic Ocean. I was suddenly terrified. What was I doing there? And, yes, there were all these snakes around. But not another human being. Not a solitary soul. Never saw a muldjewangk, either.

What's that? asked Mina

A mudgy? Water monster. Comes crawling out of the lake. Lulu told me about it. Abo legend. Same as the stories here on The Caib. Yeah, the desperate mythologies of beaten people. Then marking, marking, the usual schoolteachering malarkey.

You see, the school was taking a risk with me. They liked the idea of somebody British, even though by then I was determined to do my own thing.

Yes, I wanted to write. What a surprise. It's the usual

schoolteacher's curse. As if there aren't enough poems nobody reads.

But no, not music. Something solid like a novel. I'm no good at music. Never learned a note. And that's been the problem all along.

But what about my own painting? Sometimes Lulu and I would go behind the Murray barrage. The sun would lie like oils on the water, and I'd think, yes, yes. Get the canvas or the cardboard. Or just strips of bloody melamine. But I'd never have the guts.

And I know what you're going to say. I should have painted the sunflowers. That field of black sunflowers. The sunflowers that were poisoned. Or whatever it is they do that's fatal to sunflowers in Australia.

And no, I'm not apologising. But this was at the beginning of the internet, so you can imagine the excitement of the scene.

Before everyone became a blogger. Before the arrival of those madmen with their million word blogs. Who only make life boring. Like it already was.

Because, you have to understand, every small town has to have a freaky shop like *Hey Bulldog*. Just to make small town life bearable.

We had a counter, two or three tables for coffees, our CD racks. And piles of crap. Heaps of it. Magazines and pamphlets, the usual stuff. Really, there was nothing more to it.

Apart from some posters of The Easybeats and Kafka, *Hey Bulldog* was just an address in the back of beyond. A nest of bleached bones down a tunnel in the riverbank.

It wasn't the outback, no way. Yet it was fairly remote. Buses took a while. But the roads were wide and public transport pretty good, I'll say that for the Aussies. The trams in Adelaide were a joy.

Next door to *Hey Bulldog* was the Goolwa Central Motel, so we had a bar nearby. Kept by a Dutch couple. Good people, who understood what we were bothering about. Grasped that you had to share the madness.

They were refugees from Amsterdam so knew everything about insanity. And, that's all we had to do. Link The Easybeats with Kafka. Made for each other, weren't they? Then depend on the culture and a normal human appetite to do the rest.

Yes, there were some good people about. I'll always remember the mango man. He drove a pickup, and, yeah, it was packed with mangoes.

He carved those mangoes into flower shapes, then skewered them. His wife took the money, two dollars a mango, I think, and then she spread the fruit with relishes. Good business, it seemed. The couple hung around for three months. With an endless supply of mangoes. Until one day they disappeared.

We knew the fruit wasn't local. And the way that man used the machete, indicated foreign skill. He looked Greek. Maybe Lebanese.

Most days I would buy Lulu a mango flower and watch her devour that fruit, mango juice on her throat and fingers. Those mango petals yellow as buttercups.

IV

Yes, the appetite. Look, I'm not pretending it was the sixties. This was not so long ago, for Christ's sake. Trailblazers we were not. You might say I'd woken up late. Mad Max with a hangover. And the house already on fire.

I was an art teacher pretending I knew about nineteenth-century British painters who sailed off to Adelaide.

But the shop was still real. And the town needed it. We

allowed people to breathe. As we're trying to do on The Caib.

Just finding out if people still know how. To breathe, that is. If there are people left who still need their lungs. It's not certain, you know. Maybe we've lost that capacity. Maybe the species is changing.

Goolwa means 'elbow' in the local language. Lulu told me that. It's a place at the mouth of the Murray, one of the biggest rivers in the country. Down in the south. Deep south. Think of New Orleans without *mardi gras*. Think of The Caib but facing Antarctica.

Yes, we're talking about remoteness here. About the soul's isolation. What do you think it does to the soul to know the next country is unexplored and uninhabited? That the next country isn't really a country with history and culture. That it's an unpenetrated frozen desert. Or that your own country is only badlands and spinifex. That's thornbushes. Hundreds of miles of thornbushes.

Some people can cope with that. Others go crazy. In the front of *Hey Bulldog* was a rickety porch. In the back was a garden with quondong trees.

Those are wild peaches that the native people used to eat. Wormy and stringy, I always thought. But we had solar lights and lit tea candles and played music until there was nobody left to listen.

I remember Bach's *Goldberg Variations* at three in the morning. Lulu was curled up like a kitten in the indigo dust. Lightning in the sky and the CD on repeat play.

But there was nothing worthy about *Hey Bulldog*. What I recall playing most in the back yard was 'Wonderful Land'. As a tribute to where I found myself. This enormous country, where every river was hundreds of miles long, every patch of countryside a lethal wilderness. Where nothing had familiar names.

But out in the garden, as if I wasn't tired enough, those foreign stars would still be puzzling me. Somewhere above the candlelight.

Lulu had told me the names of the constellations. But Australian stars were like Australian bands. Or Australian writers. Somehow not important. Or just too different. Or maybe important but in a different way.

Around Goolwa there were islands. Kangaroo Island and Granite Island. Then the ocean, then the Antarctic icefields. Their unimaginable cold.

So *Hey Bulldog* made a difference for thinking people there. A difference for people who somehow felt left behind. Somehow abandoned. Somehow betrayed. It proved they weren't alone and forgotten. That there were others who shared their madnesses.

Yeah, that's what *Hey Bulldog* did. It shared the madness. The madnesses of composers and painters, and insisted in its temporary way, that the public try some of this weird stuff.

That it could be good for them. Might be a necessary medicine. If you were brave enough. To try it. For all that ailed you. For any gutrot. For any worldwarp. For any soulache. For the migraine where your soul should be.

I used to walk out in the evenings after *Hey Bulldog* closed. Well, after I'd locked up. Then I'd ask Lulu to tell me about the planets and stars. But first, it was the birds.

What's making that song, I'd ask? Because one particular bird had two voices. So, two personalities. As if it was a choir of birds. What's making that song? And why is it singing in the darkness?

And she'd laugh. You mean the magpie lark?

Yes, that must be it, I'd say. One bird with two names. And two songs.

And I'd listen to this music that the magpie lark would

create. This black and white bird that hid itself in the river willows. In the Murray while the torrent still flowed, even though the drought had set in. Common enough, I suppose. But not a lark. And not a magpie. Yet both. A sound like a waterwheel lapping the current.

Yes, the magpie lark. If ever Australia had typical music for me, it was that bird.

Sometimes I catch myself listening for it on The Caib. And have to remember that's it all over for me in Goolwa. And I'm never going back. That I'll never hear the magpie lark again.

Woman, was it? Girlfriend like Libby? Not that little Lulu?

What do you mean? asked Parry.

The reason you left Australia? laughed Mina.

In a way. Maybe.

V

But let me tell you about Lulu. We'd go as far as the lagoon. In summer the river would dry up. Became a crust on a black wadi. And that sticky water crawling with insects. With black shadows on the water until there was no water at all. Just the ink of shadows.

So on our walks, I told her about those British artists. Especially the women painters. What a bunch they were. Mad, indomitable. Didn't know any better. The problem with us, we know so much better. We've been forcefed on knowing better. But not those artists.

Well, once we went as far as the sandhills at the river mouth. I can remember Lulu pointing to Mars, red as a cinder, low over the dunes. A red hot particle, a grain of sand itself, that was Mars that night. Glowing above the evening river.

The estuary was green in the dusk. The estuary with its

herons and hawks and frogmouths. Its moths bigger than a man's hands. A whiteman's hands, Lulu pointed out.

She was a native girl, you see. But there I was, not understanding how rare Lulu was. How incredibly rare was this girl. A child of nature, as the song says. Unique.

So what did I do? To my shame I spent too long talking to Lulu about bootleggers. About specialists and programme collectors. All the damaged types who congregate around a record store. All those obsessive-compulsives hanging about. On the margin of any enthusiasm.

Hanging around in the space I'd created at *Hey Bulldog*. Polishing my floorboards with their dirty trainers. Bringing in that brickred Murray dust, thick as talcum powder.

Of course, it was really about music. Because music is always the core. It's music brings young people. And if that music is seething with sex, you're halfway there. Most of the way.

But it was even more fundamental than that. In Goolwa, at the end of the world, it was all to do with belonging. A place for nurturing. That's what Lulu sensed.

And yes, for too long, I talked to her about the things that didn't matter. And of course, now I'm doing it again on The Caib. Searching for similar sufferers. Fellow fanatics. Fed by the same delirium. Hunting out the same addicts.

But I tell you what. I don't regret it. All those collectors? The people who stapled the poetry pamphlets together? Who trawled through old suitcases full of flyers and posters? To check who was top of the bill ten years ago in a back bar in Adelaide? To work out the set list of a forgotten gig? No, I don't regret that.

Because it mattered. It mattered like crazy. It mattered as the most important thing in the world. I kid you not, there was a kind of holiness about the people attracted to *Hey Bulldog*. A powerful innocence. Remember how the song goes. How it goes. *Some kind of innocence…*

123

Anyway, they were searching. For meaningfulness. Which is what young people do. Or the dreamers before they're warned to stop dreaming.

No, it wasn't all mistaken. So, who told you about Mars? I asked Lulu.

It's in books, she said. Wonderful books.

I'll always remember that phrase. 'Wonderful books.'

I looked for Mars in the encyclopaedias and the almanacs. Sand-coloured Mars. Bronze as a hornet.

Or one of those maybugs we used to see on The Caib. Cockchafers, we called them. Droning through the dusk like electrical charges. And they'd collide with you and hold on to your shirt with their talons. Sticky as gel.

Are they still around, the maybugs? They used to detonate like grenades in the girls' hair. Like big seeds. Funny how it all starts to come back. After it all falls away.

VI

I remember a girl I knew. Somehow she was covered in flying ants. I was about seventeen and we were in the dunes here one August. We used its river of sand as a pathway. Suddenly, her hair was alive with ants. Black ants, crawling black ants. Thousands of ants.

And this girl tore off her clothes and ran off through the sand. Her hair was a torrent of ants. Skinny and pale, skinny and pale, her hair smoking, her hair fiery with ants. Down to her knickers and the sand flying, her foal's legs skinny and pale, skinny and pale.

Yes, racing down to the beach. She ran through the roses and I can still see the rosepetals floating away. Those creamy rose petals stuck to the soles of her sandals.

I found her on the shore under a log the tide had brought in. A treetrunk bleached white. There she hid, like driftwood herself.

Her name was Elisabeth. Shortened to Lizzy. But we used to call her Dizzy. *You make me Dizzy, Miss… You make me Dizzy, Miss…*

And Lizzy died. Young. The first one of our lot to do so. You always remember the first ones to die. They put a spell on you, the first ones. With their intolerable wisdom. Their outrageous bad luck.

Yeah, little Dizzy. With the rose petals stuck to the soles of her feet. I can see her as if it was yesterday. She ran past me with no clothes on. Like that picture in the Vietnam war of the naked girl burned by napalm.

Maybe I'm confusing them. The girls, the ants, the napalm. But I still remember it happening. I still need to know it really happened. And that it happened to me.

ELEVEN

The last time Parry met Libby was in Botanic Park in Adelaide. They came out of the tropical house with its tree ferns and lotus flowers. Then wandered along the Torrens under the Moreton Bay figs.

Parry had considered ordering bicycles, but had thought a walking pace more appropriate.

He was feeling better and after a month was allowed to drive. 'Stroke victim' he thought. Fifty-five, that was all he was. Crocked at fifty.

But nothing catastrophic. Yes, he could have died. But Parry already understood that. All he'd have to do was moderate his behaviour, and admit extinction to the equation. Which, yes, was a relief. But everybody had to come to terms with that.

Now, there were pins and needles in his right hand, a stiffness in his wrist that would take months to heal. If it ever did.

He was thinner too, as the anti-cholesterol medication took effect. But to Parry, this seemed speculative treatment. Surely he had not been overweight. His problem was hereditary high blood pressure. This had resulted in his father's first stroke. The doctor had indicated as such when Parry attended his Australian medical in London.

'Watch that,' was all he remarked. But had never been explicit about hypertension.

Stratospheric blood pressure, Parry now said. It runs in the family.

This was his usual explanation. Yeah, he thought. Blame something they can do nothing about. Implicate your precious genes. Your sluggish blood.

This line also became useful in his arguments with sports lovers. Parry knew the irony of his situation.

Who's crocked? Jeez, not the arty Brit? Yep, the sports-hating Pom who had studiously avoided the track and the pool.

Meanwhile, the red meat-eating, beer-guzzling gang who cruised every tavern in Gouger Street and made their HQ amongst the pillars of the Sebel Hotel lounge? They wandered through life untouched.

He had already told Libby he was going back to Britain after the last three months of teaching. Under the lianas and banana vines, curling like electric wires, her hair looked blacker. But her lipstick was an unnecessary flourish.

The zips and buckles on her trousers gleamed. But they had no function. They unlocked nothing and led nowhere. Stiffness returned to his right hand. His fingertips seemed cold.

Parry remembered their one night together. How feigning exhaustion he had turned away. Her nipples were grey rosettes.

She was thirty-four but already used up. Yes, Libby lived in an arid country. In a city like a gridiron. Hot as a griddle.

An Adelaide springtime was short. Like her strapping sons, it was sucking her dry.

If it had not been for the swamphen, he would have made excuses, cut and run. But in the undergrowth beneath the trees on the river walk, he had seen a bird. A plump, stupid-looking creature that gleamed in the foliage.

It's the same colour, Parry heard himself saying desperately. Same colour as … you know…

I know what?

Your lipstick.

And Libby had stared at the bird. And looked away.

Hardly, she said. It's turquoise.

Oh. I think so.

They're always here, she said.

Yes. I thought it was an ibis, said the schoolteacher in him. Sacred bird for the Egyptians or something. But it's a purple swamphen.

I didn't. Know that.

Well … he laughed. And took her hand. But the stiffness in his palm that morning felt uncomfortable.

Yes, his fingertips were icy. Sometimes, Parry wondered whether he might be disappearing from himself. A slow dissolution.

So what are you saying? demanded Libby.

Nothing. Only that it's a purple…

But I didn't know that. Jesus, you're a genius at pointing out the things people don't know. The things they are supposed to understand. How irritating is that?

I didn't mean…

What did you tell me in Goolwa? asked Libby. That Stevie Wright was a junkie. I didn't know Little Stevie was a junkie.

Why are you supposed to know that?

Because it's my country, asshole.

Sorry.

My culture.

Look, I'm sorry.

I'm not stupid, you know.

Of course.

The Easybeats are my history, said Libby. So why do you want me to feel stupid?

I don't want that.

Listen. I know those are black swans on the river. That they

128

fight like fury. But I'll own up to not getting the purple hen.

Swamphen, laughed Parry.

I could be here with Travis and Vincent. And they might ask me about that bird. Ooh, it's the same colour as your lipstick, mummy. It must be the incredible purple swamp chicken. Oh sorry. It's extinct.

Can we sit down? Parry asked her, gesturing to a bandstand on the rise above the river.

Look, said Libby. I better head off. Have a nice life. Oh, I forgot to mention. I'm leaving too. If it's good enough for you… Three more months and that's it.

Your career?

Never wanted a career, did I? It's time I started behaving like an artist. Get something achieved. A recognised body of work.

Is that what artists do? Parry smiled. But the woman was walking away. Expensive shoes and expensive clothes, he thought, watching her go.

Libby's hair was dark swansdown. When they had gone to bed that night in Goolwa he had cupped her scalp in his fist. Soft as peach fur, its bristling pelt. Now his fingers were frozen.

I could have died, he said to himself. Could have died. But maybe I did.

TWELVE

I

It was an October day when Glan and Serene had appeared out of The Ghetto. Parry remembered what he was playing the first time he spoke to Glan: Chet Baker and his band, with 'The Wind'. Evocative music, maybe too lush. Tainted by Hollywood.

Strange to be playing a tune like that so early. The couple had been hanging around the shop for days. Then one morning, Glan had asked Parry who was it happened to live upstairs.

Parry remembered that *happen to live* line. It made him tense.

Um … I do. I suppose.

It's all flats up there, isn't it? Or so my mother says.

Again, an odd configuration. *Or so…*

Storerooms, mostly, said Parry. They're pretty small.

Well, we're looking. Aren't we? said Glan.

Yeah, agreed Serene. Looking, looking.

For a flat?

Anywhere. See, we need a place. Don't we?

That's it, said Serene. We need an Anywhere.

Well, let me think, said Parry. And he noted how his own words first created the possibility. And then the likelihood.

II

When they left *Badfinger*, the young couple were smirking. Parry had escorted them upstairs, shown off a room already half full of boxes. Then apologised for the state of his bathroom. They would all have to share.

No problem, said Glan.

No, no problem, breathed Serene.

Parry looked at Serene. Her purple rinse. Yes, he foresaw bathroom issues. And discounted them.

Glan and Serene would bring their bags that afternoon. Now they were returning to an address in Vainquer Street. A tiny cash deposit had been mentioned.

All that part of The Caib had seen better days. The pubs were being auctioned, some of the gardens were ghostly with buddleia. There was a house in the street which Parry used to visit. Severin had lived there. Parry remembered looking at a moth one June afternoon. A moth as big as a bird.

A humming-bird moth, Sev's mother believed it was called. A moth that drank nectar through a long mouth. Almost a hypodermic.

The boys had stood with Sev's parents, regarding the creature. That term, Sev's family had moved away. Sev with his knife, his knowledge. Tough little Severin. Who never came back.

Parry could imagine the terraced house that Glan and Serene wished to leave. Perhaps the rent was going up. Possibly the neighbours were druggies. Either way, Parry didn't believe Glan's story, plausible as it was. As to payment, nothing was clear. They'd sort it out at the end of next month.

Yes, it was asking a lot. But the couple wouldn't stay long, and Parry was used to sharing his space. The green glow of the shop in Goolwa, now the Caib's marine chill. Tough times, he said to himself. It was good to live through tough times.

And it was surely exciting to live with young people. That had to be correct. Something was needed to keep the elixir flowing.

OK, here's the plan, Parry decided. They could all choose the *Badfinger* music together. And he'd prepare the list. Serene could pick first, next Glan. Then Parry would add something classy. Not Chet, not Hank, but maybe Duane Eddy under his Arizona skies.

Duane? Are you crazy? he smiled to himself. Nothing like subtle enough. Perhaps go back to Chet and *My Funny Valentine*? Or a melody, maybe Coltrane's *After the Rain?* Why not? Everybody's got to learn some time.

And surely the couple had their own favourite tracks? They could play Parry's CDs upstairs. Make toast, drink Australian wine. He could tell them about the vineyards he'd discovered around Addy. Now, that Fox Creek Shiraz had really stood out. Sparkling, yet almost black. Blood on the lips. A real discovery.

Yes, something in his collection was sure to please Serene. To impress Glan. But Parry remembered the moth. How all four of them on that June afternoon had listened to the moth's wingbeats. Craning over the verbena. Straining to hear the breath of mothwings. Their sultry murmur.

Yeah, something classy that would have Glan following the rhythm. Or Serene whispering under her breath, tapping those purple fingernails as she brushed the crumbs from her lap.

Well built, wasn't she? Yet kind of … *lissom*. Yes, make Serene smile for once. In her skintight purple leggings. In those worn-out purple boots.

III

Parry wondered how he had been affected by his trauma. If some Antarctic current had come north and momentarily chilled his blood. He seriously considered it.

Black ice from a rogue floe. Like some gang of growlers out of the Weddell Sea. Or a numbing infusion through the southern ocean. Gripping his mind, roughing him up.

What element of his life, natural and unique, had been erased? How might he know?

But, as he regained confidence, Parry thought the incident might have been beneficial. It was making living richer, because his intelligence was stranger. Surely his mind was different now.

Parry believed his thinking was clearer. Yes, his mind was being salvaged from the murk of himself. His thoughts were more peculiar. Slower, that was true. But possibly more original.

Yet one thing was clear. The next trauma might kill him.

If teaching wasn't what he wanted, he had to find whatever else proved inspirational. Or tolerable.

In Goolwa, behind the antique sunscreens of *Hey Bulldog*, he dreamed intensely.

Several times his dreams featured his parents' allotment. This had passed to newcomers years previously. In his dusty shop, or brooding over Chinese tea served in the motel next door, he had time to consider his old life.

Teaching was ending. A natural conclusion. Good riddance.

But the future left him unmoved. Yes, the truth was he had been an inadequate teacher. He resented the time necessary for the mundane tasks. And had grown frustrated too easily.

He'd had little to say about the English painters who were his subjects. Little to say, but possibly resentment for the clarity of their lives. The element of heroism.

Those artists were adventurers. They came to an unexplored

new world. There were opportunities for such people, even if they journeyed reluctantly. Whereas Parry was repeating himself. As only a teacher might.

But if teaching in Australia was unsatisfactory, he was uncertain of what else he wanted.

After the illness he was determined to use this thinking time. Here was, he convinced himself, a unique opportunity.

But his attention drifted. He had ideas of starting an Australian diary. It would be devoted to his last months in the country. But he found himself unable to concentrate.

Then why not a sketchbook? he wondered. Scratchy charcoal lines, depicting some of the local birds. Or, better, people's faces? He could depict Lulu and Libby. Maybe that gawky boy with the aquiline nose from 13P.

Parry went as far as buying a drawing pad. But he didn't sketch. Instead, down by the Murray, he followed the paddle steamers. While in the motel bar, or behind the shades of a somnolent *Hey Bulldog*, Messiaen or an inaudible Philip Glass on the DVD, he brooded over his incident.

IV

And paid attention to his dreams. Several times these involved the garden, where Dora Parry had been happiest.

Where Jack Parry too had been at his ebullient best. The man cracked jokes, describing typewriters and coffee percolators. All these things were going to transform people's lives. And it was where Jack had been able to be funny.

But no, he didn't believe the stories he recounted, his son understood that. That was why Jack Parry was funny. Paper knickers would never catch on. The world would have to learn to do without miracle chocolate drinks. Or the unsellable self-cleaning shower curtains that filled the car boot.

As to dreaming, perhaps it was Jack Parry who was responsible. His son recalled him describing the boundary wall that separated the plots from the churchyard. This was nineteenth-century construction, built with Caib stones.

Parry himself always marvelled at the colours there. Of gold lichen on grey limestone. Golden and grey. Grey, gold. The power of that juxtaposition thrilled Parry in his druggy Australian sleep.

Such a gold. Rich as a double yolker. Or the yellow of mustard in the spice market on Gouger Street. And the grey always worth a look. The same grey as oystershells in drifts and sandbars along The Caib. The stacks of shells on the isthmus of the mussel bed. Or the buried shells his mother dug out of her plot.

It puzzled Parry why he had started dreaming of such things. Lichen and liverworts and their fossil pollen. Those grey roses of the rock. There was also an ice-white encrustation, as intricate as frost, that flourished over the allotment walls.

This moss to the young Parry was old as the limestone itself. The lichen leaves seemed to belong on the seabed.

After dreaming, he resolved to combine that gold, that grey. Yes, grey and gold belonged together. Their marriage was necessary. While he dreamed, the rightness of the idea filled his mind. But the moment vanished when he woke.

That's it, Parry thought in the Goolwa Motel. But there was an air of abandonment in the bar. Or perhaps Goolwa would always be like this. A town that waited for something to happen.

Regulars were hard to come by. He noted Jann was polishing glasses already clean. Then driving out a red hornet that had flown into the bar. Toon invited him to the greenhouse to look at a new cannabis plant hidden amongst the tomatoes.

V

He remembered arguing with his father. One June day, Jack Parry had complained that air pollution was killing their potato plants.

Yellowing already, he had protested, feigning outrage. Hardly in flower and the leaves failing. Can't be blight. Or, if it is, it's industrial. I blame The Works. Nothing can flourish while that bloody poison factory is open.

Do you mind? laughed Parry. My job starts next month. Handy money, you usually say.

Even killing the moss, said Jack Parry. Moss that's been on the walls a thousand years.

But how, Parry asked himself in Goolwa, might he paint his limestone dreams? He wasn't an artist. He hadn't earned the right.

So instead of art, Parry brooded over the behaviour of his body. The treachery of his brain. Wryness, he was aware, became a new characteristic.

Maybe I'm growing up. At last. Hallelujah. This he muttered to himself one morning in the motel. He had been sipping from his green glass. That wineglass, an old rummer, would stand on the counter awaiting him, leaves of green tea, like seaweed, sunk to the bottom. He would take it to a window seat before beginning in *Hey Bulldog*.

At last what? asked Jann.

At last I'm convinced. I'm a genius.

Is that all? I thought you were already sure of that.

Neither Toon nor Jann inquired of Libby, whom both had met. They were gentle with him. Which worried Parry.

He wondered whether he gave people the impression of

ruination, this thin man in a shaft of dusty light. But decided not, he had been struck down and was getting over it. That was all.

Sipping tea, Parry did not look unwell. He was lean enough under the Aussie tan.

The dreams continued. They were not unpleasant and he became convinced they were caused by his medication.

You'll be on those tablets forever. That was how colleagues in school responded when they learned the medicines' names.

Little blue jobs? Like Viagra? Get used to them, Ripper.

Yeah, forever and ever. That's a prescription for life, Ripper.

Hey Ripper! What's it like when you realise GlaxoSmith Kline owns your arse?

VI

One of the dreams Parry recalled was about the church next to the allotment.

This was a limestone fortress. Its pulpit was incised with the flagellation of Christ.

Parry had often viewed this artwork. He was convinced that the artist was local and had deliberately made Christ and his persecutors identifiable.

Jesus and his assailants would have been men of The Caib. Fishermen, boat caulkers, labourers from the quarry.

Part of the legend was that this Christ was not being assaulted with whips but sheaves of stinging nettles. Hard as he looked at the stonework, he could see no evidence for this.

Yet Parry accepted it. The power of local art, when there was so little of it, was considerable.

He had always felt a bond with the sculptor. And marvelled that this artist had flourished half a millennium before his own life. In his Adelaide school he had shown film images of the pulpit, the graveyard, and even the allotment.

Fearing the children's reaction, dreading they would be bored, he was delighted with the response. But showing the films had disturbed Parry. There were strangers tilling his parents' garden now. The raspberry canes had been rooted out. The blackcurrant bushes he had loved to smell in the rain, in misty rain, to breathe and savour and breathe again, had been transplanted.

Sometimes he had kept a pocketful of dried blackcurrant leaves with him in university. Or during his holiday labouring job at The Works. These leaf shreds became an indigo dust, fine as tobacco. Finally a turquoise smear like fountain-pen ink.

But some of Parry's dreams shocked him. One morning he had woken in the Goolwa dawn and shed tears.

Yes, there was the pulpit, its stonework deeply chiselled. But the Christ represented was a scruffily bearded Parry himself, still a teenage schoolboy. Jesus Christ was Richard Parry, aged sixteen.

And the two figures who whipped him were Jack and Dora Parry. What had they used for the flogging? Parry could still feel the blows. As in the dream the welts appeared on his limestone skin.

Not stinging nettles. The weapons looked like the lotus flowers Parry had noticed on his visit with Libby to Botanic Park.

Parry laughed through his tears. He found it hilarious but continued weeping. He was the only man in history to suffer whipping with golden lotuses.

VII

The next morning, Parry dreamed once again. He and Libby were outside. An immense plain stretched round them. There were tussocks of grass but overall the earth was outback red.

It was hotter than anything Parry had experienced in Goolwa. Hotter than the country he had visited west of Adelaide.

They were out in the desert, anxious with thirst. The sky was black and The Caib's sulphuric moon hung in the sky. But Parry was resolute. There was a job to do and he had to see it through.

He and Libby were riding in a cart pulled by oxen. At least, Parry imagined these were the creatures. But he had never seen such huge-horned animals before.

There was a whip in his hand, this time a real whip. He used it to encourage the oxen further over the plain. Libby said nothing. She was coated in dust and wore her hair in a grey plait. She did not want to be there but did not protest.

The pair came to a red boulder. Parry jumped from the cart and walked around the stone. He was convinced at once it was made of iron.

The boulder belonged in the cart. All Parry knew was that he and Libby had been commissioned to take the iron stone into Adelaide. It was a meteorite and valuable, his headmaster was convinced. The money might make life comfortable. Or different.

All Parry had to do was lift the meteorite into the cart. Then transport it back to Adelaide. That was what the school had demanded. He saw himself stoop to raise the iron onto his back.

When he awoke he felt he was shivering with delirium. It was the coldest morning he had known in Goolwa. Outside he could sense the Murray sliding in olive-green sheets towards the sea. And in the room was a smell of smoke. Or maybe it was brakes on a train.

Parry lay wondering. If the smell was part of a dream, why was it there now he was awake?

VIII

'The Backs' had been the schoolyard name for the alleyways behind the fairground.

Most of the fair's entrances were blocked. But there were one or two possible ways in. The alleys took the curious, or the lost, past a pub called The Catriona, with its abandoned extension. Then behind the ghost train, known as The Kingdom of Evil.

From there, was a path into an area of levelled dunes and blown sand. Then north into Vainquer Street.

As a boy, Parry had used the name 'The Ghetto' himself, not understanding why. All he knew of ghettos was the Presley song, one of his big comeback numbers. But 'The Backs' was clear.

Yes, Parry said, on returning to The Caib, and eventually joining the gang at the Paradise Club, the lanes were filthy.

The place was filled with rotting mattresses, with mud in frozen ruts or piles of garden waste, broken bicycles, children's toys. And endless polystyrene trays.

Yet some of the Vainquer houses maintained a dilapidated charm. Many were now flats, or bed-and-breakfast businesses. Somehow the couples, or usually the widows who kept them, hung on.

And if you looked hard you'd notice the street retained evidence of the past. There were ornate finials, high garden walls. The few Vainquer shops made do with what trade there was. As did the pubs. Nothing is harder to break than habit.

But even in Goolwa, Parry had heard of the town's problems. The Caib was the place where young people killed themselves. As simple as that. And as brutal. The town of hopelessness, it was called.

There had been a Panorama programme shown on ABC which Libby and some of the Australian teachers had seen. Libby had even written to him at *Hey Bulldog*.

Isn't that where you're from? she asked. *I'm so sorry!*

Parry had shrugged it off.

Our turn, he had said to the parents of The Black Cockatoos, who mooched around the shop while their children rehearsed. The Cockatoos were a band created by schoolkids. They rehearsed in the evenings.

Yes, our turn to be famous. That's our fifteen minutes. And already almost over. Who's next?

IX

One night in The Paradise, Parry had asked Mina directly.

How can there be hopelessness here? It's tough. But not that bad. Things don't make sense.

Mina was frank.

Might as well blame the sand for blowing down Cato Street, she said. Or the sand for being sand. Look. Think of your parents. Were they hopeless? Course not. They were grafters. Had to be in those days. I remember your mother with her sunflowers that grew out of the dunes.

You know, she added, we used to live by the allotments in those days. And I'd spy on you from my bedroom window, twti-ing down behind the curtain.

Great tall sunflowers they were, some of them orange. But mostly the yellowest things you could imagine.

Then, in the dark, when I was sure you wouldn't come, I made dens. And yes, I'd pick the sunflower seeds off the ground. I remember one year your mother planted this especially long row. Sunflower Street, you called it yourself. A real street!

Yes, Mina added, I had a den in the kidney beans. Could squeeze right in. Because it was the sand I loved. When it was still hot. Hot sand's the best feeling in the world.

You're right, laughed Parry. I used to cycle down to the gardens through the fairground. Watch Hal and the others outside The Cat, if it was a warm night. Just smoking, chewing the fat. With the last of the gamblers having a final try.

And, you know, I'd wish my father would go out for a drink. To break the mould. Give my mother a break. Like other men. Stop … hanging around. He could be a teensy bit tragic, could my dad. But he never tried it.

And then I'd move on to the allotment. Sometimes it would be gone midnight when I was watering. Couldn't see, but I knew the water was rolling like mercury over that hot sand.

Yeah, that water in lines of mercury. Silver in the dark. Just the sound of the crickets and the water on the bean leaves. Then the water on the rough old corn.

And I'd have this other den, said Mina. A den amongst those red flowers. Big red plumes, they were.

Amaranths.

Whatever.

Yes. Amaranths. *Immortal amaranths*. Ever read *Paradise Lost?* I never did. Beautiful they were. My mother won a prize, once, for amaranths. Boring vegetable, though. Bit like spinach.

And I had dens too, Parry added. Yeah, tried in the sweet corn. But those leaves were rougher than sunflowers. Like sandpaper. Brutal.

But I remember the hot evenings when the bats were out. And those great green crickets. Four inches long, those crickets were. You must have seen the crickets if you lived by the allotments. Famous for crickets, those gardens.

Can't remember, said Mina. But you seemed a happy family. With your dad on the road selling paper knickers.

Well, she added, we had to laugh. And God knows what else. Your dad once sold coffee to my mother, by the way. It was horrible. Packets and packets of the muck. Still got it, I think. And that special dried milk. Which was worse. But what about you? Why have you turned out so well?

Have I? smiled Parry.

No, love. Just joking. You're a fucking disaster. But hopelessness doesn't come into it. And it never did.

Then why…?

Are they killing themselves? Well, Professor, remember what you said. It's all a failure of imagination.

How?

Because they can't imagine what it means not to exist. To be extinct. Look, you said that. These kids think they're going to wake up from a hangover. But they're not. Death's not being drunk. Death ain't no dream.

My daughter used to have a Greenpeace sticker on her window, Mina smiled. Took ages to scrape it off. *Extinction is forever*, it said. And all of us have to learn that. Not easy. But we have to do it.

X

Look, said Parry. My dad…

What?

My dad never sold paper knickers. Admittedly, he tried. It was a possibility. But it didn't work out.

Your dad earned his crust. He made us laugh. And you're seeing him soon, aren't you? Season of good will and all?

Yeah. I have to. Have to.

Then Parry kissed Mina on the brow and poured her the dregs of the Paradise red.

To sleep, he toasted. Maybe tonight.

And maybe not, said Mina.

How are you?

Not great. Didn't sleep at all, last night, Or was it the night before. Nights tend to blend into one. I think I dozed about dawn. You know, I've regularly had this trouble. But maybe it's something else.

Parry looked at her. Yes? he asked.

Well what's happening to you? Soon?

Death?

No. Sooner.

Enfeeblement? laughed Parry. What a great word that is.

Jesus, never heard it used before, said Mina. What about *decrepitude?* There's another beauty. No, something sooner. Happening to you. That you can't escape.

Don't know. But go on. Sicken me.

Mina finished her wine.

You're going to be sixty, lover. Sweet sixty.

Oh, so…

So this might be what's keeping me awake. Because…

Because you are too. You're sixty, Mina. But I knew that. Everybody knows that. Mina's going to hit the big six. Congratulations. When's it happening?

Two months. February 24.

Oh, another one soon. Fflint is too. He's sixty in March. And Gil coming up. They detest the idea. Say so on Facebook. Then there's…

Who?

144

Never mind.

No, who?

Dizzy. That's Lizzy. She would have been sixty on April 10th.

Yeah, well I'm another, the woman shrugged.

It's not so bad. Can it be that terrible? You're not seventy.

Sixty's old.

And you never thought at twenty it could happen to you?

Sort of.

Then don't worry. You look great. No, I'm serious…

Mina raised her eyes. Forget how I fucking look. Christ, men… No, it's, it's … *Alys*. Listen, I just know she's going to ignore it. The whole event. So the next two months is a kind of counting down…

Will she remember, you mean? said Parry. Will she care?

Yes. And here I am. Ticking off the days till Basement Booze shuts up shop. Ticking off the days till my birthday, the days till the next quarter for the rent is due. And sometimes I wonder, what kind of life is this?

Parry looked around. What about Alys' father?

That's the problem. Alys sees more of him these days. I know she stays over there sometimes. Look, she's met his new partner. And she's younger, she's…

It's up to Alys, said Parry firmly. To do the decent thing.

But how would you know that?

How would I know when I've never had children, you mean? Look, anyone would think that. Anyone. Kids or not. Alys has to do what she has to do. Like the rest of us. Simple as that.

XI

Parry stood on the corner of Nuestra Senhora del Carmen Street. He thought the cold was in his veins. In his marrow. In his pocket the tips of his fingers felt dead. The air was as cloudy as the seabed.

A cat crossed the road in front of him. A black cat with fog in its mouth.

He looked closer. No, a white bird. A white bird still alive. The cat ran into a gwli.

XII

He rubbed the mist on his brow. Then tried to shrug the black frost from his shoulders. He'd been talking to Mina in Basement Booze, but was now back at *Badfinger*.

He looked around.

He had unpacked the photo of The Easybeats, but knew he couldn't use it. Too obscure. Not even the singer, Stevie Wright, could expect to be famous now.

But, so what? he asked himself. Maybe he was tired. Repeating himself. Maybe *Hey Bulldog* had been a success because no one recognised the bands, no matter who it was Parry decided deserved attention.

It wasn't the scene itself. No, the idea of that scene. That's what Parry needed to sell.

Yes, market *Badfinger* in the right ways, and people would start to call in. As surely some already had. And maybe Glan and Serene could help it become what was needed.

The rent required was affordable. At least for the next coming year. Parry had signed a year's contract on the lease of the shop and was told he was lucky to get that.

Originally, the tenancy had to last five years. He knew the owners didn't want short-term usage. But he imagined any client was better than none.

Because The Caib now seemed inert. Both Caib and Cato streets were full of empty premises. It seemed unlikely the fairground could reopen.

In the fog it was impossible to imagine crowds on the sand. Or the fragments of funfair music that had once blown across town.

Parry always remembered Jean Michel Jarre's *Oxygene* as a segment of that soundtrack. Its first five notes were seared into his history.

Hard to think, Parry thought, that The Ziggurat might reopen. Even when he was a child it used to rattle like scrap iron. Perhaps there was more hope for The Kingdom of Evil.

But Parry knew he should never write off The Caib. The fair had flourished since the war. Its absence come next summer would be unthinkable.

Despite the weather, there were still drinkers at The Cat. Today he knew there would be smokers outside the pub, hunched against the saline dew, sharing rollies. Their silhouettes would be grey within the pollen of the fret.

Yes, their sandy footprints should still be numerous enough. The Salamander and The Ritzy had closed, people said. Pozzo's was surely on the way out. But it didn't take much to reopen a club. The Caib still lived.

Come February, the Irish and the travellers who had haunted the town would make their reappearance. The Poles and Lithuanians had vanished, but there would always be replacements. Yes, carpenters and mechanics, painters and decorators.

What was that boy's name? Parry asked himself. Yes, *Wat*. And Parry smiled as the theme of *Oxygene* played once again in his mind.

Used to sleep under the rides, didn't he? Real dark gippo. Dangerous and beautiful Wat. Girls used to love him. He'd coax anyone to buy him chips with gravy. And when things were really tight, Wat lived on *White Lightning* and garlic bread scrounged from bins in The Backs.

Because where else was there for people like that? Where other than The Caib? They had nowhere to go. Did they make the fairground. Or did the fair create the people?

And where else for Glan and Serene? The couple had started to help in *Badfinger*. That routine would begin again after the holiday.

It was important to make them earn their keep. Parry had noted Glan's broken shoes, Serene's lack of a decent coat. Which was strange when he considered the charity shops in the town. The weekly carboot sales.

Maybe secondhand clothes were too much of a giveaway. But the pair needed to look better than they did. Flashier, more outrageous. With no money spent. Yes, shabby chic, they used to call it. The pair somehow lacked essential style.

But Parry could change that. Glan's hair was now mauve. When he'd first arrived in town, it had been a different purple. Yes, the kid had pretensions. Glan and Serene must be part of *Badfinger*.

At the end, in Goolwa, Lulu had dressed to impress. She made her own poverty a fashion statement. Parry bought the girl presents from the market: plastic beads, ridiculous polka dot dresses.

He asked her to walk and throw back her dark shoulders. To hold in the tiny jewelled plate of her belly. Anything, he said, to show you're still alive. That you're thinking about being alive.

That was how you talked to young women, Parry reasoned. They would always respond.

Once he had bargained for a tie-dyed top for Libby. Green and mauve, it was like the quartz colours he remembered from The Horns.

Yes, she had smiled. But just remember I'm a mother. Of sons. I'm not one of those schoolkids you like too much. And sons can be clever about things like that.

THIRTEEN

I

I could play, said Glan. Or sing.

I'd like to hear you play, said Parry. In fact, I'd love to hear you play. Or sing.

Yeah. Course I could play.

You can play, said Serene. I've heard you.

Just pick up the axe, said Parry. Try it now.

Axe? laughed Serene.

Yes, I could play.

Lots of times, said Serene. I've heard you.

Go on.

Later.

Why later?

Why not later?

Yeah, why not later? asked Serene.

Maybe I will.

And maybe you…

Give it a go, said Parry. Don't be like me.

Oh no, said Glan. Not like you.

No, never like you, echoed Serene.

Don't wait too long, is what I mean.

You're some kind of a writer, aren't you? asked Glan.

No. But I like the idea of writing. There's a difference. I was going to write a novel in Adelaide. Had everything worked out. I was also determined to be an artist. But teaching is hard graft. Believe me, it is. So all I mean is, take your opportunities.

Glan finished his wine and reached across Parry for the bottle.

What opportunity is this, then?

Badfinger! said Parry. It's staring you in the face.

Badfinger? laughed Serene. Why d'you want to call it that?

I can organise things from here, said Parry. Gigs. At least I'm good at that. We had a great scene in this place in Oz. Workshops, classes.

Workshops? laughed Glan.

Classes? said Serene. You mean school?

Nothing like school. We just created this interesting situation. Yes, scene. Just me and this girl and a few others. Where people played music and gave talks. We did it because we could. Because it…

What? laughed Glan.

Fulfilled a need. We were likeminded people. We just came together. Fortuitous, really. Fate. Do you two believe in fate?

And Parry smiled his question at Glan. The boy was already tipsy, with red spots on his hollow cheeks. It wouldn't take much, Parry thought. No, not much.

Fate?

Yeah. Surprising conjunctions. Certain people meeting other certain people. And certain things happening because of it.

He looked at Serene, curled on the couch. At her long thigh, the black triangle of her knickers.

Hey, he said. Put this on next. And he slid a CD towards the girl.

Not another one? said Glan. His voice was slurred. Parry wondered whether the couple had been drinking earlier in the day. They had shared a bottle of red wine. But possibly had taken something else.

It's poor old Tim Buckley. Who deserves a listen. As a songwriter Buckley was, I suppose, an ambitious type. Sort of left his audience confused. Didn't work in a straight line. Jumped about.

Sounds like you, breathed Serene. Glan had closed his eyes.

Oh yeah? Do I jump about?

I bet you jump about, the girl said, smiling.

Parry looked back at Glan. The red spots on his cheeks were splashes of rouge.

Tragic family, explained Parry. Tim Buckley's son was also a performer. So both men were singer-songwriters. But he drowned. That's Jeff Buckley, who drowned. Maybe the son was even more talented. Who's to say?

I bet you could tell us, said Serene, stretching her legs. Yeah, I really bet you could. And who's that blond bloke down in the shop? They say he's dead.

Dangerous trade, music, said Parry.

Yeah. He's supposed to be dead an' all.

Oh yes. Brian Jones. Of the Rolling Stones.

This was a photograph taken in Marrakech. When Jones was alive and all things seemed possible. Before he became the bloated angel.

Christ, Jones, thought Parry. That horny bastard. Five kids, wasn't it? Impossible charisma.

Look, he said quietly. I'm right when I say take your chances. Because time passes so quickly, it's frightening. Those chances will be gone like ... blue lightning goes.

Blue lightning? smiled Serene. Oh yeah, you're some kind of a writer. Aren't you?

Whatever we had, there was a scene going for us. In this little town in Oz. Doesn't matter how it ended. Doesn't matter if its moment passed.

No, it ended when the drought ended. When the rains fell.

And those rains fell with a vengeance. But our scene made a difference to people's lives. That's one thing I'm sure about. Certain of it.

II

Glan'll play, said Serene. Or he'll sing. Sing and play. I've seen him. Loads of times.

The boy was asleep now. In the darkness, Serene's hand seemed to rest between Glan's thighs.

Who was that girl, then? she asked.

Parry was becoming uncomfortable where he sat on the floor. He was too close to the electric fire, which provided the only light in the room. The threadbare rugs he had inherited were scattered with plates and CDs. On the walls were some of the photographs from *Hey Bulldog*.

That was Lulu, he said quietly. She went out in the rains. And I lost her. Yes, I lost her. Lulu vanished. Never saw the child again. But I'm certain she didn't drown. Lulu was too clever for that. The night she disappeared I called till I was hoarse.

Lovers' tiff, was it? smiled Serene.

Then the next day I called all day. Then the next day. All day. Every day for a week I shouted. And then after four weeks the rains finally stopped. Stopped dead. Like turning off a tap.

I remember the exact moment the rains stopped. The air was stilled. But by that time it was a different world. Changed utterly.

The river was full of red silt. Red dust from the desert and red scum on the treetrunks. Red beards of weed. I'd drag my hand in the water and the skin would be speckled red. As if I had a disease. Some sort of fever.

In the evening the river would be the colour of blood, with all these drowned animals going past. Cows going past. Hundreds of snakes going past. Knotted snakes like rootballs. Ever see sunflower roots? The snakes were like that. Hissing bundles. Like bundles of fire going past.

Parry eased himself on the rug.

I used to have a job in The Works. You know, it was the same problem there. Only that was sinter. Black sinter dust so thick it might have choked a man. Someone died once. Smothered by sinter. Fell in. That dust was thick as flour.

My father was in The Works, said Serene. And his brothers.

Glan was sleeping now. A boy as beautiful as Brian Jones must once have been. Parry remembered the heart-shaped face, the stony eyes. Jones too had drowned, but in a swimming pool.

Sad and uncool, Parry thought. He had felt betrayed by Jones' death. How absurd was that? Hardly Shelley, was he? Never composed a song. Barely wrote a verse.

A selfish life that the culture pretended was a fiery martyrdom. Yet doused too soon.

No chance of a place at The Works now, said Parry. All the apprenticeships have finished. All the … *opportunities*. So that's what I'm talking about. Starting your own scene. Or being part of one. Those kids in Goolwa caught my drift. They understood. Come on, chicken. What's to lose?

Serene hugged her right knee, then held out her glass in invitation. Her teeth were black in the firelight. It seemed there might be blood on her lips.

III

Parry continued to insist. One afternoon he pushed Glan up the narrow stairs to his room. He walked behind the boy with his hands on his hips.

Well, the hair's okay, said Parry, looking at the mauve veil. Possibilities there.

Then he'd told him to take off his grey jersey. Next, the brown shirt.

Glan had stood with elbows pressed into his ribs. These were blue and prominent.

On the ivory boy, Parry breathed, *the colour of life had deepened.*

You what?

Just a poem. Don't worry.

Poem..?

Parry also noted scars in the milky skin of Glan's back.

Hey, what are these? he asked quietly. Then he had wetted his forefinger and traced the most prominent laceration.

Looks like someone's taken a whip to you, young man.

Oh yeah? whispered Glan.

Has anyone? Been beating? You?

Can't remember, the boy said quietly.

Yes, Parry repeated. What *are* these?

And he had smiled. As if in apology.

I hope my fingers aren't too cold for you.

Then he turned Glan round to face him, noting the red spots on his cheeks. The blotches were present every time he had seen Glan drink wine.

Are you ready for my shirt?

The boy's chest was cold. His nipples dark rosebuds. When Parry next inhaled, Glan smelled to him of the fret. Of salt and mist and the wet sand that drifted from the Cato Street outfall.

Maybe the dank Panasonic cardboard that otherwise filled the room. And something else.

Such weather, he said, still holding Glan's shoulders. Oh boy, where did it come from? This weather?

He could see the veins' blue traceries in Glan's neck. A pulse was beating there.

You must have brought it with you, smiled Parry.

Oh?

Bad weather birds. You and Serene. Only joking. By the way, where is Serene?

In town, somewhere, I think. The reading room in Cato Street. She likes to read, does Serene. She reads in bed.

And do you? Like it? Reading in bed?

No. I just fall asleep.

What does Serene read?

Dunno.

Might she read to you? Some couples do that.

She doesn't read to me.

Just cwtsh, do you? That's a narrow bed. Not much room for two, is there?

No.

I'm sorry about that. Have to see what I can do. Hey, I like that cologne?

Cologne?

Yes, that works. Devastating. Yes it is. Reminds me of … *blackcurrants* …

Black…?

Parry smiled as Glan flicked back his hair. Its purple streaks were darkened with mousse.

Oh yes. My absolutely favourite smell. Works for me.

Thanks. It's new. First time on.

So just relax, purred Parry. Look. Sit here. On the bed. Here. I'll clear a space. For us.

He relinquished the boy's cold shoulders.

Listen, he said, I want to tell you something. It's a story my mother told me a long time ago.

Ready? Well it was my parents' wedding day and the weather was like this. Freezing, unusual even though it was February. There was snow in the air, big flakes she told me, great soft flakes of snow, the type of snow that sticks to your skin, the snow that sticks to the world.

Now my mother's wedding dress, I've always remembered this, was hand-embroidered. A local seamstress had sewn the designs of tiny sunflowers into the bodice, into the train.

Everybody knew my mother loved sunflowers. She's grown them since she was a girl. It was the obvious idea. She was a gardener, my mother. Loved her garden. But Dora Parry was no pressed flower. Oh no.

It was February, remember. So when my mother and my father came out of the church, they had to walk around in the snow. To speak to all the guests. As the married couple must. As they should. Though I wouldn't know, I've never married. Have I? Not yet.

Then, after a while, my mother noticed that when she moved, her dress clinked with ice.

You see, the train of her wedding dress, all the hem of her ice-coloured wedding dress, was frozen. It was making the sound of bells. Tiny bells that might have been sewn into the wedding train. Into the hem. Like they sometimes sew mirrors into dresses.

Yes, the ice chiming there, that's what she heard. The chiming of icicles amongst the sunflowers. On her wedding day.

Oh, but you're cold, added Parry, his fingers again upon the boy's skin. Then he squeezed Glan's shoulders once more.

What's that? asked the boy.

He was pointing to Parry's bedside table. Glan reached over and picked up the pebble. It was round and grey with a central core of white quartz. Within the white quartz was a ball of red quartz.

Oh, that, said Parry. I've always had that.

But it feels hot, laughed Glan. How can it be hot? It's cold in this room. It's always cold here, but…

It looks like it might be hot, said Parry, but…

It's like an eye. Looking at you. A red eye.

No, not…

Is it always there? Looking at you in bed? asked the boy.

I don't think about it, laughed Parry. I don't, really. I think I found it somewhere past The Horns. There's a tiny cove and beach. Behind the sand is a low cliff.

If you can climb a little way up you see this quartz formation. Pink and white and black, it is. Like Italian marble. But the climb's not easy. Why would you bother if you didn't know it's there.

Not sure how I discovered it. Simple curiosity, I suppose. It's well concealed. That quartz is a frozen cataract. You can imagine it molten and hot, oozing like icing sugar. Yes, about ten-feet long that outcrop of quartz.

I think the eye as you call it was with other pieces of quartz on a ledge. Washed up by a high tide. I climbed there, put out my hand and found it.

When I jumped back down it was in my hand. A round pebble I'd never seen before. I opened my palm and there it was. And I've kept it. Don't know why.

Glan looked a last time.

But it's hot? he said.

I think, said Parry, that it reflects whoever's holding it. So you must be hot yourself.

He reached out again to touch Glan's chest.

But the boy freed himself and picked up his shirt and jersey. Somehow they had fallen to the floor.

IV

Parry didn't own an iron or ironing board. He agreed to take Serene to Mina's upstairs flat while Glan was sleeping off various indulgences. He stood with the girl under a painting of a ship that had run aground.

How do you manage? she had asked.

Suppose I don't, he said. Trust the spin dryer to do the job. And generally look crumpled.

Typical, the girl said. I know for certain Glan's never ironed a single thing.

Why is he in bed so long?

Oh, you know…

Yeah, I know. The weather doesn't help. Can't tell if it's day or night. Never used to be like this.

You were born here? she asked.

Yes. And did the usual. Worked in the fairground. Sold tickets for The Kingdom of Evil. Cleared glasses at The Cat. Then holiday jobs at The Works. Despite my old man.

Oh?

He hated the idea of The Works. Of thousands of men all clocking on at the same time. Shift patterns. Bit of an individualist is Dad.

Still around, is he?

Just about. Read the riot act a few times if he thought there was any likelihood of me joining the wage-slave crowd.

So you became a teacher?

Don't sneer. Teachers are the best people. They believe in life chances, in … *improvement.*

But you're back where you started?

Nothing wrong with that.

But this place ... the girl said. The Caib's become ... *notorious*.

The word surprised Parry.

We're always on the telly these days, she added. She might have said 'famous'.

He looked at Serene, a pale child with a purple rinse that needed attention. Hippy chick without the music. Silver stud in her nose. Fish hook in her eyebrow.

She should have an Incredible String Band album under her arm, Parry considered. But that had been another time. Another world.

In fact, maybe Serene looked like Licorice from the Incredibles might have done, thirty or forty years previously. Another winsome child. Yes, long lost Likki, who had vanished off the planet. Blame drugs or booze or scientology. Something was going to get you.

Like others, Parry had researched the missing Licorice. The lack of information had proved depressing. Yet perhaps also exciting. The Caib was a place, he'd always known, where people disappeared.

But that was true of life, he reasoned. As he became older, he understood better those who didn't want to be reminded of their pasts.

He'd watched a recording of Little Likki McKechnie during the Incredibles' Woodstock performance. So overawed, so unutterably bad, it was the reason their part of the film was axed. Another lyric soul howled off by the uncomprehending.

He had even told Lulu to watch Licorice on YouTube. Lulu who had never ironed in her life.

Now he watched Serene place a purple sleeve on the board.

Yeah, everybody vanishes, Parry told her. Whether they want

to or not. We should all know about the glorious departed. And realise by the time they disappear, most people are unrecognisable. Especially to themselves.

You were an art teacher. Weren't you?

Saw a job advertised in Adelaide. Amazed myself by getting it. The idea was, this high school course would tell students about the British artists who'd come over since the nineteen hundreds.

In reality it was everything except that. I ended up teaching paint, creative writing, colonial history. All sorts.

Clever, aren't you?

No. I thought I was filling in until the proper job started. Then, too late, I realised that was the proper job. But that's teaching for you.

Parry watched Serene unbutton a blouse.

You're good at that.

Thanks. I like ironing. My mam taught me. You should learn. Ironing's a skill. Can't stay creased all your life.

My mother used to say my school shirts were like sunflowers, smiled Parry. Because sunflowers explode slowly into blossom. Uncrumpling themselves along the way. Until they're perfect and miraculous.

Perfect and…?

Next time you see a sunflower, pay attention.

Serene shook out a purple shirt.

You look good in that, said Parry. I'll say.

Glan likes it best of all my clothes. It's quite…

Daring? asked Parry. Kind of see through. Perfect for summer. But beautiful material. It was great when you wore it last week. I could see you shivering.

We were finding out where everything is in the shop. How the till works. How to cash up. So when we actually start work… Anyway, I was getting ready to look presentable.

That's right. Treat this as a real job. Which it is. As a chance…

Glan said the money was okay. Considering.

It'll have to be, laughed Parry. Considering. It's real money. And for that I'm expecting real work.

Glan said everything you told him sounded like an interview.

Too true. Life's one long interview.

I don't think Glan's ever had a real job, confessed Serene. He dropped out of the schemes.

Yeah. That's clear. But you're better prepared. Aren't you?

Maybe. I'm two years older than Glan.

And you can iron.

I can do loads of things.

Cook and sew and make flowers grow?

Is that a quote? Mina says you're always using quotations. She said some women would hate that. It might make them feel stupid. But she doesn't care. Now excuse me, sir. Have to do this.

Serene was wearing black leggings. She peeled them off and placed them on the ironing board.

Her legs were sturdier than Parry imagined. Thighs whey-pale.

Nothing worse than wrinkly leggings, she laughed, sprinkling water from a bowl over the material. I hate that. Don't you?

And don't worry, they are clean. I'll wear them tonight before they go in the wash.

Look, you and Glan can come with us to the Paradise Club. That's what we called it in the past. Glass of wine. Or juice. Get to know the locals.

Well, if you're buying. I like that.

Like what?

A man who spends his money. There's nothing worse in this

world than a mean man. And maybe that's a quote for you Mr Teacher, and maybe it's not.

And Serene smiled at Parry then, a look of mischievous radiance. His eyes lingered on the blue tattoo on her belly that disappeared under the elastic of her knickers. Yes, good figure, he thought.

Okay, she said. We'll come. If I can wake Glan, we'll come. So get your money ready. As long as your date doesn't mind.

Mina's not a date, he laughed. Whatever that means these days. What should the valiant middle aged do? Surrender to the fog? There's plenty who do that on The Caib.

Outside the flat was a flare of white sodium light. Every second lamp in Caib Street had been turned off. The road was deserted.

Then the door opened and Mina came in, smacking her new lipstick. When she saw Serene she gave Parry a wry smile.

Quick work, she said. Five minutes and the kid is down to her scanties.

Serene scowled but Parry noticed she hung another shirt over the ironing board, and positioned herself behind it.

She stood under the wrecked ship, which he knew was *The Vainquer*. There were hundreds of wrecks around The Caib. And an incalculable host of the drowned.

FOURTEEN

I

Never known mist like this week, said Nia across the bar. It's killed trade. What there was of it.

Oh, I've seen it before, said Fflint. Remember the cricket?

Parry thought back. Failed to find a reference.

We were all there. Up at The Horns. The tide was as far out as it gets. And that little bastard, Severin, had the idea we should play cricket. Yes, cricket. Remember?

Not sure, said Parry.

I swear you were there, Fflint insisted. You have to remember. Already had the ball. The bat was a piece of driftwood, wickets scratches in the sand. And you had this idea to field on the boundary. So it was impossible to see you. Remember that?

Trying, said Parry.

You'd have thought it ironic, of course. Sev was bowling, I was batting, the girls were fielding close in. Everybody else was lost in the mist. Like ghosts we were. That's what you called us.

Me? asked Parry.

Yes, friend. You called us the invisibles. By then the sea was so far out it just seemed like an idea of the sea. That afternoon the mist was so thick you'd need to be in the sea to know there was any sea at all.

Ironic? wondered Mina.

Oh, heavily into irony, weren't you? accused Fflint. So chummy here has to put himself at long on. Or third man. Or whatever it was. To make his ironic point.

No, said Parry. I was always slip. That was my specialty. And bowling leg spin, of course. I played once in Oz in my teaching days. Before the shop. And yes, I confess I was terrible that day. I never promised to bowl, did I? I was seriously out of practice, that day over there. Thirty off the over, as I recall. Against one of the suburb teams.

Cricket in the mist, said Fflint. But it wasn't as thick as this week. And no salt in the air. You must remember.

The memory seemed important to Fflint.

Maybe, said Parry.

And then it lifted. In a minute the mist was gone. Just blowing away. A white cloud, then rags of it, disappearing over The Horns. You could see it … disintegrating.

And yeah, when the sun came out it was hot in seconds. So we stopped playing because the girls wanted to go in the sea. That's your mum, Nia. Leading the mutiny.

Yeah, Sian and Lizzy. Waste of time really, as there was absolutely no surf. But the boys agreed because they wanted to see what cozzies the girls were wearing. Or more especially, Lizzy and Branwen.

Not my mum, then? Who's still gorgeous. But that Lizzy who died? My dad told me about her.

Lizzy Jeffs, said Mina. She was just blossoming. Coming out of a quiet time. You know, when a kid can go one way or the other. Stay introverted and cramped by shyness. Or just start dazzling. And Lizzy was beginning to dazzle. Before her illness.

Meningitis, agreed Parry. I'd had it too.

You had that as well? asked Fflint.

As well as what?

As well as this other bloody thing. Whatever's brought you back to the cold and the mist.

You accusing me of being a hypochondriac?

No. Of being ill. Twice, soothed Mina. Being ill isn't a crime. But I didn't know you'd had meningitis.

I think I was in a wood, said Parry. With my father. Wasn't the type of place where I'd expect to find Jack. Now my mother was different. Somehow, she belonged amongst trees. Anyway, I don't know what we were doing, but I felt this headache starting. Really quickly it was, like a steel band around my skull. Then tightening all the time.

By that afternoon I was delirious. They sent me in an ambulance to the old isolation hospital. But I can still remember the headache. And the dreams. All these dream animals, parading as if they were taking turns in a circus.

First the dream lions. Then the birds of paradise with impossible feathers. Yeah, a dream circus.

Serene told me about your dreams, said Nia. Seems you woke up your young lodgers a couple of nights ago. Scared them too.

Not sure about that, said Parry. But I do remember the lions. And the fantastic birds.

People pay good money for things like that, said Fflint. You know, not so long after the cricket in the mist, that bloody Severin gave me one of his little red tablets. *Depth charges* they used to call them. Took me a week to come back. To come down. So I've stayed strictly booze from then on.

Parry smiled into his wine. It's the dream time, isn't it? At least for me. We all go through The Dreaming. In our own ways.

At least that's what I picked up from talking to Lulu and her mates. But those aboriginal kids were confused by it all. By The Dreaming.

So coming from The Caib, as I do, I think I'm a sand

dreamer. But you know, I've sometimes dreamed of jellyfish. Maybe my life is part of jellyfish dreaming.

Mina looked at him and proposed another drink.

Hey, shouted Nia, and everyone looked up. *Jellyfish Dreaming* could be the band's name. We could announce it at the gig. With an electric fanfare. Or you could all write a special song. Yes, jellyfish music! I like my idea.

Now she had returned to The Caib Nia seemed determined to make a success of the Clwb. As far as Parry knew, there was no partner. Nia had wedded the language she rarely spoke at home. Neither of her parents was fluent, although Sian Vine still took lessons.

Same all over, he had often thought. In Goolwa, Lulu had been completely ignorant of her native speech. Maybe her grandmother would have spoken a few words. Now here was Nia Vine trying to turn back the tide.

II

Jack Parry was a loner. A humorous man yet still a loner. But his son recalled one older friend, Yonderly, with whom his dad was close. Yonderly collected tools for Africa.

He lived in George Street and the tools were stored in Yonderly's workshop. This was a green shed opposite his house across the back lane.

On one of the occasions Parry had visited, he had found three men employed, restoring the donated tools. Stropping, stripping, gauging. One man was learning to clean the throat of a huge wooden plane.

Such work, the boy had thought, as he watched these volunteers busy with wire wool and shifting oils. Each face rapt in dedication. Cocooned in concentration.

Nothing here, he realised, was too insignificant to be considered for improvement. A blunt saw, a cracked mallet.

These tools were collected from local shops, or saved from the scrapyard. Dull shears and blunted mattock left Yonderly's workshop renewed.

Parry remembered a scythe from his first visit. This was a huge implement with dangerous blade, awkward handle.

He had seen Yonderly himself select a whetstone from a baffling selection. Then he began loosening the tool's rust. The scythe itself was wrapped and bandaged like an invalid, so careful had Yonderly been to protect his volunteers.

Usually, Parry's work was to roll up unending reams of carbon paper. Under a frieze of women who touched themselves and licked their own fingers. While, outside in the sun, carbon smoke hung in ribbons, the yellow plastic shimmering in its lake.

So when Yonderly had pointed out the scythe's sap-blackened chine, the cracked snaith, Parry had found himself speechless.

The boy did not know those words. When Yonderly said *chine*, then when Yonderly said *snaith*, those were the first occasions Parry had heard the words. And the last.

But such a sound was *scythe*. How that word had unsettled Parry. It flashed in his mind, that scythe's iron chine.

Amongst the grasses' seedheads, the yellow rattle and smoky mugwort, Parry gazed into a world the scythe revealed only to himself.

Look at that beast, Yonderly had said, unwrapping the scythe's swaddling.

A man peens a scythe blade, he said. Yes, peens a chine. Peening is sharpening. Or hammering. The finer a man peens, the sharper the metal.

They say the best peeners could get their blades thinner than cigarette papers. Even finer. And hammered out on a scythe anvil.

Ever seen a scythe anvil? No, nor me. In all the years I've had this shed open, I've never found a single one. But comes a day. Comes a day...

I love this work, Yonderly would announce. I say to the boys, we can never know what will be brought in. Simply never know. What might be delivered. Think of everything that's waiting for us. The possibilities.

Jack Parry had been there to see the scythe unwrapped. His son had expected comment. He was not disappointed.

Well, we must all be safe now, the father beamed. The Grim Reaper's lost his big knife. Hallelujah! Let's have a party, tell the girls. But what a nasty piece of work that shears is. Could take a man's head clean off.

Although he had not seen one used, Parry imagined a scythe's strokes, its sighing amongst sap-heavy stems, as dusk's dew settled on the swathes.

Yes, Parry had once thought. Was it the tools he loved? Or the words for the tools? In those days, he had been going to write.

Even in Australia, he had still been eager to compose, enthused as he was by Gouger Street market.

No better work, was there? Not painting, no, not painting.

But he saw his mother once again. Her face to the earth as she breathed in the white coriander flowers, tiny as watchwheels. As she burrowed in the limestone tilth. Yes, gardening was considerable work.

But in Yonderly's workshop, there had been incense in the air. Parry thought now it was the perfume of the words themselves. All the lost vocabularies that might find restoration.

On one of his walks Parry passed what he thought was Yonderly's house. He found himself in the back lane, searching out the workshop.

But there was no green shed there. Or nowhere that Parry could recognise. He looked around a cratered yard, hoping for evidence of tools that had awaited repair.

Not a screwdriver, he grimaced. Let alone a twisted caib on The Caib.

Haven't thought of Yonderly for forty years, Parry realised. Yet maybe his house was in Lily Street.

Yes, perhaps the old man never lived in George Street at all. In this mist I'm getting my orientation of The Caib all wrong.

And Parry had paused in a cone of streetlight, tasting the pearls that crusted his stubble. In that district of town not another soul stirred.

Must be close to high tide now, he had thought. Yes, almost high tide. The shoulders of the swell were rubbing against a world he called home. Somewhere, the glow from a pub door shimmied like mercury. An attic light was switched on.

He closed his eyes and tried to recall the workshop. Wires and wheels. A forest of dead dials. But more powerful were the smells of the different oils that had suffused the benches.

And on he walked, a puzzled man, doubting himself. The workshop could not be found. The fret clung like thistledown. Air was thick around him.

And he thought once more of his mother. A pinch of ash was all he had held, watching it blow back from the Caib cliffs. A spoonful over The Horns, across the lagoons. An urnful dug into the allotment. Now kept by strangers.

Ash grey, ash fine. To stick to the lapels of his second-hand suit. To rest a moment upon his lips. A powder like the mist that had grown over the town and hung in a pall.

Yes, people disappear, Parry said to himself, the rime cold on his lips. Everybody disappears. Eventually. So why shouldn't places vanish?

III

What did you do there exactly? asked Mina. In this marvellous shop? Down Under?

She and Parry were together in Basement Booze, sharing mugs of coffee. A man came in and asked about cigarettes. There was a woman with a gauze of mist in her hair, looking at the Polish beers.

I can get these for nearly half the price in B&M, she told the room.

Mina looked tired. Obviously after a poor night. But she shrugged and clinked mugs with Parry.

You really want to know? he asked. It's pretty dull.

Try me.

Sorted the stock that I brought in from Gouger Street Market. Tapes and CDs and second-hand books.

Think: posters of David Bowie, poems by DH Lawrence. Or was it the other way around? All these boxes of paper, I suppose. Anything that people might have stored. Bills of lading, news cuttings. Rubbish, mostly.

But anything that could make *Hey Bulldog* seem cool. Or vital. I was trying to give the impression that something was going on. You know the song? *There's something happening here…*

Must have passed me by, love. But I understand you. And doing it then was easier then doing it now. So opening *Badfinger* is…

Half-baked? Suicidal? A stroke of genius? Who's to say? But yes, we need a website. Will ask Gil.

Parry paused. Or is Gil past it already? Might ask a twenty year old. Glan must know something. As to money, this first year we'll make a loss. And a loss next year. But I can cope with that.

Mina clinked Parry's mug once more.

Maybe we'll also try clothes, he said. A cool second-hand dress agency, if we can squash it into *Badfinger*. Use upstairs. Use my bedroom. And try Serene as a model for the frocks. Good figure, hasn't she? Kind of classical.

And Glan too. He's got great cheekbone structure. I can picture him in a vintage dinner jacket. Or something tweedy. With leather elbow patches.

Hoi, Svengali! Cool down.

I mean it, laughed Parry. They're a couple with er, stylistic possibilities.

First time I saw them together in the shop, I thought, yeah, that could work! Didn't even know what I was looking for. Just that I was looking. For something.

Yes, I like Glan's sneer. Seemed a bit shifty on first acquaintance, okay. But combine that sneer with his vulnerability. His rock 'n' roll insouciance. Mix it up and you've discovered something. What everyone is looking for.

He's a hard little bastard, said Mina. I'll say that about him. Maybe the girl's all right. Yeah, great tits. And small waist. Lucky madam. But Glan is a user. And he's using her. Plain as day.

Maybe it is. Maybe he's using me. Maybe Lulu was using me. Maybe I was using Lulu.

Look, I used to tell Lulu what to wear. Just a skimpy top, I'd say. Flaunt those shoulders, I'd say. You know what I mean, Lu.

Soon the boys were queuing for a gander. Their dads, too. This was Goolwa, remember. Not much else was happening. Farm boys who wrote their names on dirty pick ups? Older brothers who collected stamps? None of them with the Net. Remember that, the world without the Net? Stone Age. I was doing them all a favour.

And here's me thinking it was art, said Mina.

Course it was art. It still is art. Everything's art. I just helped the art along.

And little Lulu cut the mustard in Goolwa?

She was a natural. As to Oz, *Hey Bulldog* was only open eighteen months. Not long enough. It was still in the experimental stage. And now, years later, I'm trying again. One last throw of the dice.

Was it expensive over there?

Not really. I didn't own the place, after all. Just a dusty little shop, wasn't it? A shop with a garden we tried to use for unplugged nights.

Paying the rent was the big expense. And the rates. Making sure most of the bills didn't get out of hand. But there weren't proper wages. I never drew a salary. Lulu had to organise her own tax, her own insurance.

Then Parry smirked.

As if! he said. It never occurred to me to talk to Lulu about tax. She just wasn't that kind of person. Too young for a start. The whole idea would be ... *preposterous*.

IV

How old was she really, and don't lie.

Sixteen.

Sure?

Well, yes. Call it sixteen. Maybe seventeen.

You're unconvincing.

Maybe twenty-five.

Oh yes. Who could ever believe you, mister? I never do. You're dangerous, you are.

Then call it seventeen. I think so. No, I know so.

Sure?

Believe me. She was. Sixteen. She was twenty. Might have been eighteen. Honestly. Not that it mattered. She was like … *family*. And I've never had a daughter, remember.

Like me, you mean?

Not having children is crucial, said Parry. Sometimes I wake up and I think I'm still in Oz. Must be summer, I think, I'm sweating so much. I'm clammy. Christ, I'm soaked.

But it's dread I'm feeling. Yes, a kind of sickening horror. And you know what it comes from? It's not having a family. That's what.

But little Lulu was sort of … expendable? suggested Mina.

Well … who isn't? After what happened to me I know I am. But, yes, being honest again, she was expendable. Yet that's not the word. *Hey Bulldog* was just an idea, remember. A conception. The trick is, always get others to do things for you. So they own that idea. And one day they'll fight for that idea.

But you liked her?

I loved Lulu to pieces. Wonderful kid. Yeah, she slept in the shop. Amongst the stock. Wherever she curled up. In a nest on top of the tapes and posters. Sometimes in a hammock in the garden.

And you miss that life? Don't you?

Too true. But it feels like a dream. I've entered the dream time, God help me. And there's no coming out of that.

Out of the Dreaming? That's what they call it, isn't it? Over there?

Yeah. The Dreaming.

So tell me about it, said Mina.

Parry smiled. It was … the right thing. For a while.

Or is that called hindsight? Look, I gave Lulu money. Of course I gave her money. *Hey Bulldog* didn't cost too much, and I wasn't really spending my salary.

So I started paying for Lulu's clothes. For everything.

There was this haberdashery in Goolwa high street. Real old-fashioned place. Corsets and stockings and petticoats. Used to be a girl in there I liked. By that I mean she had an interesting face. And, I wanted to rescue her.

So I brought that girl into *Hey Bulldog*. She came in once, I think. Picked up a Miles Davis album and … *giggled*. Without hearing a note. 'Bitches Brew' I think it was. Bit different from The New Seekers, which was on the jukeboxes in town.

And that was it. The girl must have had really ancient parents. You see, some people are doomed. Nothing can be done for them.

It's not their fault. It's just life. Anyway, Lulu hated the shop that smelled of mothballs. So I took her to Gouger Street and let her choose whatever she wanted. Free rein.

And I paid for it all. For Lulu's soap and for Lulu's shampoo and Lulu's perfumes. Even for Lulu's tampax. Which reminds me.

Oh dear.

Yeah, story coming up. Lulu was already friendly with an older girl. Another native girl. Another sweet face. Sucker, aren't I?

Once I came back from Gouger Street and found Lulu tipsy as a wallaby. I couldn't believe it. Or, perhaps I could.

Anyway, this other girl had recommended her party trick. You know, the alcoholic tampon trick. Soak your tampax in vodka, then tonic, then insert.

But forget the tonic. Because tonic's expensive. And Christ, it worked. Better than Lulu ever expected. I had to put her to bed. Again. After she was sick. Again.

That's nonsense, laughed Mina. It's a bloody myth. But who'd be a parent?

Not me, it seems. What was funny was her telling the tale. It all came out. You see, I found the tampax applicator in the bathroom. I even warned her about toxic shock. Now that really frightened her. And me.

So who'd be a mother? said Mina.

Not that the kid cost much. She wasn't used to luxury.

Lucky though, I'd say. Wasn't she?

Lulu made her own luck, said Parry. And boy, she had good luck coming to her after that rough time in Addy. Now, where was I?

V

You must think I'm naïve, said Mina. Look, you're just a man. You're alive. No need to apologise.

Well, sorry anyway. And sometimes Lulu drank beer and sometimes Lulu drank peppermint schapps.

Sometimes Lulu even smoked the Dutchies' draw. That bloody head-spinning skunk the couple next door cultivated in their motel garden. Worse than white widow, that stuff. Once Lulu smoked so much skunk she was sick. Yeah, again. The kid slept for fifteen hours.

After you encouraged her?

That time I was really worried about her. Again. But Lulu was a force of nature. She pleased herself.

And yes, Lulu told me about stars. We'd go out for walks down to the Murray. She'd peel off those old khaki keks she wore and dive in.

Yes, it scared me. Before that she'd always say, look at this, look at this, Richard! And she'd put my hand on this line of black moles in the small of her back. Above the right hipbone. Her constellation, she called it. Like Orion's belt, she used to say. But upside down. Her black stars. Above the scar.

Ooh, do you think I'm a black star, Richard? she'd ask. Am

I a black star to you? Or a brown star? Because people are like stars, aren't they, Richard? Some stars become red and some become blue. But like people, most stars are in the middle. Yes, yellow stars.

And Lulu would tell me the names of the stars in Orion. The stars I can never remember.

Oh, she was a golden arrow, Lulu was then. Lulu who could just … *vanish*. And I was always sure she'd drown in the Murray.

So I'd wait and I'd wait until I couldn't stand it any longer. And then I'd have to wait some more and wait some more before I heard this *whoosh*, this wonderful *whooshing*. Yeah, this *swooshing* sound.

And there she'd be, Lulu spitting out the Murray's red water. Lulu boasting about how long she had held her breath this time.

Over two minutes! Richard. Two minutes fifteen. A record for the stinking old Murray with its waving weed.

And let's go and have a cold beer, Richard. Let's get a Dr Tim's out of that fridge of yours. It's been there for two days now. Should be cold enough, Richard. Even for a hot old Pom like you.

So let's have a Dr Tim's in the garden and I'll test you on your Arabic stars. Yes, I'll test the schoolteacher. I'll give the schoolteacher marks out of ten.

And then you can give me a cuddle, Richard, because maybe I'm missing my mother tonight, Richard. Maybe I'm missing my mum.

Mina shook her head. You just make it up. Admit it. You could say anything and we'd have to believe you. Because who's going to check up. On you, Mr Parry? How could we ever find out?

True, I suppose. But doesn't everyone? Make stuff up? And

believe me, the kid needed comforting. You're a mother. You know.

Yes, said Mina quietly. I know.

Once, I went in too. Dived in the Murray. Scared me, the water was so murky. But warm after the first shock. Cloudy as blood, it was. Sticky as spunk.

Mina shook her head.

That river came out of the heart of Oz. The parched red heart. It was like an old sclerotic artery. And I was part of the bloodstream. Couldn't be more different from here. You ever swim in The Chasm?

No way. I'd have to be crazy.

But in the sea?

Not for years.

Yes, swimming's hard to imagine in this mist, said Parry. But look, there's a silver light out there now. Over the sea. Isn't that strange?

But we all used to go in the sea together. The whole gang. Especially Sev. But even Fflinty. And that was in the dark, too. Skinnydipping up at The Horns. We must have been mad.

Don't think I ever dared, said Mina.

But your daughter paints those wrecks, doesn't she? The ships that sank around The Caib?

Used to. Paint that is.

She's talented, said Parry. If traditional. All that titanium white for seafoam. But I like *The Vainquer* in your front room. And *The Cato's* pretty … *dramatic.* Yeah, all these storms. The whole coast's a graveyard.

That's what they say, said Mina. A shipwreck every year, it used to be. So my dad told me.

Where does she live?

Alys? asked Mina.

Yes. Your artistic daughter.

178

Followed her father, didn't she.

While you're working in Basement Booze? said Parry. And living in a flat over the shop.

That's me. Smuggling vodka and fags up the back stairs. Wanting to do the accounts by hand when it's got to be spreadsheets and pricy accounting packages now. Tragic, aren't I?

You're a heroine, laughed Parry.

Can't compete with the supermarkets, can we? There's talk of a three-month extension. But it'll be a miracle if we're saved.

Testing times, said Parry.

And here's you opening a business, selling, exactly … *what?*

Dreams, laughed Parry. Believe me, I am. No, to be truthful, old records and CDs. But dreams are the real niche market.

Romantic, aren't you.

Look, *Badfinger*'s giving people something cool. It's just an experiment. And, like I said, it's tough all round. My pension's paying for it.

Pension? laughed Mina. Christ, what's that? I deal in real life, honey. While you're still dreaming. Yes, you're still in the dream time.

I'm as real as you, said Parry. Look, I'm not a philanthropist.

See that display? asked Mina. That bottle of red wine on top costs fifty quid. Been here since I arrived. Before we close, when it's even harder to make a living, I'm going to smash that bottle. Or pretend to. Then you can come over to celebrate. I'll do a bolognaise.

It's a date. And Alys has talent. Tell her from me. Remember, I used to teach art.

And you can tell a story, said Mina. But that Lulu girl had you round her little finger. Didn't she?

Parry looked away.

So you'll have to finish the story. About what happened.

Because something happened over there. Didn't it? Something that scared you home.

Look, if everything's a story, said Parry, the best stories are the ones you work out yourself. But the very best stories never run in straight lines. Don't you agree?

Course I do. But with stories like yours I've just no idea what to believe.

Believe it all, said Parry, grimacing at the coffee. Every word.

VI

In summer, cycling was difficult in the fair. There were too many distracted visitors. Often, Parry had to dismount.

But winters were different. He remembered one ride clearly. It was a freezing day in the first week of December. He passed the Kingdom of Evil and the Ritzy. Then took the sandy road into the aisles of caravans. Even dog walkers were scarce.

But predictably, the allotments were busy. Parry had decided upon one job only. Cutting down the sunflowers, then burning them.

That summer there had been a remarkable crop. Twenty had survived, the latest version of the Parrys' Sunflower Street.

The tallest of the flowers had originally been twelve foot high. Now they were laid low in ruin. Seedheads in rotten honeycombs.

When he arrived he noted a rat climbing the tallest stem. Sunflower season was over in barely six weeks. But decline extended months.

Parry opened the allotment toolbox, never locked. He decided on an antique machete for cutting the stems. Then a caib for digging out rootballs.

It was satisfactory work. Lopping, cutting, hacking. The

sunflowers were dry now, and soon their faces were restored to a final corona. The pyre released a barrage of sparks.

And hadn't someone come over? To complain about the sunflower fire? Yes, a stranger. Parry couldn't remember seeing him before.

There's laws about fires, the man had said. Think of all the pollution you're causing.

Sorry, smiled Parry. But if I put them on the compost they'll never rot down. And if I left these alone they'd be here next summer.

Black skeletons, he thought. Sunflower ghosts. So all in all, he added, sunflowers are a bit of a problem.

Don't belong, do they? the man had said.

Oh, we love them, said Parry. Especially my mother. She's the guilty party here.

To me, they're aliens, the man had said. South of France? Fine. Put a spell on old Van Gogh, didn't they? But too exotic for The Caib.

Doesn't your heart lift? When you see a sunflower? Mine does. Spuds and beans get predictable, I think. And we can't grow caulis. Peas are unreliable, too.

The man had paused.

When you put it like that, he considered.

Every one's a miracle, said Parry. Twelve feet, fifteen almost, these sunflowers. They shouldn't be here. But every May, they begin. And from about now, my mother collects the seeds. To plant the next generation.

Parry kept smiling. There was sunflower ash on his brow. One of his shoes showed sparks from where he had rearranged the blaze.

Watch it, don't set yourself afire, the man had said. Parry noted that word. It wasn't local.

Thanks, said Parry. But I'd be sorry to see them go.

Seen you in The Works, haven't I? the man asked. Over in the sheds?

That's it.

Lonely place, out there, said the man.

I'm used to it now, said Parry. Where no one bothers you.

FIFTEEN

I

I always thought, said Parry, that they looked like tears.

He pointed close to the quartz. Then stroked the rock.

Or maybe drops of milk, he added. Yeah, stone milk. But become crystal. So crystal milk. Looks like milk, doesn't it?

Someone, years ago it must have been, had scratched a crude eye into the limestone. The graffiti had faded but was still distinct.

The quartz was cool under his fingers.

I remember the boy who claimed he wasn't guilty. Of doing that. But I was there when the deed was done. Always getting into some kind of trouble, was Sev. Hard to believe that was over forty years ago.

Glan too touched the quartz tears. They were a series of white eruptions. Eyelets of ice.

This is part of a walk I always used to take, Parry said. Reminds me of going to the allotments on my bike. Through the fair, across the badlands, and into the caravan park.

On that walk I try to pass all the fossils we have around here. While remembering they were once alive. Which, of course, isn't easy to do.

Stone's not alive, said Glan.

Isn't it?

How could stone be alive?

You know, I always regret not doing geology in college, said Parry.

But how could stone be alive?

Because it was once … vital. That's how. Molten, unstable. That's stone. And different stones have different tastes. Different smells.

I can't smell stone, said Glan.

Go into the dunes. The highest crest. Break open one of the grey stones on top. Then breathe it in. Yes, breathe in the stone. It'll smell, all right. A sulphur smell.

Some stones are full of ghosts. Because fossils are ghosts. And then look into that stone. That stone will be packed with corals. With minute creatures. From the seabed.

Yeah, stones are full of ghosts. Like echoes in the earth. Or that's what I think.

Parry stood on tiptoe and placed his tongue against the quartz. It could have been a glass nipple within his mouth.

And this stone tastes, too, he said.

Of what?

Salt, Parry said immediately, licking the white eye. A beadlet white as a dog's wall eye.

Yes, salt of course. But also wet sand. A dead seagull. That horrible cider they sell in The Cat. The outfall. It's however The Caib smells. Because it smells like home.

Great.

You know, I used to dream about that smell when I was over in Oz. Salt forever in the air. Because we're drenched in salt here. Overwhelmed by salt. There are currents of salt flowing through this place.

Parry looked round and smiled.

Hey, he asked, you ever drank in The Cat?

Took Serene in there once, said Glan. On her birthday. Some

old bloke bought her a sherry. And she'd never had sherry in her life.

What you drinking? this old bloke says.

Sherry, Serene says. And I swear it was the first word that came into her head. Surprised us both.

Then a sherry for my friend here, said the old bloke. And I had one too. Why not, this old geezer's buying. It tasted hot. Sweet and hot.

Yes, home on The Caib, said Parry. And here's me still sucking on its icy tit. Stone milk. Stone blood. And all around us, stone pollen. The Caib's wild spoor.

Welcome home, the salt is saying. Welcome home, the sand is saying.

You know, eventually, there are some things you have to accept. Like where you come from. And you realise it will do. Yes, it will do. That you don't need to apologise any more. That the truth is good enough.

Parry paused. We used to come this way to the fair. Me and Sev. They call these lanes 'The Backs'. Godawful place, it's always been. The backs of beyond. You come out by The Ziggurat.

Yeah, past the burned-out caravans, added Glan. Quickest way into the fair. If you're not squeamish, that is. Around here is where they found two of the boys. Hanging. In these stone shelters.

It's a maze, always was, said Parry. That's why it took months to find them.

People knew the boys were here, says Glan. It was the obvious place. Only those people didn't want to report it. Because what's it matter when they were found? And they were dead, weren't they? Dead, dead, dead.

Parry smiled at his companion.

Ever wondered why these deaths are happening? he asked. I have. Seems a peculiar way of making yourself famous.

Maybe they didn't mean to kill themselves.

Maybe, said Parry.

Could have been?

What?

A mistake?

I'll say, said Parry, considering. The biggest mistake possible. But read your history, it's always happened. Years ago they found a girl buried in the sand. Dug her out of some type of tomb. She'd been burned. Sort of sacrificed. To the fire.

That must have been three thousand years ago. There's a report on it in the museum in Cato Street.

That doesn't mean she did it herself, said Glan. No young person really wants to die.

Parry looked at the bedraggled boy, damp from the salt mist. The salt was quicksilver on Glan's eyebrows. Every eyelash distinct. Around both men it was if a cloud had descended, heavy with unfallen rain.

Parry kept his hand against the limestone, feeling its chill. Even at the height of summer this rock would be cold.

In The Backs there was little direct light. Instead, there were endless passages here, some blocked by broken doors, old crates.

Ivy had pushed into the crevices. Someone must have tried to clear it, years earlier. The rock was a network of white scars.

In fact, there had always been attempts to deny access to this maze. If he was not mistaken, close by was an entrance to one of The Catriona's cellars.

Under Parry's hands the bevels of quartz lay like ridges of frost. White capillaries ran through the stone.

Like I said, it's the weeping rock. Or that's what we called it in the past. There's probably a legend about it. This place is full of legends.

Sand lay underfoot, a gauze of mist in the air. Parry realised that they were now below the fairground. Maybe directly above were the rooms where broken carriages from the Kingdom of Evil were stored. But it was difficult to be precise. Such were the complications of The Backs.

Christ, it's cold down here, said Parry. The damp gets right inside you.

He licked the salt from his lips.

Deep down inside. And to think this is the weather I wanted when the drought was on. Down under.

I could picture myself, sipping the seamist. Yeah, I dreamed about this mist. A cocktail of seamist, barman! No, never satisfied, are we? But I'm missing that electric fire.

Parry glanced round at the streaming walls.

Hey, Glan, fancy a drink? We're just feet from the back door of The Cat. At least I think we are. I'll get Mina over.

II

They had to leave the passages by the way they'd entered.

Parry first wondered whether the pub was open. But remembered The Cat never closed. Only the unfinished section was off limits.

Fancy a sherry?

Nah.

Lager then? I see they've that new German stuff. Strong.

Fair enough.

Parry recognised one or two of the drinkers by sight. Davy Dumma, the treasure-hunter, was in. But he would speak to no one.

In a far corner was a man some people called Cranc. Once he'd been arrested for cutting up jellyfish.

The bodies and tentacles had been sliced on the sands. The

police let him go with a warning. There had been debate about whether jellyfish feel pain.

In summer, some of the jellies that washed on to The Horns and Caib Caves were enormous. Parry remembered them as molten glass. Creatures almost transparent, scarcely visible. On the sands they looked as if they had melted. Pools of vaseline. A strange afterbirth. That was why some of the girls didn't like swimming after dark.

Just imagine, he could recall Lizzy saying, reaching out and touching that. I'd die, I swear I'd die.

What if it put its arms around you? And what's it made of anyway? And what's inside it?

He remembered his carbon paper job in the sheds. There had been jellyfish on that beach also, gritty from the sinter-covered sands.

What a summer that had been. The best summer of all. When everybody had a job. At least everybody who wanted one.

Even Jack Parry had boasted of a miraculous period. Money coming in before the lay offs. Before the season of discontent. Jack Parry selling his coffee and his paperbacks and his typewriter courses. And making a tidy profit.

Like father, like … thought Parry, taking in the room. Good old Jack, doing it his way. Dad, getting his own scene together.

III

Parry was surprised when Mina walked in, looking around.

Hey, you're awake, he greeted her.

Mina ignored him.

Been years, she confessed.

We bet. Didn't we? That you wouldn't come.

Glan didn't speak.

The woman shook out her umbrella but her red hair was still sparkling with salt.

And it's not raining, she complained. What weather. Mad isn't it?

More than mad, said Parry. It's suicide weather.

Christ, the woman said. Don't you know you never use that word. You never, ever use that word.

True though, laughed Parry.

Well, I suppose you're allowed as you've been away. You've sort of arrived in the middle of it. Just make sure you never say that word again.

Very superstitious, aren't you, said Parry. By the way, I always wondered about the line in that song, 'The writing's on the wall'. What's it mean?

Some things shouldn't be written down, said Mina, out of the corner of her mouth.

But you know what that boy had written? she continued. It was in biro on a strip of white cement. On the wall. In that disgusting room. The room where he was found.

I think about him writing that. Then doing it. A kid all alone. In that room. Makes me cringe.

Parry was going to ask what the boy had written. But a young woman appeared from behind the bar and inquired about their order.

Mina looked around more carefully.

Yes, ten years, I'd say. No danger. But yes, is my motto. Saying yes to everything. Yes, yes, yes. So white wine with soda, please. Large one. Enormous one. That'll teach yah.

Parry noted rime on the blonde hairs above Mina's lip, cruel in the striplight. The weather had marked them all. Redheaded woman, ivory boy.

Affects everyone, this weather, said Mina. Even him. And she

189

gestured towards Cranc who had not bothered to remove his wet jacket.

The man was staring into the fret. As if trying to detect something rubbing itself against the glass.

You know what I remember? she asked. That bench. The bench with the pink sea-serpent frame. I'll never forget that bench.

After everything that's been destroyed, I can't believe it's still here. Considering the price of scrap, I can't.

But last time I was down here, there it was. Yes, the iron sea serpent, we always called it. Painted pink. Or red. Like something that might have crawled out of the waves. Or something heading back that way.

We played here too, said Parry. Pretending it was a monster.

I'd have thought everything would have vanished down here, said Mina. But since plans for The Mall were shelved…

Too bad, said Parry.

Hey, Peter Lorre was in that film, wasn't he, asked the woman.

What film?

Twenty Thousand Leagues Under the Sea. Talking about sea monsters made me think. It was on telly last week.

But it's one Sunday when I was ten or twelve, I remember best. My dad said, watch him, he's good. Watch him. That's Peter Lorre.

So I spent the whole film watching my dad watching Peter Lorre. At the start, I didn't understand what Dad meant. But I kept watching.

By the end, it was obvious. Maybe Peter Lorre looked peculiar, with those insect eyes of his. Like a grasshopper. But mesmerised, that was Dad.

Yeah, there's an Al Stewart song mentions Peter Lorre, said Parry. Which reminds me. Let's get some Al Stewart on offer in *Badfinger*. He used to sell OK in Oz. Well, no worse than any other British folkie in a woolly jumper. Let's honour those who deserve honouring.

And when we went to Disneyland in Paris, said Mina, what did we find? One of their rides was based on *Twenty Thousand Leagues*.

Made me think about The Caib again. The sand blowing around the caravans in those little tornados. And a pink sea serpent used as a bench.

They used to show films upstairs, said Parry. A club called the Black Lite. And there'd be acts down here, singers, bands, over in that corner. Where Cranc is.

It's dead now, said Glan.

It's quiet, said Parry. I'll give you that.

Feels dead to me, the boy said. The whole town.

Then *Badfinger*'s the first sign of life, said Parry. Cheer up, people. If we could make it work in a one-horse town in Australia, in the middle of the worst drought for a century, we can do it here.

When Serene walked in, looking nervous, Parry held his arms open.

Like a family reunion, he shouted. My children!

Saw her in the shop, practising, said Mina, giving Parry a knowing glance. I said, you look great, love. Everything'll work out. So, relax.

Listen, I said, we're in The Cat. Don't know why. Come along. Just keep your clothes on this time, lady.

Glan was now distracted. Mina leaned close to Parry.

And stop giving them money. They'll have to cope on their own.

It was just a few quid, said Parry.

Happening a lot, isn't it?

They'll be working for me soon. Real jobs.

They have to be able to talk about the stock. Remember, everything on sale in *Badfinger* comes with a story. A unique history. It's not just product, so they're more than sales assistants. They have to learn. Like Lulu learned.

But no sales experience, Mina said.

They learn on the job. You know that.

Get a grip on yourself, man. You're besotted.

Nonsense.

But I don't know with which one.

Don't talk mad. Everything's under control, I promise you.

Parry was now beaming at the room. Cranc had slipped away into the mist.

Sherry? he asked Serene, who was wearing her violet blouse. Oh yes, we know all about you and sherry.

SIXTEEN

I

At the top of Nuestra Senhora del Carmen Street a pale sun, a sun greyly glittering. A sun of deadwhite coral. Around that sun a smoky aurora.

II

Above The Chasm was a drift of pebbles. All were white or grey as gull feathers. Each was unmoveable.

Round as owl eggs, thought Parry, pleased with himself, as he awoke from an Australian dream.

Above his bed he could see the moon, fat and silver. But for Lulu's catlike snores, *Hey Bulldog* was silent.

Outside, a bat had touched the window, a creature black as charcoal, a ghost sketched even darker than the night. A silhouette in charred paper.

The moon was so close it seemed all he needed to do was open his mouth to suck its pale pumice.

Bitter as quartz, he whispered. Stone milk from a stone breast. Acid leaking from a wound. *No man alive, no man alive will…*

I'm still dreaming, he realised.

Still dreaming.

Or maybe he was singing.

Yes, here I am, he had murmured to no one. Child of the moon? Another song with Brian Jones, footling away. Poor Brian. Under his cap of silver wire. His aragonite hair. Sad and just as barren. As desperate.

Parry had thought then of his music collection. He would have scrabbled for a CD, any CD that might take away the silence.

He longed for a Kerala raga he had once heard, based on a drone, the endless syllable of 'Om'. Music for the hour before dawn. When life seemed stunned. Yet all was possible.

But there had been nothing to hand. He could hear his own breathing. The whisper of his breath. The whimper of it. Which was all he had ever owned.

So Parry had lain in his moon-coloured sweat. Yes, a man woken in a strange country, he had thought then. On an alien continent. Even the birds are foreign for me in this place. It will always be the same.

And the dread stole up on him. Colder than his perspiration. At that moment the night sounds were terrifying, the inexplicable night with the Murray passing out of the dead heart. Flowing past the room where he lay.

Where a girl child moaned in her sleep, a bat-thing of a girl, a black spirit who had brushed against his window, begging to be allowed in. An urchin, a refugee, a wisp of burnt paper. Blown against the glass.

What had he expected to find? he had asked himself then. Here?

In such a place?

Where the next country is an ice desert.

Parry lay upon the silver sheet. He thought of a woman he had seen rescued from the sea. Maybe she was part of the dream. It was Sev who had pointed to the group of people. Yes, Sev who noticed the drama.

The woman had been wrapped in aluminium foil to prevent hypothermia. She had glimmered like some medieval Madonna.

The rescuing hands upon her were black, brutal. Colder than seawater, thought Parry then. As they bore the silver woman to her bier, carrying her along the beach. Silent in procession.

But the dream was not about Sev or the woman. Parry's dream had been full of fog. Yes, that was it. And he remembered the dream again. The dream with the moonlight upon him, the moon's white sweat on his belly. That pouch of moonsilver had gilded his balls and sheathed his cock. Parry groaned beneath his silver erection.

But yes, he had heard something. The sound of the fog. The call of the foghorn.

Maybe he hadn't heard the foghorn for years. Or had he? As a boy, how he had thrilled in his bed in the darkness, when the fog's music had blown over The Caib.

Yes, he thought. The foghorn was louder than the sirens at The Works. More unexpected than May's fairground anthems, suddenly audible in the back garden.

Because whenever the foghorn had sounded in Amazon Street or the Cato Street slipway, his life had become different.

When the fog had come to brush itself against his own window, it had tasted of sand and salt. Acid and milk. And in the fog everything was changed.

Parry shivered, thinking about the dream. And he tried once again to remember it. Maybe in the dream the fog was made of white stones. White, hollow stones, light enough to float away.

Yes, the fog was stones. Limestones, pale as gas from The Works. Stones bitter as the sulphur his father hated.

Dad, Dad, he thought. Jack Parry rubbing against the grain.

Jack getting it wrong, consistently wrong. His own father pissing into the wind. Dad who liked music that made his son cringe. Dad who chose unsuitable jobs. Jack Parry who planted potatoes upside down.

But they still grow, he could hear his father's voice once more, accusing Parry and his mother of ganging up on him.

Up or down, those potatoes are fine. You stick them in the ground and rose end up or rose end down they grow. So relax.

The fog was white stones. The fog was snow smeared with mercury.

The foghorn was located in a lighthouse to the east of The Caib. It was a monstrous white instrument that Parry and Gil had once thought could be used on a recording.

In fact, Gil had done something with a tape he had made. An impossible bass chord.

A holy throb, Gil had called the sound. Religious, even. Last stop on a church organ but far deeper yet.

Yes, stones, Parry thought. Those stones above The Chasm. Impossible to lift. Like snowballs children have rolled up huge. Yes, that's fog. Or a pillow over the face.

In the dream, wheels of thistledown floated past.

Yes, hollow stones. Hollow in Parry's head. *No man alive will… No man alive…*

Someone had drowned. The woman had drowned. But they were keeping her warm. Upon a bed of thistledown.

Parry lay in his silver bed. He raised his mouth to the moon's breast.

No man alive… he whispered again.

No man…

Then perhaps he slept.

III

Quietly the Arvo Part music came to an end. Ominous and eerie, it was a mistake. But it had been played so softly neither Glan nor Serene had commented. And Parry had been talking but not listening.

Through the streetlight the fret hung in pearls. 3.09am. he noted. In the dark flat a nightlight like a red star cast a glow. Serene had taken it from the Christmas decorations in the shop.

It warms your freezing room, she had insisted. This way, people on the street can see it. And you get the benefit. We all do.

Yes, said Parry. He saw it was 3.12 and felt exhausted.

Good idea of yours. It can be seen from as far off as Cato Street. Almost the only light, Christmas or not. A red star like Arcturus.

Like what?

I knew somebody once, murmured Parry, who understood stars.

You see, smiled the girl, my star shows there's someone alive. In this house.

She was wearing one of Parry's purple shirts and two of his thickest jerseys. On the couch behind, Glan was covered by a duvet.

Shows there's somebody who wants to be alive, Serene added. Someone who's celebrating being alive.

Quietest Christmas I can remember, said Parry.

But next year will be great, insisted the girl. I can feel it. Things can't stay like this. It's...

What?

Impossible. It's just ... *impossible.*

You weren't around in the seventies.

My dad's told me about Thatcher, the girl hissed. But yes it can get better.

I admire your optimism. But life will be tougher before that. No one knows how tough. Get ready for it.

Serene hugged her purple knees.

You know there's been another one? she asked.

No, I hadn't heard. But I'm not surprised. This weather can't be helping. We're living inside a cloud. Bloody fog. Feels like we're all suffocating.

Glan says…

Yes?

Oh. Nothing.

Glan shouldn't smoke that stuff if it's going to do things to him, said Parry,

Well, who gave it to him?

I just happened to share what Dai had offered me. Bit like the old days in the Paradise Club. Not that we were regular users. Course not. Hasn't harmed you, has it?

Glan always sparks out, said the girl, kissing her right kneecap through her tights. I knew he would.

Predictable, is he?

She considered this.

Maybe. But men are…

Boring?

Glan's not boring, Serene smiled grimly. I wouldn't stay with him if he was boring.

Parry hugged his own knees. A car passed in the street. The headlights shone through the curtains. He ground out the butt in a saucer.

I don't do this often, he said. Smoke, that is. But thanks.

For?

For checking up on me. Seeing if I was alive.

Well, we are living together, said Serene. And thank you for the wine. Yes, quite a night. Red wine and more red wine. Then a little drop of whisky and the last of the peppermint schnapps and Dai's draw and cheese on toast with that mad paprika stuff. And more toast. And all were most … the girl paused. Most *welcome*.

My pleasure, said Parry. But it wasn't the cheese on toast that knocked out Glan.

Did we drink so much?

Er … yes. But don't tell me that's all he's had.

S'all I know about, breathed Serene. Honestly. Glan and me can't afford to drink. You know that. But Mina's good. Passes on what she calls discontinued lines.

Yeah, bless those redundant Riojas, smiled Parry. So Mina's more than useful to know. But I saw Glan's eyes. He must have taken something else. He was tranked up like a first timer. Now the kid's out cold.

All right, she said. I do know about something else. These ones are white.

What are white?

Serene again kissed her kneecap through the purple tights.

The pills Glan takes. He had one this morning. I said not to. I said don't. Not today. Because of how they make you behave, I told him. But he only laughed.

And then I said we used to share everything. Once. But not these. Not these white ones. I can't do the white ones. I can't share the white ones. Tried a white one once. Never again.

Parry thought about his own tablets. They were white ones. Big ones white, little ones white. Big pills, little pills. The rest of his life on pills.

He looked at his wrist in the red light. 3.23.

What was it now? Six months since he had last taken his medicines? No, maybe ten. Perhaps a year. He hadn't ordered any for ages. No one had checked.

Parry considered how he felt. Every morning at the time to take his tablets he conducted an investigation. Surely, there was no change. At least, nothing to speak of. Nothing important. But then he had not felt unwell in the first place. At the beginning of all his trouble. But now, it was hard to care.

How do the pills make Glan feel?

Serene coughed. He says they make him come alive.

Parry waited. The girl continued.

Not so…

Parry still waited. Both he and Serene were bathed in the star's red glow.

Not so … anxious, I suppose, she said at last. Not so … scared.

She stretched out her purple legs towards him then.

3.27.

I'm cold, she whispered.

Time for sleep, said Parry.

You know, breathed Serene, I knew one of those boys. Those boys who did it. I remember him from school. And you'd never think. You'd never think he was that type. But the last time we met, he talked to me. Honest to God, he talked to me.

Parry took her hand in the electric starlight.

You are cold, he said.

He talked about dreams. The fact that he never dreamed. But why did he tell me that? We weren't friends. Don't you think that's a strange thing to tell anyone? The fact that you never dream?

Yeah, you're cold. Cold as the fog.

And I thought, that was the reason. For what he did. The reason why he … ended up like that.

You know, said Parry, I think I like you in my clothes.

Serene shifted on the rug. I never dream, the boy told me. He just came out with it. Said it like that. As if he was

200

confessing to something. As if he was apologising. I never dream, he said. I never dream.

Serene hugged her knees again.

You know, I love to see that star in the fog, she whispered. That's why I love the fog. The star is blurry and kind of soft. As if it's melting, turning pink. Like pink icing.

When I see the star at the end of Amazon Street, I know I'm coming home. To our star. And Glan too. Glan feels the same. I know he does.

3.37.

Parry licked the wine crust round his mouth.

Too cold to get into bed, he said. I can't stand the idea of those clammy sheets. Like they were woven from the mist.

He laughed again. Yeah, they feel like fog.

You see, we say it's our star, said Serene softly. Me and Glan. Our star.

The girl seemed beyond the borders of sleep. And when we see the star, she added, we know the ghosts can't find us.

Ghosts?

This town's full of ghosts. Didn't you know?

Parry blinked in the red light.

Everybody, whispered Serene, knows there are ghosts on The Caib. Always have been. But since the fog started, I've thought lots about ghosts. And Glan believes too.

Yes, Glan believes in ghosts. He's seen them. He's seen children like … they were made from the fog. Children glittering in the fog. Under the streetlights. In silver rags.

But it's creepy now the council's turned the lamps off. It's dark all the time. Don't you think it's creepy?

Every other light, said Parry. To save money.

But it's so dark now. When Glan got up yesterday it was dark in the afternoon.

Wake him up earlier, then.

I try. I really try. But it's hardly ever light these days. Look, will you keep it?

Keep what? asked Parry. 4.01. He was exhausted.

The star! Promise to keep the star and see that it's lit. So I can find you.

And always be the man who lives under a weird red star? smiled Parry.

Promise me.

Yeah, I promise.

Truly?

Truly. I promise. But Serene? Can … can I…?

Parry looked at the girl. At last she might have been sleeping.

IV

7.10am. When Parry walked down Caib Street the air was still wet. The fret sparkled in the single street light outside the supermarket. The first sketch of dawn was yet to appear behind him.

How had he arrived there? He couldn't remember leaving the shop.

Parry licked the salt on his lips. As he used to when crossing the beach at low tide to The Works.

Dora Parry complained the saltwater ruined his shoes. Parry would counter by saying he wore only his oldest footwear to the carbon-paper job. Suppurating daps, heel-less Clarks.

It's not that kind of place, Mum. Ask Dad.

At the end of the gwli before the shop entrance, Parry paused. He wasn't sure what was happening. Three men were struggling on the wet pavement, under the light.

He looked harder. Then had to stand back as they fell towards him.

Three men fighting. And in silence. That's what Parry noted. The three men were completely silent.

It seemed to be two against one. A security guard from the supermarket now gripped the arm of an older man in a black jacket. A third man held his other arm in what looked a judo grip. Now they were rolling around in broken glass.

The third man seemed more than capable. He had forced the second man's face into the pavement and was crushing it against the stone. There was blood on the victim's skin.

What occurred to Parry was an old phrase: rub his nose in it. He remembered his grandmother rubbing a cat's face into its own shit.

A bottle had been smashed to tiny pieces. Only the red and silver label, *Krazy Kremlin*, remained whole.

All of a sudden the three were on their feet. How quickly this resurrection had occurred. The guard and the third man, holding an arm each, rushed the second man up the vegetable aisle. They disappeared behind the delicatessen meats.

Parry moved slowly to the kiosk. There were several shoppers present but he was able to pick up a newspaper and ask the assistant what had happened.

It's his first day, she said, clearly stunned. His first morning. Only started at six. We don't even know his name.

When Parry turned, he found the third man behind him.

What was all that about? he asked.

Oh, the security bloke was having problems. So I helped out.

Who was the…

Thief? We got him. Red-handed. Someone who thought vodka is free.

You might have been killed.

So might the toe rag. But no, I'm all right. No problem. Though it's typical, isn't it? These days.

When the man turned, Parry was able to appraise him. Tall,

muscular. Despite the weather he wore only cut-off jeans and a yellow tee shirt with smiley face design.

His physique was such Parry first thought of steroids. He was clearly a bodybuilder, biceps enormous. Parry noted his shoulder had been cut by the smashed bottle.

SEVENTEEN

I

It was low tide. Parry decided to walk.

Exercise, he decided, must be good. And at that moment anything was better than worrying about stock for *Badfinger*, sorting what could be kept from his own collections.

His books were in good condition and might be of interest. Rock and jazz biographies, poetry. The stacks of review copies he had picked up in job lots.

Books must still mean something, he told himself. Okay, they weren't to Glan's taste. But the boy didn't read. Well, his loss. Blame the schools. Blame the teachers.

He thought of his classes in Adelaide. Young people, taller, leaner, brighter than him. And now they'd never grow old.

But who read today? At least Serene had thumbed through a David Bowie bio that didn't seem too dependent on cut and paste. And Bowie was literate. More than might be said of his contemporaries.

Maybe Bowie lacked the tragic dimension that was necessary for artists, Parry thought, setting off in the fret.

Yes, maybe Bowie's middle age had proved strangely anonymous. Above him in the window the star was still lit. At the junction he turned and it gleamed pink.

Maybe the fog's here forever, he had joked. But no one survived middle age, he reasoned. Not even David Bowie.

Perhaps he'd been hasty about quitting Adelaide. There wasn't pressure from the school. Compared with now, the money had been wonderful.

He might have sat back. Enjoyed all that Oz offered. Gone exploring the desert. Hunted the oldest stones in the world. Found some space.

But here he was. Sand on his boots, mist in his mouth. The jewelled air wet on his face. He'd limped home to what was familiar.

Basement Booze wasn't open yet. He smiled at Mina's handwritten sign that said no money was kept in the shop overnight. Arrows were inked towards the empty drawers of the till.

He pictured the woman in her armchair, asleep after wakeful hours.

Yes, there'd be a BBC voice low in the background, darkness softened by a halogen glow.

Parry resolved to call round later with a choice of music. 'Nature Boy', he decided, Nat King Cole's version. Mina would love that.

II

He walked past the Clwb. Maybe Nia was already clearing up from last night. There was a glow in one of the top windows, but Parry wanted to press on.

Yes, he thought. Here I am. A dog returning to its vomit. Back again. To the familiar griefs.

At the end of the street he met Fflint beside his front door.

Bloody fog, said Fflint as way of greeting. He was holding

an enormous bottle of milk and a copy of the *Daily Telegraph*. He brandished the plastic under Parry's nose.

Last us a week, this will. And the paper's for Mum. Old habits, eh? Still loves the crossword.

Mum? Of course, Parry thought. He still lives with his mother. He'd known Fflint for fifty years but couldn't remember ever being invited into the house.

He and Gil and Lizzy always waited outside when they called round. They'd all found refuge in the back room of The Lily in those days. Making their plans. Outlining the future.

Fflint's father was long dead. But Mrs Fflint was occasionally glimpsed in a downstairs window. In his twenties, Fflint himself had occupied the top storey of 1, Senhora Street. It was his studio.

Lizzy and Branwen had been intrigued, plotting an invitation, suggesting parties.

Did you ever think you'd end up like this? asked Fflint.

End?

Well…

And like what?

As a shopkeeper.

Oh. As in a nation of. No, I never thought. I'd do this. Keeping shop. But you have to. Do something. Don't you?

Yeah. Like I take photographs. Or try to.

Because, said Parry slowly, you run out of options. When you're young, all things are possible. Then the possibilities become…

Unlikely, laughed Fflint. Then impossibilities.

Poker becomes pontoon, said Parry, shaking his head. Then you realise the dealer's stopped giving out cards. You're stuck with the same old hand.

Could be worse.

Much worse. I saw the other shops on Goolwa high street,

remember. Tried to do my shopping local. Close by was this haberdashery, the whole place permeated by a camphorated calm. Like they were still selling wimples.

Caib Street used to be busier, said Fflint.

True. But around here were some hopeless shops. Grocers with dusty tins of peas on empty shelves. Delis that had never heard of olives.

Oh yes. I remember those.

Jones', nodded Parry.

Fflint grimaced in agreement. Old Jones did his best, I suppose, he said.

Hopeless, said Parry. Think the last mall I saw was Rundle Street in Adelaide. Now the girls who worked there had to be smart. It was obligatory. And the blokes. One was the only male parfumier I've ever seen. Yeah, I thought, why not? Immaculate's not the word.

Parry paused. Have you actually … rehearsed anything? he asked.

Course not, said Fflint. Everything's shambolic. As it always was. No, nothing changes.

Gil all right? asked Parry.

Same old Gil. No, not the same. Looks a bit older. Maybe a lot. Says he can cope with keyboard fillers and laying down some form of a bass line. Like Ray Manzarek used to, he said. But we were pretty ragged.

You'll be great.

Look, said Fflint, it's three numbers and then just jamming half an hour of *Dipsomaniac's Blues*. Till we get sick of it. With Maestro Gil directing us.

And Glan?

Looks the part, said Fflint slowly. I'll give him that. Which is all that counts. These days. So he shows the old men up a bit. But his voice is really weak. Maybe we can bury him.

As to his guitar playing, forget it. Just repeat A, I told him. Vamp it, boy, vamp that A. Maybe we won't turn his amp on. There are always ways…

Now Parry looked at the front door. He noted a bell and a silver knocker shaped like a dragonfly. On a plaque brass letters spelled out *Caib Villa*.

Where you off, then? asked Fflint. I'd have thought you'd be tucking into breakfast made by those kids. What's the girl's name? The one with purple hair?

Serene.

Parry dug his hands into his coat pockets and laughed.

Breakfast? Fat chance. They sleep in, kids today.

Yeah, typical, said Fflint. I saw the girl yesterday. She's working in your shop now?

That's the idea.

And staying…

With me. She and Glan are in the spare room. I'm trying to introduce them to some decent sounds. They know nothing.

Like I said. Typical. But don't scare them off with bloody John Cage. Remember you played that silent thing?

That was Gil. He couldn't believe someone had thought of it before him. But, yes, I'm being gentle with Glan. With Serene.

Parry was pleased Fflint hadn't disappeared through his front door.

Look, sure you're OK for this event? he asked. Gil's all set.

When Fflint smiled, Parry knew.

Won't be any worse than some of our other disasters, will it? Two run throughs is more than we used to manage…

Course. It can't work without you.

Well, it's something to do, isn't it, said Fflint. I was on Gil's website this week. Bloody incredible. He's got lists of all the gigs we did. Boy, the stuff we played.

He's even remastered some of those tapes we made, and put them on line. Even how long each track lasts. I'd never heard them properly before. Couldn't remember the titles.

But there they were. I could hear myself. Talk about your past coming back to haunt you. Every duff note. Made me wince. But I thought, yeah, don't knock it. This was our life. So thank you, Gil. Yeah, Gil believes in life. Maybe I'll ring him to ask about royalties.

Parry looked at the black beads on Fflint's shoulders, the pouches under his eyes.

You keeping well? he asked.

How'd you think? And added quietly. Don't know how long Mum's got. So I take it one day at a time. She's still clear up top. Like a razor. But who can say? Her friends still come in to sit. Mutual support, like.

Coming in to sit. Parry recalled the phrase. The last time he'd heard it was during Dora Parry's swift decline.

And just the two of you…?

Just us two. Waste really, a house like this. Needs a family, needs.

Yeah, said Parry. I know. See you tonight?

But Fflint wanted to talk.

D'you remember a twelvemonth back? he asked. We think the weather's poor now. But a year ago it was beyond.

I wasn't here. Over in Oz. But I've heard about the snow.

Yeah, bad, said Fflint. Colder than I've ever known it on The Caib. Went out walking. Up till then walking wasn't my favourite occupation, but I took my new camera. I'd started thinking about photography, starting lessons. Like Gil.

Who always was good, agreed Parry. Technical genius that boy. Remember he did us those album covers?

Yeah. Before we'd laid down the songs. Before we'd written the songs. Those notional album covers are online too.

Be great to have him in the Paradise again, said Parry.

Perhaps. But you know, now I walk everywhere. Keeping an eye. Keeping an eye.

So, that first day, I ended up across the dunes at Caib pool. Can't remember getting there, it's miles. But suddenly…

You were there.

Yeah. I was there. Snow wasn't too thick. Powdery stuff. But everything was just … magic. So I took pictures of the pool. First shots I ever tried. I could hardly hold the camera, my fingers were so numb.

And frozen solid that pool was. Blue and silver, like iron. Or dark blue. What's that word for dark blue?

Indigo?

Yeah, indigo. Indigo, that ice. Well, from a distance. Hard like a lid. A lid of ice. But around the edges of the pool that ice was no colour at all. Clean as a front-room mirror it was. So now…

So now you're a photographer. That's great. I wish I was.

Parry looked at the freezer dew on the milk bottle. Fflint seemed to be wearing a powerful aftershave. He was taller than Parry, standing there on the step of 1, Senhora Street. Parry looked up at his corbel of yellow teeth.

How long were you in The Works? he asked.

Thirty-three years, said Fflint. Then I took that chance.

Fflint had lost his pension when he joined a friend's pyramid selling scheme.

We all have to take risks, said Parry. What's life for?

Mum still complains about it. Me? I didn't see how it could fail.

III

From the West End of The Caib Parry descended to the beach.

He walked past The Chasm and round its boulders. Then passed The Horns and on, further west. To Caib Cliffs and Caib Caves.

He walked until he was able to take a sandy track that followed the edge of the dunes. He realised the foghorn was sounding. This week it had grown familiar. And before this week? It might have been years since he had last heard that forlorn bellowing.

Parry pressed on.

Writer? Never.

Artist? No, he didn't have the guts. The smell of paint hadn't infected him deeply enough. He'd washed away the paint stink too easily.

But if paint hadn't marked him for life, what was he?

Dunesman?

He said the word aloud.

Dunes Man?

Was that all?

Dunesman.

Possibly. But no, some kind of shopkeeper was what he was now. In a decaying town. Whose children dreamed of death. As if The Caib was cursed.

The previous night each working street light had been a twndish of pearls. Now the horizon was a milky wash. To the south the sea was still retreating but its horizon was white in the sand. Headlights went past. Then a figure loomed out of the fret.

It was a young woman, and Parry noted her Dr Martens, laced in yellow and green. For some reason he thought she might have been a nun.

He looked back into the mist and found nothing certain. Distances were reduced, directions blurred. Like his own eyesight, he thought grimly.

This had been excellent until two years previously. But was declining. Parry hated wearing glasses, though it was imperative now. Yet glasses meant reading wasn't the same. Somehow it felt mechanical. Maybe it was easier not to bother.

But when had he last read a book? In Australia, he realised. Soon after he'd become ill.

He remembered sitting behind the sunscreens in the shop, Lulu bringing endless mugs of green tea. For all he remembered, the pages might have been blank.

He blinked at the fog. Twenty yards away, he reasoned, he would have been invisible to anyone passing. This was how people disappeared. Molecule by molecule. A thinning of the self.

Yet he was comforted. The salt in the air tasted like his own sweat. He'd come back for this. Exactly this.

He'd loved the Murray, the olive shoals and shouldering swell of the river as it roiled through Goolwa. But it had proved impossible to stay. And there could be no return.

IV

Parry examined his hands. His hair was grey and his skin rough as rocksalt. He was a man abandoned under the limestone sky.

Because there was nothing else to do, he walked on. Now Parry could see only ten yards ahead. He knew he was taking a risk. The rocks were wet and covered in weed. He inched down an inlet colonised by barnacles, crushing some underfoot.

In the nearest pool were pieces of driftwood, pale as chicken bones. He edged closer and saw a plastic bag filled with what might have been chicken meat. He moved on.

As a boy he had been familiar with this place. It was where

cuttle-coloured sandwort grew amongst the lagoons.

But that was a world of summer bathing, October heatwaves. Now, the tide was out. Every surface steamed and spat. Once he had climbed here, scaling the cliffs' buttresses. Yes, he had known every ledge, every fissure. Known where to step and how to reach.

Parry understood if there had been light he now would have seen seams of quartz. Creamy veins and purple outcropping. Livid as flesh.

But the stone was wet, indistinguishable from the pools. This new world, the only world that mattered, was grey, oozing salt. Some of the rock here seemed to have melted: once liquid now solidified. Darker sections might have been lava.

He reached out a hand. Yes, as he had expected, there it was. A fossil. No, as he had *predicted,* a fossil where it had always been. A life shadow, a tumour in the stone. White scirrhous in whiter lime.

Slowly he descended, feeling the calcite under his hands. But not a gleam. Not a flicker shone through that sea mist. Parry felt invisible, Even to himself. How quickly he was disappearing.

A gang of gulls were screaming at each other. One had scavenged food and the others were harrying it. The victim dropped its prize which was lost in a pool. The chasing birds flew back into the fret.

Around him seawater stood in hissing pits. There was salt on his eyebrows and in his hair.

And there Parry paused. Amongst the limestone misshapes of The Caib. A man of salt, ghost in the gwter. His own heartbeat part of the day's sibilance.

V

Parry recalled other expeditions. First The Horns, then the whole ragged coast. Severin used to come sometimes. How old were they then? he wondered. Fourteen? No more than fifteen.

Parry guessed Sev might have been younger than the rest of the gang. But when he thought about those explorations, Severin was usually implicated. Always the blond kid, freckled like a dogfish. One incident stood out.

Parry and Severin were wandering around The Horns and the limestone lagoons. It must have been a hot day because both had been swimming.

They knew this could be dangerous. Some of the rock pools were deeper than suspected. But no, there was no one else around, Parry was sure of that. No trogs, no girls.

That's right, he thought. They had been looking at the rocks, wondering about undiscovered fossils.

Closer to the tide line the boys had come upon several moon jellyfish. These creatures resembled grey breasts, surprisingly large. Within the jellies were organs that might have been brains or hearts. A violet life pulsing. But almost certainly they were dead.

Let's look for starfish! It was surely Sev who made the suggestion. It usually was. And Parry was pleased to have a task.

Yes, the weather had been perfect. Both boys had no trouble matching one another's finds. There were always starfish in those days, Parry recalled. The usual yellow, but sometimes the rarer red variety, clinging to the rock.

The yellow were always dead, the others living. And yes, breathing, if you looked hard. If you dared investigate. The starfish were breathing.

Three, Severin had called. The boys were in the gutters

under the cliff. Wading through pools, in earshot but out of sight.

Three, Parry had responded.

Four, Sev had shouted. Five.

Then Parry was underwater, marvelling at the warmth of the pool. He was feeling around the base of a boulder, in the coralweed and sand.

Where no one else has ever explored, he thought. Where no human hand has reached.

Then he moved into shadow. The water immediately grew chilly. Yes, he thought now, there's a geology of water. In fact, there were places under the cliff where the sun has never shone. Then the water darkened and Parry recoiled as if he touched something alive.

Near here was a fissure in the limestone. Parry imagined it was thirty feet deep, an easy, if vertical, climb. But at the top Parry had always hesitated above the drop.

It was a simple jump, yet he always performed it with closed eyes. A limestone buttress, with a scattering of ammonites. Nothing to worry about. But every time he closed his eyes he imagined never opening them again.

Now Parry leaped. And the world was dark. But once again his feet found purchase. Safe, he said to no one. Till the next time.

When he finally emerged from The Horns, he called out his tally.

Still three, he shouted. And heard his words echoing.

Still three. Three, three. You *win, win, win.*

But there was no response from Severin.

Sev, Parry called. Hey *Sev. Sev, Sev.*

The Horns were silent. Parry shivered in the chequered sunlight. He tracked back to where Sev had been starfish-hunting.

You know? he called. I got my hand on a fish. Big as a bass. Huge.

But Sev wasn't there. What Parry found were the yellow arms of a starfish. Cut clean off. Four starfish arms. They reminded him of sliced peaches in a tin of fruit salad. When Parry looked further, he discovered two other starfish cut that way.

Severin always had a penknife with him. He was forever cutting his name into treebark or driftwood. The white SEV his familiar signature.

But that week in school, it was Sev who confronted Parry.

Why did you do that? he asked in a classroom.

Do what?

Chop up those starfish?

Parry had laughed outright.

No, that was you, he said.

Fuck off, said Severin. You cut them up. With your knife. You've always got that knife. Haven't you?

So have you, said Parry. You've always got a knife. It was you.

No, you, said Sev.

You.

You.

In the end, they had laughed. Was it shortly afterwards, the boy had disappeared from school?

Anyway, so what? he remembered Sev now saying. And Parry had concurred.

Yeah, so what? he said. S'only starfish.

But Parry always remembered that afternoon. The blood heat of the brine. His hand upon the fish's body. The black swash of darkness where the lagoon water suddenly chilled. The shadows behind the shadows.

And yes, Parry could see himself staring down at the bottom of the pool. Transfixed by a starfish.

Parry imagined summoning the courage to immerse himself. Touching that creature, half hidden in sand. And yes, he could see his own hand. Reaching down through that sour tarn, almost as warm as the brackish Murray, the river where he and Lulu swam in Goolwa.

His own hand was reaching out, his hand with the knife in it. Stretching, with his old penknife.

But that wasn't true, thought Parry. And he shivered in the fret that blew over the gorse. The breeze was more noticeable today, bringing the mist in from the sea.

Parry looked around. There was no feature he could distinguish, no clear direction. All the world was a milk-in-water whiteness. He pressed on with his impossible thoughts.

VI

Jack Parry hung on. His two strokes had occurred when he was seventy-one. Everyone thought they would have killed him. But Jack Parry persisted. Jack Parry had refused the invitation to the dark. That's how his son saw it. So Jack Parry had lingered in the same room of the same nursing home for eight years.

Dora Parry had died aged seventy, two years after her husband's illness. Their house was sold to pay for Jack's care. He was partially paralysed and required a surgical hoist and two nurses to move him from bed to armchair or his wheelchair.

If he had used the dining room, Jack would have encountered an immense sea view. There was also a field visible behind the building, where horses were kept. Often, new foals were to be seen there. Jack Parry's few friends imagined he would enjoy the horses.

His son had once taken him outside in a wheelchair and they had gone to the fence. One of the foals had approached and pushed its muzzle into Jack's lap. Parry recalled its nostrils flaring, the hairs red as copper wire. An orange tint in the matted mane.

But after the first two years, his father had insisted that his meals be taken in his own room. Parry thought the old man might have been afraid of some of the other residents.

Scared by their impairments. Intimidated by how much they had been reduced. The silent, the tearful, the dribblers. The incomprehensible gibberers.

These last were known as 'the shouters'. Jack Parry had once been a shouter himself, his family was told.

What does he shout? asked his son. He knew the question was wrong. It should have been, who does he shout for? Or, what does he shout about?

But, as everyone said, at least the other residents could be companions. His father might learn from them. Surely, it could be comfortable there. At least bearable?

When Dora Parry was alive, she brought in yoghurt pots filled with the soil of their allotment. She also brought a velvet bag of sunflower seeds collected the previous autumn. He could see those seeds to this day. White as a cat's teeth.

Go on, she had urged her husband. Dib them in. Right in.

And, as deeply as he could, he had pressed the seeds into the soil. Dibbed with his left forefinger. Jack Parry's right arm was paralysed.

But no matter how much he was coaxed, Jack Parry remained adamant. He was determined to avoid the dining room.

Maybe it was a mistake to agree, a manager had once confided in Parry. But he seemed so unhappy when he met the others.

Now, usually we wouldn't pay attention to that. But the fact is, your father became hysterical. He was sobbing. He wouldn't stop.

The other residents certainly scared Parry. Especially the shouters. Yes, he understood why those people shouted. It should have been obvious to all.

Abandoned, weren't they? High and dry. Yes, worse than marooned. Shipwrecked on the shore of their old age. And worse again. Betrayed. That was surely it. Betrayed by life itself.

Some of the old men and women wailed before drugs or futility knocked them out. But the shouters and the shocked-into-silence shared a secret, Parry knew.

There was a poem he half remembered. *Into the heart a wind that chills.* Something like that.

That's the challenge, Parry thought. Live with this. If you could. If you dared. Live through this.

Life was a test. Like something mechanical, you would be tested to breaking point. And everybody broke. The lucky ones were those who shattered outright.

VII

Where am I? Parry wondered. The air was cloudy as the seabed. There was a mesh of rain in the air. Within a rock pool at his feet something glinted. It was a crab shell, white as a cranium. Floating on the pool was a yellowing gullwing.

Lost, he laughed to himself. Lost at home.

He recalled climbing the cliff above The Horns. Every dint was a tarn rimmed with rock salt. A cup of crystals.

Hadn't he and Sev thought they were lost on that occasion? They'd even boasted about it. Fflint had been predictably scornful.

But everybody was lost. Weren't they? The secret was not to stay lost.

Parry stepped over a ditch the departing tide had gouged into the beach. Everything was saturated, the sand, the air, the limestone. All bubbling. All breathing. He pulled his coat closer.

VIII

He thought he might have been near 'The Mine'. This was an iron sphere wedged in a cleft west of The Horns.

It had been there longer than anyone could recall. Must have been from the war, they thought. But surely a mine, a real mine. Like a huge sea anemone. Raw ingot. Unhealable sore.

There was a pattern in the iron, a series of ornate *vees*. These might have formed a word, Parry thought. An eroded inscription that made no sense. VVVVVvvv. He had pondered on the meaning, with Sev or Gil or whoever else was prepared to walk that far.

Sometimes he had stood on the sphere, trying to dislodge it. The mine was wedged in the crevice. A blister on The Caib. A bloody welt. If the current couldn't shift it, what use muscle?

IX

The air was slurred with sulphurous fret. Parry recalled coalsmoke from steam trains, grey billows and a burning smell.

And it returned, the memory of a gang of kids trespassing on the line. A squall of coke flying from the firebox...

...No, he realised, he hadn't walked so far west for years. The way now lay along the dram road that led to The Works. If the tide was right, he'd taken this route himself. On the way to the carbon paper job.

He reckoned he was close to The Tramlines. This was an area of quartz set in red sandstone. A series of white lines he and Sev believed they had discovered. And so named.

He remembered a painting he had thought about on his walks to work. The problem was posed by the colours of mother-of-pearl, and how they might be recreated.

Fool, he smiled wryly. Painting wasn't copying anything. Painting had to combine spontaneous joy with hard-earned technique.

Make a mess, he'd told his classes in Adelaide. As much mess as you can. Because life's a mess. Isn't it? A human mess. And what's art but describing what's it's like to be human?

Those classes, he smiled. The first step was choosing their music. Art master as disc jockey. That was how he'd befriended Libby. She'd come into his class because Mozart's clarinet concerto was too loud.

Yes, sorry, he'd said. We were all getting carried away. Especially Wolfgang.

No, painting to music's a great idea, she had said. I'll try it myself. Let's have a look at what CDs you're lining up. Mostly Bluenote I expect, from what was on last week. Oh, some Indian things too, I see. And who's Etta James?

No, he'd never been a painter. Never had the guts to try the big canvas he had once imagined. One hundred feet square. It would be his depiction of the morning sky of The Caib. *Mother of Pearl* could be the title. A hundred different colours, most of them greys. The most delicate painting imaginable. Doing the dawn justice. Yes, *Mother of Pearl*.

It was to be the cover of his first album, he grimaced. The image on his first book. And that book's title?

Dunesman.

He said the word again.

Dunesman.

Dunes Man.

Yes, mysterious enough. Intriguing. Surely. And of course, it might still be done. It should still be done. He wasn't old, after all. The right side of sixty. Mina swore he might pass for five years younger. Maybe ten. As if, he smiled, it mattered. But it did.

Now he licked the salt on his lips and kicked over a crust of sand. There was a gull in the rocks nearby. As Parry approached he noted it didn't fly away. Rather, it rose and came back to the beach, landing awkwardly.

He saw there was a nylon fishing line caught round its leg. Attached to the line was a lead sinker.

Sighing, he went through the motions. Come here, kitty, he called. Nice kitty.

Parry approached the gull and it flew away before falling back. He made his rescue attempt three times. Three times the bird escaped. Soon the kittiwake was lost in the fret.

EIGHTEEN

I

He couldn't locate The Tramlines. Thirty minutes later he was leaving the dunes and the dram road behind. Then slipping through the back fence of Rhidyll House.

Nearby in the grounds, two pale horses, the colour of the fog, were standing together. Two smoky smudges against white render.

Rhidyll had been built thirty years previously as a bar and hotel. Then become a nursing home.

Parry rang the bell and was admitted. He gave his hands an antiseptic scrub and signed the visitors' book. Jack Parry was, he was told, upstairs in room 33.

As ever, he thought, climbing the stairs.

For some reason Parry knocked, then felt foolish. When he entered, the light was on. The first thing he did was switch it off. Then he looked at his father and switched it back on.

Jack was belted into his armchair with a double tray on castors before him. There were crumbs on the tray and uneaten bread on the floor around his chair.

Morning, Dad. What about this fog, then? You ever remember it worse? I've never heard that foghorn used so much. Such a sad sound, Dad. Like a wounded animal.

Parry crossed to a radiator and warmed his hands.

Feels raw out there, Dad. Never known it so bad, have we? And you, Dad? You're the same colour, I'd say. The colour of the fog.

He regarded Jack more closely. The old man seemed to have shrunk since his son had last seen him. His cheeks were limestone's grey roses, his pyjamas and dressing gown too big. They were covered in toast crumbs.

Parry turned away and looked down at the two horses. They were old animals, manes and tails tinged with sulphur. Both had remained motionless.

I bet Mum could have told us when the fog was worse. If it was ever worse than this. Yeah, Mum could have said.

Jack Parry had anaemia and was due for a transfusion. It was thought he was bleeding internally. His face was white as paper and unshaven.

Still waiting, aren't we? smiled his son. Hanging on all over Christmas and now into New Year. But they'll give us a date soon, Dad. I know it'll be soon. Bound to be.

Parry ran the hot tap.

Wow, boiling as ever. So where's that razor of yours? Not that you look bad. Not half bad. Ever grown a beard, Dad? Might have suited.

But no, Mum wouldn't like you all whiskery, would she? Mum was old school. Still, I think you look pretty modern myself. Yeah, cool, Dad. You look cool. Ever been called cool before?

He examined his father's pale lips. Found a comb and dragged it through his hair.

Haven't had this washed for a while, have you? As bad as mine, it's so greasy. But yeah, you look modern with that stubble, Dad.

Parry scanned room 33: television, radio, CD player. An anonymous painting above the bed that he had meant to remove. And resolved, once again, to do so.

There was a framed photograph of Dora Parry on the bedside table. Beside the door was a photograph of The Horns at sunset that Parry had organised. Close by was another of what had been the Parrys' allotment.

In one corner was a mechanical hoist, used for moving his father from bed to armchair. Jack's wheelchair was nowhere to be seen.

I'll take you out for a walk, soon, Dad, he said. When it's warmer. Haven't been for ages, have we? For ages.

II

The last time Parry had seen his father was two months earlier. He had walked into Rhidyll House and a nurse directed him to the main lounge.

They're all in there, he'd said.

Who's that? asked Parry.

Everyone.

He quickly realised it was a birthday party. One of the residents was one hundred years old, that day, November 13.

Jack Parry too? his son queried, disbelieving.

Let me see … let me see. I'm sure, yes. Jack too. We're honoured. Aren't we! And you are?

There were twenty Rhidyll residents present, only three of them men. At first, Jack had been difficult to identify, as he was slumped in his wheelchair. He failed to acknowledge his son, who pulled up a seat beside him.

Morning, Dad. Or is it afternoon. Look, sorry I haven't been over. You know how it is. You know, Dad.

That morning, or afternoon, Jack Parry did not say one word. Even when Happy Birthday was sung, along with early Christmas carols and choruses of the Hokey Cokey.

Everyone present was offered a glass of sherry, including Parry. Who somehow commandeered three.

Not drinking, Dad? he asked eventually. Look, we can go upstairs if you like. If you don't fancy any more of this party.

Jack had remained mute. But Parry thought it was an improvement. For the old man to visit the lounge boded well.

He still preferred to eat alone in his room, but his birthday appearance indicated a thaw.

Parry was delighted by this, and decided to visit his father more regularly. Such had been his intention.

December arrived, then Christmas. Today, all he remembered of the November visit were verses from 'Hark, the Herald' and feeling light-headed when driving home from Rhidyll. With the assistance of a nurse, the three sherries had become five. Or was it…

Later, Parry had found himself in the back bar of The Lily, inexplicably buying drinks for Cranc, Davy Dumma and George from The Cat.

Then he'd phoned Mina at Basement Booze and arranged to meet at the Paradise.

III

Yes, he continued, we can get one of those taxis with its own lift and go into town. What about a pub lunch? Or fish and chips at Eddies'? But remember the old Paradise Club? Maybe we'll go there. I'll plan a party.

Parry hated Rhidyll House and knew his father felt the same. Care for Jack was paid for by the sale of the family home. At the time, the son had thought nothing of the money he had lost.

Yes, like a film star, Dad. Maybe Humphrey Bogart in *The*

Treasure of the Sierra Madre? Remember that one? Or *The African Queen*? All those leeches Bogart had to pick off his own skin? Burning them with a cigarette? Like little pieces of black rubber. Gave us both the creeps.

Or did the girl do it for him? Yeah, who was the actress now? Lauren Bacall? No, Katherine Hepburn, of course. I'm sure it was her. She played that stuck-up Englishwoman.

Or was it a rich American. Yeah, Hepburn. It was great to see films like that on a Sunday afternoon, wasn't it? When we were all together.

But Mum wouldn't like it, would she? The unshaven look? So, do you think I could do this? I'll try my best. Maybe Katherine Hepburn gave Bogart a shave in *The African Queen*? Did she? Should have been in the script.

Parry was surprised to be allowed to shave his father. Jack submitted to the lathering of his cheeks and neck, which his son accomplished with his own fingers.

It was a disposable razor but keen enough. Jack Parry's cheeks were simple to deal with. But above the lip, under the nose and chin, was more of a challenge.

Parry nicked his father two or three times. He could feel the cuts himself but as yet they weren't bleeding.

All right, that's it, he smiled with relief, towelling his father's face.

Maybe I should have shaved myself. Usually I only bother every other day. Like the lights in town, Dad. Only every one in two or three is switched on now. To save money.

Means it's dark by three o'clock. And the fog not due to lift. That's what I've heard. Boy, you can smell The Works from here in this weather. Holds all the fumes in. The fog's like a pan lid. Almost as bad as it used to be before the clean-up.

Hey, I'll put the kettle on, Dad. Fancy a cuppa? You can have the rest of that toast with it. What about that? Yes, you've made a mess with that toast, haven't you? I said you've made a mess with the toast.

But no, we won't call a nurse. We can clear it up ourselves, can't we? We can do that. And I can make fresh.

Because I'm being spoiled just now, you know. Got this young couple staying over, and they do bits and pieces.

Yes, there's Glan and his partner, Serene. Good-looking girl, Serene. And purple hair, dad. You should see her long purple hair. Like that woman who used to live in Senhora Street. Remember her? Only her hair was red. Not purple.

And Glan, he's all right. Even though he drinks all my wine. Worse than me for red wine, Dad.

You see, Glan and Serene will both be working in *Badfinger*. Started already, really. You know, my shop? *Badfinger*, it's called. I'm training them. Giving them work experience. Selling books and records and CDs, Dad. All sorts. We sell all sorts there. Just what The Caib needs, people say. Something for the kids.

You see, it's difficult for young people now, Dad. Bloody hard. Maybe impossible, we're making it so hard. Much tougher than when I was their age. When I was as old as Glan. I had it easy compared with them.

As to *Badfinger*, it's on Caib Street. And I'm living in the flat above the shop. Yes 33, Caib Street. Like you're in Room 33. In this mansion in the sand. Coincidence, eh? No, the flat's not huge. But there's a spare room for Glan and Serene.

Look, I'll boil that kettle in the kitchen. Be back in a sec. Oh, coffee or tea, Dad? Feels like coffee time to me. I know, make it strong.

Hey, I walked all the way. How about that then? Up off the beach and over the rocks. Over the pebbles, Dad. Across the scree.

Way past what we used to call The Tramlines. Not sure how I'll get back. They've stopped so many buses round here.

But I thought it seemed quiet downstairs. No crises for once? No birthdays with sherry? That's a relief. And yes, I can do more toast. No probs.

Oh and Dad, another question for you. What's pink and rose and all the greys and all the whites and all the blues until the blues get as far as indigo?

Kind of a riddle, Dad. Well, it's the sky, isn't it? The sky around here. Yes, The Caib sky. When you can see the sky that is. Mad as the mist, eh Dad, that's me. Mad as the mist and snow.

IV

When Parry pushed open the door of Room 33 he was holding a tray with two full mugs of coffee and a plate of buttered toast. An alarm was ringing down the corridor.

No porridge, he smiled. But if you don't fancy this, don't worry. Though I do. See, I remember where the nurses keep their bread. And their butter.

Because they like a bit of toast at night. Don't they, those nurses? Oh yes, I recall. Though I know it's been a while, Dad. Yes, I admit. It's been a while.

Jack seemed in the same position as when his son had left the room. Parry put the tray down and checked his father's face.

Pretty smooth, though I say it myself. Not a bad barber, am I? Just wipe off this little bit of soap.

Parry thought his father might have bled, but the shaving cuts hadn't opened.

Dig in then, he ordered. I'm starving after that walk. And maybe the fog's making me hungry. So another question, Dad. Does a morning of foul and filthy air stir the appetite? Answers on a postcard please to *Badfinger*, 33, Caib Street.

But I can see you've lost weight, Dad. Haven't you? Yes, you've really lost more weight. And no colour, Dad. There's no colour in you at all. Like this weather, Dad.

Parry sipped his coffee and gazed down on the two horses. They were standing together, still immobile.

What are those horses' names, then? The nurses must know. You should ask them, Dad. Ask the nurses. Find out the horses' names.

Jack Parry sighed and looked at his son. Then he glanced away again.

Listen, said Parry. I was thinking about this when making our breakfast. Thinking about something in Australia. A simple little story like I used to tell my classes.

You see I was working in a high school in Adelaide. Teaching the children about art and painting and music. About all sorts, Dad.

But I also rented a shop in a little town about sixty miles away. Just to create some sort of a scene, you see. Somewhere for young people to go.

To hang out, Dad, is what they call it. Like I'm doing now on The Caib. At 33, Caib Street, Dad. Somewhere for the kids to hang out.

Yeah, we'll see if it works. We'll see. Make our assessment next June, say. But we'll give it a full year.

Oh yes, have to try it for at least one year. Probably two. Because I know trade will be ragged at first. Everything will be really, really slow to begin with.

It always is around here, isn't it, Dad? You know that. Yeah, like a glacier melting. Like limestone being laid down.

Parry took a draught of his coffee. You know what limestone's made of, Dad? Lilies? That's right, sea lilies. Year after year after year. One lily on top of another lily. Uncountable years. Uncountable lilies because there wasn't anyone around to count them. Was there?

Well, I don't think there was. And those lilies died every year. Until there were enough lilies to turn into stone. To turn into limestone, dad. To become stone.

V

Parry looked out into the fret. A nurse in a blue tunic was brushing the mane of one of the horses. The two horses were standing close together. Almost nose to nose. Their breath was the same colour as the fog. Despite the cold, the nurse had bare arms.

Big numbers, Dad. And of course, they're beyond me. I should have worked harder at my physics. And my geology. Shouldn't I?

But I thought about this in Goolwa, when I went to live there. Because I lived in a shop in the high street, Dad. Like I'm doing here at number 33.

And in Goolwa I worked with a friend who loved stars. She used to tell me stories about stars. How many stars there were and how far apart those stars were.

So one night, I said, come on. Let's sleep outside. Give me an idea of what you're talking about.

Be nice to see stars, again, eh, Dad? Don't feel I've seen a real star for weeks. Where's old Orion when you need him, Dad? Or Venus, burning over the dunes?

Okay, you know me. I might have had a glass of wine or a bottle of beer. Well, it was warm, that night in Oz, after a hot day. And there was a clear sky and no light pollution. So we took a blanket each and a bedroll. No, no sleeping bags. And we camped out.

The weather was dry, bone dry. See, it was a drought, Dad. No dew or dewfall, no river mist, no sea mist. No fog. And we lay down on the river bank, the bank of the Murray river. The current sliding past, only a few yards away, Dad. Two or three yards away.

You know, I felt I could have reached out my hand and touched the water, that black river water. Black as tar, it was. A slow torrent of oil.

And the current was low, Dad. I could smell the river. That old Murray, hurrying past. Yeah, I could inhale it. Like I can smell the tide here on the slipway. Sewage and sand and salt and seaweed. The smell that will follow me till I die.

So why am I telling you all this, Dad? Because I was thinking about someone I used to teach with. Libby, Dad, you'd have liked Libby. Had an edge to her, did Libby.

No, she didn't do or say the obvious. Libby was the headmaster's wife, Dad. But she wasn't crushed by it. She was still a functioning human being. No side. At least when I knew her.

But she told me a story about breaking down in her car, miles from anywhere. Way west of Adelaide, Dad. Out on the Nullabor.

Seems she waited all night and no other vehicle passed. Hard to believe, but that's Australia. The country's empty. And so big you can't comprehend it.

And Libby comforted herself, she told me, by looking at the lights on the dashboard. You know, green and red lights in the dark. The alternator light, whatever.

Libby looked at those lights all night. Like stars, she told me. I thought they were stars, she said. And when she woke up in the morning there was a police patrol car pulling in to the roadside.

Good job, because her battery was flat. Took her back to Addy after giving her a jump start. Told me the officer first made a pass and Libby obliged. But that's the type of thing she would say. Looking to shock, Dad. Hoping for a reaction. To make something happen.

VI

But what about my other friend? Hey, you following this, Dad? We lay down in the sand. And listened to the Australian night. That Australian summer night.

I've often thought of doing it here, Dad. Sleeping out, now that I'm back. Should have tried it last year. So roll on next July.

But remember when I camped with Vine and those? You know, Gil and Sev and Fflinty. Gil's around somewhere, though he's stopped teaching.

But he still plays, Dad. In fact, we might do something together soon. He's talking about that *Dipsomaniac's Blues* he once recorded.

And the girls used to stay out too. You know, Sian and Lizzy. Yes, that Lizzy. You and Mum were always asking me how it was going with Lizzy.

How's what going? I'd answer.

Oh, you know, you'd laugh. She's a smart girl.

Yes, I knew she was a smart girl. But there was never any hope of that. No hope at all.

And you know what happened to Lizzy, Dad. And even if she'd been fine, if it hadn't happened, people drift apart. It's natural, Dad.

Yes, all of us used to sleep out at The Horns. Or up at the Caves. Only no one ever got any sleep. We talked and kept talking. Drank a bit, too, I suppose. No, can't deny that, can I?

And remember that geography teacher who used to camp in the dunes? Lol, mad old Lol they called him, but that's kids for you. Lived in that villa, *Mattancheri,* on the front. The roof tiles are coming off now, it's a real state. But everyone still loves it.

Well, most summers Lol slept out in some hideaway hidden in the sand. Built a bivouac and lived off the land. Whinberries and blackberries and mushrooms. Dogfish if he could catch them. And samphire that the French call 'babies' fingers'.

Yeah, lived off the dunes. Or by raiding bins on the caravan site, other people said. Interesting life, though I don't know how he'd have coped in all this fog. Probably fine because he always talked about ghosts. Because we're all like ghosts out here, Dad. It's weather for ghosts.

VII

So in Goolwa, me and this friend, we lay down. And counted the stars. Some silver, some yellow. And a few stars red. And we looked at the summer lightning, Dad, and I thought of those seams of quartz you find all over The Caib.

Purple, green and white, Dad. Make a great flag, those colours would, I've always thought. For when we announce the republic, Dad. The republic of The Caib. But skydust was what we called those stars. Yeah, our heads were full of skydust.

And we listened, Dad, because it was impossible not to listen. Impossible not to overhear the night unwrapping itself around us.

Just the two of us and that Australian night unwrapping itself like a huge birthday present. Moans and groans and murmurings, Dad. All manner of muttering. Even the grass was muttering, Dad. Even the reeds and the wind in the reeds.

There were sploshing and swimming sounds. And once an explosion of water as if something big had fallen in. Something as big as a man. I asked Lulu if it was an alligator and she laughed.

And always the sound of the earth breathing, Dad. The earth under us, breathing out, breathing in. And the river sand beneath us, still warm from the afternoon. And the earth ticking as it cooled. Like an engine, Dad.

Remember how I used to go out to listen to the engine on the old green Austin? As it cooled after you came home from work.

I'd sit outside and breathe in the petrol smell. Counting the ticks the engine made. You know, like a cockroach clicks or a cockchafer crackles when it lifts its wings. Or one of those Australian waterbugs that look like they're wearing armour.

And I used to think, one day, one day… And Mam would come out and say don't sit in the oil, don't…

And there we were, Dad. Looking into the skydust. Meteors going over us, white and gone. Satellites shooting over us like chalk marks on a blackboard. Hey, once a teacher… But gone for a million years, Dad. Gone a billion years. But not gone forever. Can you imagine a billion years, Dad?

And maybe I can blame that old Austin for my life. Remember, you used to keep stuff in the boot? All the things you sold, the packets of coffee, the dried milk?

VIII

Parry looked out into the mist.

But best were the books, Dad. I loved the books you drove round and tried to sell. Scores and scores of paperbacks. All thick and glossy. Books about murderers and serial killers. Yeah, shock and horror stories. Or ghost stories, or real life stories like the siege of Stalingrad.

The worst histories in the world, Dad. And the worst books. But at one time I used to love those books. And that's what I'm still doing, I suppose.

Finding books. Finding records and CDs, putting them all together and trying to make sense of it. Some sort of scene.

Even when the kids don't want a scene, Dad. But trying to enthuse them, Dad. Trying to make them enjoy what I enjoy.

And cannibals! That book was about cannibals. The one about the siege of Stalingrad. Why do people like cannibals, Dad? I just had to read that book. Every word of it. So I blame you, Dad. Blame you for everything.

And when we were tired and it was dawn and the stars were printed on our eyeballs, all we did was scoop sand away to fit our hips. And I suppose we fell asleep. With that skydust in our eyes.

IX

Parry continued to stare into the fret. It was the colour of a bale of barbed wire. There might have been pinpoints of ice in the air. Bright as mica.

Not sure of the forecast, Dad. But it has to change. The Caib's getting strange.

The horses were still nose to nose, their breath the same cloud. Once again he listened to the foghorn's bass.

They'll be coming round with the medicine trolley, I expect, he said. They never let you forget those pills, do they? Measuring our lives with what the doctors prescribe. Getting desperate if we miss a dose.

No, don't listen to me, Dad. I'm a bad influence and I know it. But the doctors even want me to take tablets now, Dad. To accept my medicine. Like a good boy. Forever.

Well, don't tell anybody, Dad, but I haven't been co-operating. I'm experimenting with myself, see. A big, scary experiment. And I think in the year since I took the last tablet, I've been better.

Yeah, God's truth, I've stopped yawning, Dad. Stopped these enormous yawns. I'm just generally fresher and lighter, Dad. More optimistic. Like I used to be.

No, it doesn't mean I'm not going to die. Does it? But I think refreshed is the right word. Or maybe restored. In the way I feel. Yeah, maybe it's a year. I'm not sure now.

So I was able to walk over here, Dad. Through the foggy foggy dew. Like I did going to The Works, burning the carbon paper, Dad. Remember that?

But this fog, it's like The Works is pumping it out. Manufacturing fog, Dad. Now there's a thought for us both. All part of the great conspiracy, Dad. It would explain a lot.

And yes, remember you drove right into the site, once, Dad. And they let you through. Couldn't believe it, could you?

Looking for Richard Parry, you said. Took a long time to find me, my duty being stuck out in The Sheds. No one had a clue who or where I was.

And I felt bad about you seeing me at the incinerator. With all that filthy ash, floating about. And no mask. Of course, I never wore a mask.

So this is it, you said. This is it. When you looked around I didn't want you to feel disappointed. For me. No, I didn't want you to feel that.

But what a place, Dad. The benches with the rusted vices? All those mountains of scrap metal that were stored in the sheds, spilling everywhere?

And all the computer paper that we'd salvaged from the print-outs? The tons of paper we'd saved. Waiting to be collected.

There was even that bulldozer that had seized up. It hadn't moved in ten years, they said. With all that white bindweed tangled in the tracks. When we pulled the flowers out they went on for miles. On those long green vines, Dad. With the sap that stained our skins brown.

I was ashamed of that place. Even though you were bringing the letter that told me I had another job. More money. Real prospects.

And then we walked into the shed and you asked me where I actually worked. I wasn't sure what to say. Everything was obviously derelict.

The sheds had been abandoned years earlier. But we didn't know what The Works' long-term plans were. There were holes in the roof where we could see the sky. Even in the heat, there were pools of oily water everywhere.

And all that bindweed. Its bitter white rosettes. Growing out of the bulldozer. Like an enormous wreath, it was, Dad. Yeah, that bindweed. Flowers the same colour as lightbulbs, I always thought. Same colour as this fog.

And when you walked into my shed and looked around you saw my bag on one of the benches. And you know what you said, Dad? You looked at where I worked and said 'so this is it. This is the magician's table.'

I've always remembered that, Dad. And I still wonder what you meant. Whether you were being your sarcastic self. Or if it was a compliment.

Because I'd had that birthday present once. A real magician's table. All the props for magic tricks, the bunches of plastic flowers, the handkerchiefs.

And yeah, you recognised my bag, full of the books on painting I was reading. And *Melody Maker*, of course. I was addicted to that. Every Thursday. Boy, Thursdays were special because of *Melody Maker*.

And all around us were the tools and cables, thick with rust. The carburettor I thought was a metal heart? All those valves and tubes, Dad. What a place, eh? There was ivy coming through the broken windows. Over the pin-ups of girls that had hung there for years. For a forgotten shift, Dad. From another time.

And I opened the letter right there but I knew what it would say. That I'd found a better job. But still in The Works, Dad. It was months before that teaching appointment came up and I moved on.

I'd been having my lunch, Dad. Sitting out in the sun with the boys who worked with me on the carbon. Daf and Bran in his big steelies, and Mazza. Remember them? Not sure if you ever met them now. No, I'm not sure.

Bran never spoke much. You know how I try to make up what people say, Dad? Suppose I'm a ventriloquist, really. But seeing that Bran never spoke, that was difficult. Next to impossible. Because Bran never spoke I started to make things up in my head for him. Yeah, a ventriloquist. That's my art.

And Daf, Dad. I think about Daf sometimes. What happened to Daf? I wonder. What happens to people? Do they just disintegrate? Like pixels on a screen, Dad? Pointillism, you know. Maybe I could have painted that way. Dot after dot. And that's how people disappear, isn't it? Dot by dot by dot.

I remember that acid Daf showed me. Why no vats for the vitriol? Why those vials? I picked one up once and disturbed the sediment. Like a glass of brown fog.

Well, me and Daf and Bran were sitting on a heap of sinter, passing round a bottle of water. Warmer than piss, the stuff we drank there. Yeah, the three of us coughing the carbon smoke out of our guts, our clothes stiff with carbon dust. Used to drive Mum mad, didn't it. She always asked why I didn't have overalls.

Then you came out of the shed, and said, well congratulations. At last you can move on from here.

And I felt ashamed, Dad. I saw what you must have seen that afternoon, as you drove out through those pools, Mazza doing his impression of a chimpanzee. Everything you'd warned me about, Dad. The terrible life of work.

Because you were right, Dad. I'd say you were spot on. The less we did, the less we wanted to do.

So in the end we couldn't be bothered with anything. Because by then everything was too much trouble.

I used to burn that carbon paper. And watch as it became nothing. Just an oily scum at the end of the shift. All that work, reduced to dust. With the smokestink in my clothes and in my hair…

You were right. I used to bath all the time. Scrub myself raw. With that piece of pumice, Dad.

With the black stone. So, yes, I should have listened. To you, Dad. Should have listened to you.

I suppose that's all I wanted to say. But no, I'm not going to take my pills again. I want to see what happens. In my experiment.

X

Parry examined his father. The old man was paler than he could recall. Jack looked away but then he turned his face back into the room. An alarm was ringing down the corridor. It had been ringing a long time.

Parry looked outside once again. Into the limestone fog. The silver air.

There was a silence. Then Jack Parry spoke.

Gramps and Nana, said the old man.

Parry immediately turned round.

You what, Dad?

Gramps and Nana. Nana and Gramps.

Who, Dad? Who?

Jack Parry sighed. Then, slowly, he spoke again. Sighed and
spoke.

The horses. The blind horses. They're taking them away.

NINETEEN

I

Parry stood in the shop, talking to Serene. Glan was upstairs, sleeping.

At the drought's height, he explained, Lulu became ill. She was working in the shop every day. As school was off, I was in Goolwa most of the time. We'd organised a rock group for local children. The idea occurred they might busk in the main street.

The kids seemed to love it, their parents supported us. We were building up to a festival. At last it seemed *Hey Bulldog* was capturing local imagination. Writers, musicians, even a ukulele band, had promised to perform.

Lulu had designed a poster, black and red. She'd painted a red-tailed black cockatoo. Just a few daubs. But an evil-looking creature. Something devilish about it. Not a local bird, but no rarity either. Lulu could mimic its cry.

So the band became The Black Cockatoos. At least, that was one of their names. And they sounded like cockatoos. That typical echo you hear when they're flying.

But it was obvious that Lulu was ill. It was horribly hot, and her skin was dry. Soon she was vomiting. I bought a thermometer in the pharmacy and immediately her temperature went up to 103. Scared me.

She lay in my bed but couldn't keep her clothes on. The

weather was impossible. I placed bowls of water around the shop, trying to cool the air, bathing her face, making her drink.

I'll never forget the worst day. She lay in the green light behind the sunscreens. A child on fire before my eyes, delirium's honey-thick sweat in the pool of her throat.

A green demon she looked to me. A gap-toothed green child, speaking an incomprehensible language. The alien in my bed.

I'd sit with her and bring ice and towels. Or make her take aspirin. While outside on the pavement and down the street, The Black Cockatoos were rehearsing their set. Just a bunch of children singing in the dust, ragged versions of *Louie Louie* and *Anarchy in the UK*.

Their parents were there too, laughing, drinking beer. Two of the dads used to coach the kids. The rest of us listened to those children sing about being an Antichrist. Being an anarchist. You know that song?

Nuh … no, said Serene. Don't think so.

There they were, explained Parry, The Black Cockatoos. Twelve year olds let loose with mikes and amps. Then coming back to the shop for milk and biscuits.

Wasn't that what I'd wanted? What I had been working towards. Making a statement. Some kind of cultural manifesto.

But I'd wonder, there behind the sunscreens, in the afternoon glare, at the hottest hour of the drought, the worst drought of the century, what on earth had I done?

To make everything worse, there was Lulu. Her hair matted, an old Adelaide Crows shirt, just a sodden rag, on her back. Yeah, blue, red and gold, that shirt. Someone said it was an original. A first edition. Like a book.

What a day. That worst day I'd wring her shirt out like a dishcloth. And listen to Lulu's madness.

She was talking about her grandmother. Or telling me she was unravelling. Her whole body, as if it was wool, or thread, somehow unravelling. Like taking strings off a guitar.

I thought I knew how she felt. Because I was unravelling too. Listening to these baby punks in front of the motel. Their parents were determined to make a session of it, egging The Cockatoos on, spraying beer around.

And then, to crown it all, an official delegation arrived. Because of the racket.

But all day long, on the worst day, I stayed put. I sat in the shop watching ice melt in the ice bucket and ice water running down Lulu's face and belly. Lulu might have been my wife. And I should have wept.

Because I knew then I was mistaken not to have had my own children. It dawned on me as clearly as any lesson could. That I had been a fool. That I had been selfish.

There in the green afternoon. The afternoon of fever and anarchy. With a green child whose brow was burning under my palm. With a kid whose shirt was black with the froth of delirium. Yes, a child who was accusing me. While the other children, the antichrist children, told me I was guilty too.

Yes, there behind the screen I should have wept. But I don't think I did. No, I don't think I wept. As I never painted.

Instead I sat there while the ice melted. And watched Lulu pull the strings out of herself. And then, on the hottest day of the worst drought the country had ever known, you know what happened? Can you guess?

Er ... don't think so, murmured Serene.

The ukulele band arrived.

245

II

The mist hung outside the Paradise Club. The friends were huddled in a corner by the bar.

Ever seen a film called *Storm Boy*? asked Parry. Made in the momentous year of 1976.

So what were you doing in '76? asked Mina.

Good question. Trying to work out all the punk stuff. Still listening with Gil and those to bands who played twenty-minute drum solos. Deciding I was good at art history, and that maybe I should be a lecturer. See, I was delusional even then...

And what happened?

Applied for jobs but they didn't quite ... take. In the meantime, I decided to go back to The Works. To tide me over while I waited.

That carbon paper job?

It paid, love. Dad was right. Dead end work like that has an effect. It's comforting, you're never challenged. You understand exactly what the job means. Often it means nothing.

After college, I just walked into The Works one Monday morning. They said welcome back, what took you so long? It was that easy.

And you stayed for...

Four years. And eleven months.

Burning paper?

Look, it was a real job. Ridiculously well paid. After a while I moved to other duties, but, yeah, they were all pretty menial. Compared to history of art lecturing. Which I never did. Or compared to studying. Or teaching. Which I was good at.

After a while there was a clerical job on offer at The Works and I breezed in. Too bloody easily.

A month later I remember the department's Christmas party,

trying the Grand Quiz. One of the questions was about the jobs people did before they became famous.

You know, like Kenny Everett, the disc jockey, working in a bakery. He used to scrape burned sausage rolls off the baking tins. These days people haven't a clue who Kenny Everett is. Such is fame.

Wanted to be famous did you? said Mina.

Parry paused. Didn't we all. Or should I say don't we all? And isn't that the trouble? We've been infected by the sickness.

And then you trained as a teacher?

Eventually. Could have stayed at The Works. They liked me there. But teacher training seemed the better bet.

You were all teachers, you lot, said Mina. That John Vine, Gil, Sian. All bleeding the country dry with your pensions.

It's different for the rest of us, she added. I'll be in Basement Booze till it closes. Which children, is only three months away. You're not supposed to know. After that, everything's a mess. Look, how old am I?

Thirty-two, said Fflint, through his glass.

Not so bloody old I won't have to try the Job Centre soon. Now they've changed the pension dates.

So, said Mina, it'll all be meaningless retraining. Then travelling to somewhere that's ninety minutes away by public transport. Then ninety back. It scares me.

That's why I've started *Badfinger*, said Parry. Christ, some places have to stay open. Caib Street's a disaster area.

But you don't pay, do you? said Fflint. You're running on volunteers. What's the good of that?

We offer expenses, insisted Parry. And listen, we're providing the experience of work, the community of work.

Yeah, I know the shop's small, he went on. But all it needs is vision. Okay, and a business plan. Don't tell me I should have stayed burning carbon.

Look, every record and poster in *Badfinger* has its own story. What I say to people like Glan and Serene is, learn that story. Make it your own. Come on, let's see *Badfinger* thrive!

Like your place in Oz? said Fflint.

Anyway, said Parry, you should try and catch *Storm Boy* somewhere. It's set in The Coorong. All sand bars and pelican beaks.

Now, The Coorong's near where I lived in Goolwa. The pelicans in the film had names. One died only recently in Adelaide Zoo.

I think it was on one afternoon, said Mina. When I had flu.

But you asked about the weather, shrugged Parry. That summer was so hot, we even called off school sports events. Rarely done over there. Then autumn stayed dry and everything was … *ominous*. It was one dry year after another in a disastrous series of dry years.

Libby used to tell me how worried everyone was. Because she was worried herself. But I was obsessed with starting *Hey Bulldog*. With finding stock, organising volunteer rotas and then rehearsals for The Black Cockatoos.

So it didn't really register with me. The weather, I mean. Yes, the whole state had become arid. A drought's not unnatural in South Australia. But I had to learn a drought can last years. And that's when it dawned on me that things were bad. That the country was in a crisis. But how was I to know? I'd arrived almost at the end of everything.

III

By then the ground was parched. Withered, I suppose. The look of a famished land.

Rain was expected, but rain wouldn't fall. Simply would not fall. And everyone was desperate for rain.

It was like an illness, a starvation of rain. People were rain-sick, cattle were crazed. It was the rain famine and I'd turned up in the middle. But as I said, it was difficult to tell, being an alien there. Because sometimes I felt an intruder, trespassing in another life. Which it was. Another life.

When it was windy there was too much dust. I remember the dust on the counter at *Hey Bulldog*. I could write my name, clean it off, then write that name again an hour later. Which meant dust all over the stock.

There was dust in my eyes and dust in my throat. Veils of dust drifting down the dirt roads around Goolwa. Some dust red, some dust grey. Riverbeds had disintegrated into dust. And that dust turned the sunset purple. Yes, tall indigo skies. Like a psychedelic album cover.

And you know, I could taste that dust on my tongue and the same dust sharp in my fillings. Ever seen a young trout with those red stipples on its belly? Or a foxhound with red sprockles on its paws? I looked like that trout at the end. A white man in a white shirt painted with crimson dust. Only this dust was brick-red.

We used to catch trout in Caib stream when I was a kid. Silver and red those trout. I can still remember tickling trout in the shallows.

IV

I'd already decided that anything was possible in that country. I spent my life being amazed. Yet though I depended on Lulu to tell me things, weather was unimportant to her.

For months, I was obsessed with the shop. Or the idea of

Hey Bulldog. Once, we went to the library to look at astronomy books. To find The Pistol Star. But the real reason was for me to visit Gouger Street. To have another look at the market.

I was always trying to learn things for the shop. There was this café in the market and we ordered bowls of broth. Tofu, Chinese cabbage, something spicy like horseradish, which we'd grown on The Caib. Cheap, easy to make by the gallon. I thought, maybe we could serve food. Start a café.

Well, I remember Lulu's face. Grinning at me over the bowl, as she slurped her soup. Wild girl, making these sucking noises. So other people started to look. And the more they stared, the worse she behaved.

She had freckles, did Lulu. Darker on a dark skin. Like cappuccino chocolate. Not that she was black, nothing like. Lulu was mixed race, sandy-coloured. No, weak molasses, if you follow me.

That time she was ill she had this awful yellow tinge. Anyway, her hair was black hay. Yes, straw with a kink which she made even frizzier.

In the mornings she'd be walking around in these curlers she'd tied herself. Just rags, and a fag stuck on her lip. Her language first thing something ripe.

Yeah, Lulu, that little star. If she wasn't talking about stars, that is. Because stars were sanctified. Stars were sacred. On and on she'd go about The Pistol Star. How enormous it was. And what stars meant.

You what? I used to ask. No matter how big they are, stars don't *mean* diddly squat. Stars can't *mean* anything. Stars simply *are*. Nothing means anything. Or the other way about. But however you cut it, it's the same.

That surprised her, I think. But it's what I believed, and still do. Is there a holy principle in physics? I don't think so. Just things we haven't discovered.

But it's exciting to look, I understand that. Yet at the end, packing up the shop, all I remember were those copies of *Astronomy Today* that Lulu never returned to the library.

That was the hardest thing to do. Pack up *Hey Bulldog* without Lulu. Not knowing what had happened to her. Giving her things away. Her mug, her clothes.

What was I supposed to do? Lulu had vanished but nothing was resolved. There was no closure. Lulu was the missing particle we were looking for in the heart of the atom.

At the end, only Lulu could make sense of the country for me. She could be out in the desert still, for all I know. Gazing up at the skydust.

V

You see, people came and went. It was hard to keep track.

Once this woman arrived with a refrigerated display case, run off a generator in the back of her car. She was selling oysters.

Where you from, honey? she asked, when I ordered the first oyster, showing me her soy, her lemonjuice.

Oysterville, I laughed. So these better be good.

And they were.

Later I took the woman into the garden of *Hey Bulldog*, and begged a bottle of sauvignon from the motel. We drank it under the jacaranda while Lulu ran around, lighting incense, putting Bach on the CD.

And how about you? I asked the oyster woman, looking at her brown knees, torn vest. She smelled of oysters, too, cutting open the last oystershell from her fridge.

Addy, she laughed, lips salty with soy. There was a young poets' reading that night in the shop and I invited her to stay. Scared her off.

VI

Sometimes we'd go next door to the motel. If I had Chinese tea, so would Lulu.

What's my title, boss? Lulu would ask. What do I call myself on the phone?

No one ever rings us, I told her. So don't worry.

But if they do? she insisted. When they do call.

How about Development Officer? I'd say. No, Deputy Project Manager. Is that serious enough?

Stupendous, she'd say. Yes, I like that. And she'd sip her tea, and pronounce *Deputy Project Manager* till the Dutchies left the bar in disgust.

Well *Hey Bulldog*'s a project, I'd say. In fact, a hell of a project. In the wrong place, of course, but plenty of people find themselves in unlikely places. And make the best of it.

And I'd ask her what we had sold that day. This was when I was permanently in Goolwa. I'd given up Adelaide by then. So I was tidying up, preparing. For departure. Even if it took ages.

And I realised I'd already been out there for five years. But in the end, I was back in the UK within six months.

Album by Nirvana, she'd say. You know, the first Nirvana. With the Irish boy and the Greek boy. It was called *Pentecost Hotel*.

Good girl. I'd say. Yes, I'd taught her well. Who bought it?

Sophia, she'd say. Who else?

Sophia lived in Goolwa on a farm outside town. She wanted to be Joni Mitchell. Or Kate Bush. Strummed a black Fender Dreadnought and wrote her own lyrics. Helped in the shop sometimes, too. One of our merry pranksters. Sophia was headed for college, and maybe Europe. Smart kid. Budding poet, God help her.

And? I'd ask. Don't tell me that's everything?

Well Blagger came in and wasted my time. Then Myra came in. And wasted my time. Steve came in next. And wasted my time. Kept looking down my front. Should I wear a bra, boss?

After Steve, this old bloke comes in. And asks if we had the *Oxford Book of Australian Poetry*.

Dunno, I said, but told him he could check the shelves. You see, that's what you always said. Get the customers to do it themselves. To feel involved.

Anyway, seems we didn't have it. But he found a pamphlet he liked. About the paddle steamers. Just a few pages stapled together, but he coughed up ten dollarinos.

Then ten minutes ago this girl asks if I knew about Carinda. Turns out to be a tiny place in New South Wales. Much smaller than here, she says.

Never heard of it, I said. Must be a long way away.

Oh, she says. You know David Bowie went to Carinda and they made a film of him. In Carinda.

No, I said. But I'll check. So I'm checking with you. And there it is, boss, the report from *Hey Bulldog*'s Deputy Project Manager. Can I have a pay rise now, boss?

So I told Lulu, yes, it was on the news or maybe YouTube. David Bowie had arrived in a forgotten town, smaller than Goolwa, more insignificant than Goolwa. To make a video of 'Let's Dance'.

Okay, maybe I laboured the point of Bowie as an Outback explorer. But Lulu understood why I was making it.

Bowie in Carinda was unthinkable. But since the unthinkable had already happened, it couldn't happen again.

And yes, I suppose I felt a bit peeved. Wasn't Bowie famous enough? Anyway, Lulu knew I was leaving. That I was getting ready. But she disappeared before I'd said goodbye.

VII

No. No rain at all. But everywhere a rumour of rain. A Chinese whisper of rain. That became anything but rain.

I'd look at the sky as if I was a meteorologist. Like everyone else, I studied clouds. Yes, those Australian clouds, huge and gold-rimmed in the evening. Grey and pink at dawn.

In fact I thought I should have been painting clouds. Because surely there had never been clouds like those before.

Most of us were weather experts at the end, me and Lulu and the Dutch couple included. It was all we talked about.

I would get up early, before six. For years I'd been an early riser, because that's what school demanded. And I'd sit in *Hey Bulldog* behind the sunscreens and look at the shadows of the shrubs and potted plants we grew in the garden.

Which was my garden. I'd rescued it from the undergrowth in ten-minute stints. Yes, it was my garden. Though I never felt much like a gardener. Over there.

That was where Lulu lit her tea candles and we stayed smoking. And talking, talking. Where kids like that singer, Sophia, might strum that black Dreadnought and read her mystical couplets. Where some writer could freeload on my wine and a pizza from the motel.

Yeah, druggy rubbish, I suppose we talked mostly. But important to me at the time.

I can still see those shadows trembling on the green walls. My walls, that I was leaving behind. Walls someone could turn into a hairdresser's. Or tourist information centre when they'd arranged for the rent to be knocked down.

Lulu used to do these finger puppet shapes in the morning when the light was right. Seems blissful, now I think about it. So here's a toast to the *Hey Bulldog* gang. All those who naturally gravitated to that scene. Hey, no matter where you are now, you too had a role.

Actually, I had an email from Goolwa last week. Seems the shop is still empty. But waiting for a possible tenant to make up her mind.

And I thought, yes, another sign of these times. As if I needed one. But at least I put my hand in my pocket and paid for something I thought could make a difference. And maybe it did. For a while.

VIII

There was a painting I liked. Pinned up, not even framed. Called '*Chronicle of Light*' I think. Whoever the artist was, and I'm sure they were local, they'd done something wonderful.

I nearly said perfect. But *perfect*'s never the word, is it? Yet at least I liked it. They'd shown the Murray in spate before the years of drought. Olive waters, but gilded. Yes, like the light you see around The Caib.

And you know, sometimes I look at the light here and it breaks my heart. I call it the limestone light because it's laid down in layers. Like stone or paint can be. Photon by photon. As if there was, or there could be, a geology of light. But yes, limestone light.

And if I see it, then I think that everybody else must see it. Even if they don't talk about it. That limestone light. Which shines out of the people around here. Even though they would laugh at the idea.

Like you're probably laughing now. No, they'd never admit to it, the limestone light. Rather shrug it off as an embarrassment.

IX

It might have been only one room and I'd have been happy. But *Hey Bulldog* was three rooms, and it felt like home. And I was making my stand. As I'm doing now.

Yes, it felt like home. Whatever home is supposed to mean. In the morning I'd sip a cold coffee and maybe play something so low it was hardly audible. Say Steve Reich. Or a raga, all drone.

Or maybe I'd put on some Bach harpsichord piece. Sheer sunlight, that music, like the concerto in D minor. And I'd look at the shadows moving and hear the breath of Bach. Then I'd think, no it's not so bad here. Even with the ants it's not so bad.

X

Lulu would be asleep somewhere unexpected. She was a cat who curled up anywhere. But even at the end, when I was in Goolwa permanently, I would walk first thing out to the Murray. To smell the low tide, smell the high tide. And realise how different those tides were. Just like The Caib.

The tide here reeks on the slipway. It smells of weed and salt and rot. Of rottenness. But it's different when the waves creep up the breakwater. Slapping against the stone steps and over your shoes.

That's when you know the water's perfume is in your hair. And on your skin. There forever, its stink. The stink of The Caib.

When they die, that's what people from here take with them. The filthy perfume of The Caib. Its salt pollen. Because it's here now. The Caib on our eyelids. The Caib on our lips. Its smell no other smell. Its taste no other taste.

Taint, is that the word? Good enough, I'd say. Because we're tainted by life on The Caib. Yes, that taint is the giveaway. It's what identifies people here. Like the sand in our shoes.

XI

But whatever the tide at the Murray mouth, it ran under a dirty white sky. My sky. Or darker still, almost pewter. Gunmetal without the sheen.

Yes, I'd gaze at clouds that became greyer. An ominous sky with clouds massing in the south. Like a photograph I saw once, of cancer cells under the microscope.

So I'd walk down to the Murray and say *for God's sake now.* It must be now. As if I might predict rain to the second.

Here, I know how rain smells. Blackthorn flowers in the morning. A salty January dawn.

Over there was different. By the end we were all pleading. But no rains fell. There were weather systems passing over and I thought, yes. Right about now. Those owl eggs are ready to hatch.

Then, one Sunday morning, something woke me. I think I'd been drinking into the small hours. Wasn't supposed to, but who is? These days? And maybe I was starting to feel cut loose. A state of disassociation.

When you've been used to school it's hard to adapt to change. You realise your need for routine. That you're uncertain when deprived of it. That you're bereft.

All that time us teachers spend complaining about the job? Meaningless. We're institutionalised. We're timetable addicts. Without the direction a proper job brings to life, lots of people go to pieces.

XII

But forget the red wine or Australian whisky. That Sunday my head was as clear as it's ever been.

Not a cloud in my mind. I was sharp and primed. I almost said ready, but ready for what I've no idea. Outside there was complete silence. Yet I knew. I knew.

Lulu was snoring. Curled like an ammonite in the limestone. In the dirty sheet. And sucking her thumb. Yes, Lulu always sucked her thumb. And I never knew from one night to the next where she'd fall asleep.

It was night, or at least still dark. But I'd heard something. I got up immediately. Naked I suppose, and walked through the shop and opened the front door. I stepped out on to the street.

When I woke it wasn't quite raining. By the time I opened the door I could hear pittering on the skylight. Big drops. Fat, slow drops. Like blood. Drops so big they exploded around me. Great sticky detonations against my shoulders. On my belly and on my neck. And I knew then the weather had changed. But maybe it wasn't a serious change.

Because if the rain came from the south it would have been cold, travelling over the southern ocean. Maybe up from Antarctica.

Like when the wind blows east on The Caib, and the sand seems to go the wrong way. Because we're used to sand travelling east, not west. The same direction the trees point. The way people on The Caib lean into the east. Have you noticed that? Because that's what the wind on The Caib does for you. Deforms you from birth.

XIII

I'd felt it before, that southern rain. Just once or twice. And I'd hated it.

Cold as quartz, that southern rain. You know, if I was a musician, I'd write a song about it. Minor key, a bit wistful. The mood darkening as the rain grows colder. As you realise that southern rain from the southern ocean means winter coming on.

But this was warm rain. And that's why I thought it felt like blood. Rain from the interior, where there never was rain. Where the rain didn't belong.

This was red rain. Miraculous red rain that left rust on my skin and a ruddy film over this silver Hyundai parked in the street.

You know how sometimes everything you see stays clear? And you know you'll never forget it? It's rare but it happens.

That was one of those moments, when I saw the silver car. And the silver car made sense. At last I was seeing that car for the first time.

It had been parked by the shop all week but I'd hadn't really noticed it before. I can remember the car radio had been disconnected and was on the front passenger's seat. That there was a yellow tee shirt in the back with a smiley face design. Used as a rag.

As soon as it rained I saw rings of red dust around every raindrop. Yes, a blister of dust, like sand bubbles when the tide goes out. And as I went into the street I looked up and saw red rings on the skylight. All these red Saturns.

Cleaning that glass in *Hey Bulldog* had always been a problem. It was old and pitted, a breast of antique glass that must have served a purpose.

Originally, I'd been determined to make it a feature. God

259

knows that high street needed something distinctive. But cleaning was always the issue. There was moss on the outside so the green stains were never removed, no matter how we scrubbed.

Getting up there was impossible, I thought. But maybe I was wrong. I should have given Lulu a bunk up and a scrubbing brush. Or I should have scrambled up the outside. But I've never been good with heights. Or that's the excuse I made.

But think about it. Everything might have been different. Lulu would still have been living in Goolwa. And I'd be selling books and pop-art collages in *Hey Bulldog*. On a dust-blown high street. In a town where David Bowie didn't make a video for *Let's Dance*. Where my ghost and Lulu's ghost drank green tea in the Goolwa Motel. While talking about stars and music and our customers, and how fame was bad for you.

As ever, we wondered whether there was anyone left who wasn't phoney. Because we were the real thing. Weren't we? We were the last of the pure. The founders of a new age.

XIV

When I went back inside, I said let's celebrate. Lulu was asleep but I still called out, commanding her.

Let's celebrate the rain.

Rain? she grunted. Rain?

Rain, I said. Red rain. And I pulled the duvet back from the bed. This worn old rag with Elvis's face on it.

But the fat Elvis. The stupid Elvis. Not the beautiful Elvis. The rhinestone Elvis. I pulled Elvis off the bed and grabbed Lulu by the wrist. She was wearing those disgusting khaki shorts and some old vest and I dragged her to the window. I said, all this time we've been waiting, months we've been waiting, years I suppose, so listen to it. Listen to the rain.

No, she screamed. No. I'm still sleeping. Let me sleep, you bastard.

But she stayed up with me, cursing like a trooper. Stood beside the glass in her curlers. And that's what we did.

Listened to that rain come down. Not torrential rain, not yet. But by then the light had arrived. Morning happens quickly in the south, and we looked out as the raindrops exploded. Thick as molten glass those raindrops.

And after a while we realised the rain was golden. Yes, it was golden rain falling on Goolwa that early morning. Rain full of desert dust, so it looked golden to us. We stood under the skylight and listened to the rain. With velvet hammers pounding.

XV

Of course, it had rained before when I was in Oz. But not much and I'd never paid attention. Yet even at that moment I could feel the light and the air changing.

The red rains fell, steadily. For an hour or two. We both went out, back to the pavement, drinking in that golden rain. Two fools in the deluge who knew it was a rare rain on our skins.

That rain seemed a blessing. Death of the drought, that's what the rain meant to us. Everything would be better, we thought. The land could drink and flower again. You know, the wattles and the gums, the fields of orchids.

Lulu walked around in that golden torrent, kicking through the puddles. Pretty soon her hair was hanging straight and lank. No more frizz. The rain was polishing her face and throat and that vest was just stuck to her.

I told you how clear everything was? The silver car, Lulu's drenched skin? Like a cloud had lifted. Yes, Lulu was golden that morning. Maybe we both were, gilded by a desert in every drop of rain.

Yeah, celebrate, said Lulu. We gotta celebrate. And I admit, it was me who opened the beer. Just one beer each to toast the end of the drought. Because that's what it certainly was. The end of the endless waiting.

Come on, I said.

It must have been me, mustn't it? Sometimes you have to take responsibility. So, I own up to that. But just one bottle each. That's all we had.

And we went down to the Murray and afterwards over to the dunes. We were soaked through but it didn't matter. It was momentous rain that fell on us that morning.

Other people had the same idea. There were plenty of us at the riverbank, trying to get the Sunday barbies going. Yeah, people were fiddling with the charcoal and cracking the grog.

No, you don't often celebrate rain. But this was a special occasion. I think people were beginning to believe a catastrophe had been averted.

There's a pub on the river, where they brew their own. If it was a drink I wanted, and the motel seemed too close, that was the place. A walk and its reward.

That special morning the owners were opening as we arrived. So we sat there, steaming. They put their heaters on for us, and soon we were dried out.

And no, I don't think I ordered Lulu more beer. But it all gets hazy. Maybe I had a glass of red. Two at most. They have this real juicy cabernet there, chocolate and leather. Yes, those local wines from McLaren Vale, they're worth investigation.

But I would never have bought Lulu a drink in public. Kids and booze, that's a serious protocol. Not that Lulu was a child. Of course not. She was mature and reliable. More than competent in the shop. As much as anyone else I met over there.

Okay, I'd taken her out in Addy a few times. But only for food. Usually at the Sebel Hotel, which has an ornate bar. The kind of place to make you feel good about yourself.

She loved it in the Sebel. I remember once she had shrimps in garlic mayonnaise. Another time it was just nachos with melted cheese at the bar. Wow, she wolfed it down.

But her favourite? Wedges, no question. No one does wedges like the Aussies. Real thick wedges with sour cream. Forget bloody chips, wedges are the genuine thing. We had wedges in Goolwa too, in the motel where they always looked after us.

XVI

And then that rain stopped. More people were appearing on the riverbank. Maybe I thought The Cockatoos should give an impromptu gig at the shop.

It wasn't organised. Getting the kids together at short notice would have been impossible.

But it's the type of thing we do, I told Lulu. Spontaneous and natural. That's what *Hey Bulldog* really means.

We're not your puppets, she said.

It would be wonderful, I remember saying. Lots of people would find out about the shop.

Not your puppets, she repeated. And went on repeating. Making up a song. Like she did sometimes. But over and over. Not your puppets she kept singing. Not your puppets.

Yet it was only an idea.

And that's when I realised. Sitting there by the heater, a glass of wine in my hand at ten in the morning. That I couldn't make it work.

Yes, I thought, Lulu's right. This orphan off the street,

brought up by her grandmother? She understands it all better than I ever can. Or ever will.

The public doesn't want the shop. The band doesn't want to play. And here's me, literally killing myself to make it work. When nobody gives a damn. Whatever difference it makes is not enough. I've tried and it's impossible.

TWENTY

I

When we went back I think we played *Pink Moon* by Nick
Drake. The whole of the album. Then played it again. And I
talked to Lulu about life back here. Trying to explain it.

She was virtually an adult, so she understood. Look, she was
definitely an adult. I talked about standing at The Horns and
looking towards the iron horizons of The Works. About
hearing the songs blow over from the fairground. Ghostly
songs all mixed up in the wind. And all the screaming you hear
at the fair.

After a while you get used to that. Because if you're brought
up on The Caib, screaming doesn't mean so much.

We tried some Bach too, Glen Gould doing the Goldberg
Variations. With that humming, his own extemporizations
behind the notes.

Hmmm, hmmm, hm, hm, Gould goes. *Hmmmm … hm!* You've
heard it? Gould's humming? I love his humming on that
recording.

But maybe the drink and the poor sleep the night before
were having an effect. I started to think about the end of
things.

Poor Nick Drake died, didn't he? Young as Keats and not
much older than Lulu. Though Lulu's not dead, is she? No,

Lulu's not dead. And I ask myself, aren't people allowed? To be eccentric any more?

Now that verse, that line from Nick Drake's song – 'Now we rise And we are everywhere' is on his gravestone. I know it's optimistic yet that line chills me. Why is that? What's that line mean?

Don't worry. I know what it means.

Nick Drake was shyer than a man should be. Can be. They turned *Pink Moon* into a car advert. Like everything else. The whole of music pillaged to sell... Ah, you know.

Does it matter? Well I remember telling Lulu music like *Pink Moon* can create a unique psychic space for yourself. Pompous eh? Sometimes I hear myself and I cringe.

But no, I don't care. So yes, it mattered. And maybe it still matters. This year we've played *Pink Moon* once in *Badfinger*. I told Glan and Serene about Nick Drake, even if he's dead and meaningless to them.

But so is the bloody Goldberg meaningless. A man humming as he plays the piano? Sometimes I switch the Goldberg on in the dark and Glenn Gould is there with me.

Mnmm, hm, hm he goes. *Mnmmn...* And the hairs on the back of my neck are standing up. Christ, I can smell Glenn Gould in my room. Smell that ointment he had to rub into his back and his neck. And the smell is part of the dream. And when I wake it's still there. That ointment smell.

Ah, don't mind me. I'm just letting off steam.

II

It's increasingly hazy from then on. As part of our rain celebration we were playing our all-time faves. So it must have been, let's see, Miles and Mingus and Terry Riley and JSB and… Yeah, I remember, we did The Easybeats as a homage to Oz.

Okay, maybe we might have played two CDs together. To see if they'd complement one another. Like the fairground, I told Lulu. That's how the fairground sounds.

But those poor unlucky bastards, The Easies …Life's not fair is it. And there's Lulu and me dancing round, singing

It's gonna happen…

gonna happen…

gonna happen…

gonna…

III

While the party was going on I can remember some man came out of nowhere. Telling us to turn the volume down. Yes, do us all a favour. Do us all a favour and tone it down. *Sport.* That's what he said.

Or at least I was told he said that. Because, it's true, we were inclined to crank it up. Either we'd open the doors, front and back, to create a draught. Or rig The Cockatoos' PA up on the pavement in the little square between the shop and the motel.

They called that square The Birdcage. And yes, sometimes they held gigs there. Perfect for The Cockatoos. In my mind, I'd designed the poster. Or maybe Lulu had drawn it already. *The Black Cockatoos in Goolwa Birdcage.* But tone it down, this man told me.

Tone it down. Sport.

Tone it down. *Sport.*

For Chrissakes.

IV

We weren't too loud. No, I'm positive we weren't very loud. But what I do remember is that it was raining heavily.

Yet this was different rain. This was coming the other way rain. This was going to be a long rain. I could tell that. I could easily tell that.

No, not from the interior, this rain. This rain didn't come from the red, dead dustbowl. This rain was drifting up from the south. From the southern ocean and the icefields. And I had the tune for it, my song to southern rain.

I swear I had started writing that song. I could hear it in my mind. It's there, waiting for me, that song. I've started it. I've started that song.

But that must happen millions of times. Think of all the vanished songs and poems. Those ideas lost for want of a notebook or a pencil, a simple recorder. Lost forever…

For Chrissakes, that man said. What are you doing? What are you both doing in here?

But what were we doing? Celebrating, that's all it was. That's all. Look, everybody else was celebrating. Weren't we allowed?

V

The clouds were black in the south. Those rainclouds still massing as they had for weeks. Those clouds like cancer cells.

Okay, the music must have been my choice. Lulu would have wanted Kylie. But we just couldn't have her in the shop. That day.

I only know what happened from then on by asking questions. Trying to piece the jigsaw together. And I'm still trying.

VI

I'd had a poor night previously, as I've said. And I think those pills I'd been taking were still having an effect. Sometimes they make me drowsy. Yes, I think I was taking the pills then. But I'm not sure. Sometimes it's noticeable. I might have nodded off.

No, it's time to own up. I slept. I went back to bed. I went to sleep and I remember Lulu shaking me, shaking me, saying she was getting her own back, ha, ha. And the next thing I remember she was cuddling up and she was as hot as when she had that fever.

But Lulu always felt like that. A scalding little radiator I used to call her. Hot as the earth in summer. Under those quondong trees.

Yeah, that's what colour Lulu was, the Goolwa earth. And drowsiness is the poet's condition. Isn't it? Keats was always drowsy. John Lennon's usually tired. Lulu says she shook me but I pushed her away.

But how could Lulu tell me that? I haven't spoken to Lulu since. Since that man said we played our music too loud. Not since she disappeared.

VII

No I've not spoken a word to her I'm sure I haven't but I can imagine how she felt because she must have been hungry and we never even had breakfast I hadn't thought of that hadn't thought of anything just passed her a vest in case she was cold and all I cared about was getting out to celebrate the rain and yes we were dancing this wild dancing but surely everyone was dancing to celebrate and when The Easies came on they were the loudest yes louder than the Goldberg and that man who came in should blame The Easies but what did he know yes what did he know *coz it's gonna happen gonna happen* over and over in my head yes all the time *it's gonna happen* in my head *gonna happen*. And that gold dust on her.

Oh I know what you've been doing, I said. I know it all.

VIII

Then I woke up. And I remembered.

Everything.

Nothing.

I was lying on top of the bed. The Elvis duvet was half on. Half off. I was cold. I was hungry. My throat was lined with dust.

But my first thought was Lulu. I swear Lulu was my only thought.

I could tell in seconds she wasn't in *Hey Bulldog.* I searched all her sleeping places, the nests I'd seen her use, the trunk, the recycling box, the shop window. Behind the green screens. Not there, not there. But I wasn't worried.

And when no, she wasn't in the motel either I still wasn't worried. They gave me my green tea. But I wasn't worried. I sat in the window looking at the rain. And I wasn't worried.

Because Lulu knew everyone… Look, Lulu was mixed race but she was attached to some of the Coorong people. And those people were as local to Goolwa as you could get for blacks. For native people.

Yeah, she'd come and she'd go. Come and… But everybody knew Lulu. That's why I wasn't surprised. When I woke up.

Because in a way, Lulu was always missing. That's right, Lulu was always missing. She'd please herself.

IX

She'd come and she'd… But after a while I decided to go down to the Murray and look for her. Futile, I knew. Because she always took her own time about things. Yet some kind of action was required.

And no, she wasn't in the brewpub. Yes, of course they remembered us being there. First customers of the day. Weren't we? I'd bought that bottle of cabernet. Hadn't I?

We must have drunk it together. Celebrating the rain, I explained.

Yes, they said. They could see that. *Impressive,* they said. That's the word they used. Impressive. But they didn't look at me twice. Didn't presume.

Okay, sometimes you can tell. When people don't approve. Of a white man. With a black girl. But not there. We'd never have tried the brewpub if that had been a possibility.

But I couldn't believe it was the same day. Those pills can really send you off when you're tired. I must have been taking the pills then, I was blurred with sleep. But no, it didn't seem like the same day… And God, I used to be able… To remember everything.

X

I moved on through the dunes. Then climbed to the highest crest and looked round.

White sand. White sand whiter than sand on The Caib. I had taken binoculars and looked at the few people walking in the dunes. I could tell none of them was Lulu.

Because nobody moved like Lulu. Her easy lope, her … *grace*… Though she was changing. Putting on weight. Only natural. At her age. All those wedges. Not that she was…

We'd been to the high dune before, the pair of us. The Dutchies had organised a picnic on one of the hottest days. We brought sandwiches from the motel because Lulu didn't like the look of the food I'd made.

Yeah, cheese sandwiches and bottles of beer. Very Caib. The world was trembling in the heat haze. The sky was blue and the river was … *tangerine.*

Soon the Dutchies lit up. Toon passed it round and I lay back and thought, it's not so bad here, is it? Not so bad.

When I opened my eyes I could see the stream pattern. Where water drained into the Murray. Scores and scores of lines. Like silver fingerprints. Yes, that was the best of times.

XI

As to *Storm Boy*, I found out what happened to the hero, Greg Rowe. I think he was twelve when he made that film. Dropped out of the business soon afterwards. Or it dropped him. The usual thing.

But at least he's alive. So he must have coped with being a child star. I've got a DVD and I play the film. To bring it back. How the sand moved. How the surf tasted.

And yes, to remind me of Lulu. The sand child, storm girl. I can show *Storm Boy* to you any time. I promise if you see that film you'll smell the southern ocean. You'll hear those combers rolling all the way up from the Antarctic to the Hindmarsh Bridge. And maybe then you'll have an idea of everything I've had to do.

But you won't see Lulu. So I should have made my own film, shouldn't I? Just as I should film The Caib now.

That's why from spring, *Badfinger* will show the work of local directors and photographers. Music's had its era. Wonderful and now finished.

If there are any artists at all out there they'll be editing their own films. Let *Badfinger* discover them.

You know, I've thought of giving prize money to the most promising… Just a small amount…

XII

That afternoon I was searching for someone I knew I wouldn't find. Not until she was ready. I scanned the world, but Lulu was stubborn, I always knew that. And so time drew on.

The evening was when I cried. For the first time. Because the land was impossible. The whole country was impossible.

No, it wasn't the wind making me cry. You think the wind on The Caib is hard to bear? It's nothing to The Coorong. All that spindrift flying. All that space.

It was raining steadily now. I knew it would be raining for weeks. Understood that the drought had broken and the waters would be coming downstream. Immense waters, miles of floodwater, planes of water gliding by. Coming from upcountry. Down to the sea.

And it was all too much. The Dreaming was too much, all the dreams. The sandbars and the reefs were too much.

On the Murray there are hundreds of rivermouths.

It's vast there. The Murray mouth is bewildering. It's so easy to get lost. Or to hide anything.

It's a series of freshwater lakes and saltwater lagoons. How the freshwater mixes with the salt is crucial to the balance. It's never the same, from one day to the next. From one hour to the next, it's never the same. That's why the drought had been so serious.

As I looked down from the crest, scanning the dunes and the river, I knew I didn't have the words. For Australia. My other world.

It's baffling enough on The Caib when the sand blows away like smoke and the map of what you think you know dissolves. Then remakes itself.

Yet in Goolwa, scale is immense. Change is constant. Salt swamps one day are dry crust the next. And the dunes grow and retreat, as they do here. Like lungs shrinking, lungs expanding.

Yeah, the sand's alive on The Caib. But differently alive in Goolwa. Seems I'm cursed by sand. I can't escape it.

XIII

The blacks understood the Murray country. But that had taken them thousands of years. And then we wiped the blacks out and destroyed their knowledge. And no, we can't catch up. We can never catch up now.

As to Lulu, she was a native kid. But she wasn't instinctive. No inherited wisdom. Look, she was raised on the streets of Adelaide. Her grandma taught her to smile at men on Hanson Road.

The Lulu I knew liked wedges and peanut butter sandwiches and astronomy books. She was just teaching herself, about stars, about life. If she'd kept off the skunk she might have gone to college. Maybe. But college costs a fortune these days. And yes, perhaps, I might have paid. For her future.

If I had.

If she had.

If we had stayed...

TWENTY-ONE

I

Lulu didn't have a mother. But there was a friend. That was Kath, and she might have been thirty. Maybe less. Hard to tell because Kath was fond of her grog. That booze had had its effect.

I liked Kath. Her health was going downhill but so was mine. At that time at least. So we always had that in common.

Kath was … *wry.* Know what I mean? Yeah, *wry.* I love that word. Makes me laugh. Made Lulu have fits, Kath was so bloody wry.

This Kath was friendly with some of the Coorong people. It was all fluid, a big extended family. Impossible to say who was related and who not. She was mixed race too. I'd say she had Greek hair. Or Lebanese. Maybe like Lulu.

Kath would hang around for a while. Then she'd disappear to Addy or get work in the vineyards at Maclaren Vale. Came into *Hey Bulldog* a few times, slept there occasionally. Those nights were great, Lulu getting all domestic. Even cooking for us.

What was it once? Poached eggs. Disaster. Then wedges, first time came out raw, second black. Lulu burned the fat and all we had was this mountain of bread and butter I'd prepared. And three pints of ruined sunflower oil.

Think we ended up in the motel. One drink led to another, with Kath telling stories of life at the Adelaide racetracks. You know, being a bookie's runner. Seemed believable.

But Kath also loved the market. She remembered how it was to work in the Gouger cafés, peeling spuds, washing pak choi. And maybe I liked Kath because she had no kids of her own.

Look, I never used to think about not having children. Now in a way it's crucial. The not having, that is. I believe both of us adopted Lulu because Lulu made sense.

At times we were competitive in the way that barren people sometimes are. Yes, barren. It's not a dirty word, believe me. Maybe a mild obscenity. If you don't like it try *incomplete*.

You know, if you can't bring up your own kids, you're going to help with somebody else's. That's a role you drift into. It's inescapable. Look at all those wildlife films.

And soon, it becomes natural. And, yes it's honourable. Because there's no shame in it. Oh no, there's no shame at all. It's simply a reason to carry on.

One day we piled into the car and off we went. Kath, Lulu, me. It was hot, worst of the drought. Kath told us she wanted to take me somewhere.

I was driving but Lulu was keen to learn. As ever. Well, fat chance. We were playing CDs, that Dylan track 'When I paint my Masterpiece', Lulu repeating it over and over. Not a great song. Far from it, but...

When you gonna paint your masterpiece, boss, Lulu asked, her gappy smile flashing.

Maybe I have, I said.

Then when was it? she asked.

Maybe I have and nobody noticed.

When?

Yesterday, I said. Or last year.

Wasn't yesterday, said Lulu.

Maybe tomorrow, then. Yes, it's always tomorrow. Can't be another day. Can't be in the past either. Or how do we look forward?

Yes, that's what that terrible song is about. Because how could you live? If you knew you'd already done your best?

II

Kath was sleeping. She'd given directions and dropped off. I woke her when we came to the turning she'd described, and she explained how to get there.

It was obvious what she wanted us to see. Rolling hills, once good horse country, but arid. No, worse than that. All the acacias, all the gums, had been burned. The earth was still smouldering.

The fire had started maybe a month before. We stepped out of the car and nobody said anything. What was the point? That fire stank like the sea stinks in Cato Street. Only one hundred times worse.

Smoke was still leaking out of the soil. Threads of smoke, fine and white as wire. The smoke was a pelt on that earth, a smoky fleece made up of thousands of hairs. Every hair was a filament of smoke. Smoke like … fur, I suppose.

In a few places that smoke was still billowing. Yes, there were smoke geysers in the valley bottom and along the slopes. On the ridge a tree was still burning.

I looked at that smoking tree and thought it was something from the bible. I used to go to Sunday School and I racked my brain. But the verse didn't come.

So many other verses I know, from all the hundreds of songs I've heard and learned. Even 'When I paint my Masterpiece'.

With its clunking rhymes. Why did I already know that song? Why were we playing it?

But your mind lets you down, doesn't it? There was no place for the burning tree in my memory. No, the burning bush, wasn't it? No space because of all the other rubbish.

The fire might die down, Kath said. But all of a sudden it'll catch hold again.

Because that fire refused to die. It had started a month, two months earlier. The gums had gone up like candles. When a gum burns the fire cracks like whiplash. You could smell the trees' resin that had oozed from those gums. A burnt oil smell. Like our black chip fat.

Someone set it deliberately, Kath whispered. Oh yes. It's well known.

And that's all we said. As if we were afraid we'd be overheard. By the firestarters.

Who? I asked.

Who?

That's all I could say. I was whispering to Kath but she never answered.

And Lulu? She was overcome. But she did say one thing. Yes, she made a speech. When we were in the ash fields. Where everything was reduced to powder.

Just think, said Lulu, what it's like here. After dark. The embers still glowing, burned branches crumbling away. The whole earth cracking and exploding like seeds. And the sparks alive like stars. Yes, stars like rubies. What are they, teacher?

Arcturus, I laughed. Not sure about the others…

Well remember them this time, she said. Aldebaran, Betelgeuse. And on and on. We all had to recite them. The names of the red stars. In that white field, thick with ash. Even Kath, who wore a grim little smile. Suited her twisted mouth. Even Kath had to name the red stars.

278

No, don't misunderstand. I liked Kath. She was doing her best. Better than I would in those circumstances. Being foreign in her own country. Being dirt poor. Being ill.

Jaundice had been the problem for years. You know what causes that. She had a yellow tinge, did Kath. But plenty of those people were the same.

That's how a few of the locals knew her in Goolwa. That yellow nigger. Or that yellow *nunga* if they were being benevolent. But Kath was more yellow than black. And Lulu was not black at all. Not really. Just kept her hair curly as a fashion statement. As a way of being.

As far as I know the arsonist was never caught.

III

Getting out of the car I bent to touch the earth. It was still warm.

Then in that empty place, I heard a noise. Not a bird was singing, there wasn't a breath of wind. But gradually we heard an engine. Then this Mitsubishi 4x4 comes over the ridge.

Rust-red and battered it was. With a spare tyre on the bonnet. Didn't seem right, that something should be moving. Or anyone should be alive, after such a blaze. Didn't feel … *appropriate*, if you understand me.

It passed us within ten yards. Lulu waved, but the driver, and this blonde girl with him, ignored us all. They were heading into the heart of the fire, with ash white in the tyre tracks.

Yes, ash everywhere. Ash white, ash grey. Thick quilts of ashes, intricate as snow. Like a goosefeather pillow I remember bursting as a boy.

That ash lay drift upon drift. Soon there was harshness in the backs of our throats and the three of us were coughing.

No matter how carefully we walked, we disturbed the ash. Finer than talcum powder, those siftings. And some of the tree trunks were still crowned with sparks. That fire was clinging to life weeks after it had begun.

IV

There was one stump I saw. I thought it was decorated with rubies. Yes, hot rubies in the dust. Like Lulu said.

And when we passed the tree those cinders glowed again, their fire renewed. Just the breath of our bodies was enough to bring them life. Those sparks in the dust were like red ants.

But you know what? I remembered The Works and the sinter spread over the beach and the dunes, and my father feeling betrayed. Feeling left out. Jack Parry isolated and alone because his own son had found a job. The wrong job. The easy job.

We went along the ridge and up the hill. Trying not to disturb the ash. Ash softer than Caib sand, sculpted into fantastic shapes. We tiptoed on through the tree stumps in a charred forest of sticks. There were trees reduced entirely to powder. They crumbled to nothing as we passed.

We were hardly breathing by then. Holding the coughs in our fists, afraid to disturb a spark. Unwilling to mark that ash with our footprints. Ash deeper than snow. The footprints that were leading up to us.

V

And I thought, no, nobody's walked here before. And no one will walk here again. A frost where no one had stepped. But there we were, the three of us, the first people in the world.

A young woman in dirty shorts. An older woman in jeans. A middle-aged man on medication. Together on an incinerated hill.

What did we know? Nothing? What had we achieved? Nothing. Yet we were the first and we were the last.

Don't tell me. I know we were fools even to stop the car. Fools to have driven up that dirt road.

The fire wasn't out and we had wandered away from the vehicle. Kath said there were people burned to death in a home close by. A boy had run back to the house and climbed into a full bath. He had boiled to death. His mother was trapped in a field and the fire had run over her. Run over her and run through her.

Ancient legends. Recycled one more time. Fire stories you hear all over that country. Echoes from the mythology of fire, especially the boy in the bath. I didn't know what to believe.

But I saw what the fire had done to that ground. Ploughed it and harrowed it. Then raced roaring away.

I pictured the boy and the woman, mummies made of ash, consumed entirely. Statues of salt. Nothing greedier, is there? And nothing more ignorant than fire.

But how did Kath know about that place, I wonder? We were one hundred miles inland on that hill, a different country from Goolwa and the Coorong.

And how gorgeous Goolwa seemed in comparison. Goolwa with its rivers and salt lagoons, its lakes and bayous. Its basking sharks. The Murray at its mouth was salty as a bowl of olives. Yet with all its luxurious water. Thinking about that ash makes me thirsty, even now.

Back at the car my boots were white. Kath was laughing in her strange way. She said it would be a good place to cook, the ground was so hot. The whole hill was a fire-pit.

But Lulu was quiet after her speech about stars, her face smeared white. That's what they did, you know, the aboriginal people. Daub themselves with ashes.

Some of it was men's business and some of it women's. Painting with ashes signified many things. Made quite a ceremony of it, did Little Miss Lulu. Anointing herself that way. With the gold dust on her clothes, already.

When we were walking back we passed the Mitsubishi. That dirty great Shogun covered in caked mud. And now grey with ashes. The driver and the girl were both out in the ash. This perfect pale pasture.

The man was filming and the girl, she was … she was *dancing*. In that ruined place. Where those people had burned to death. Where the fire had obliterated everything.

Wearing a red bikini, the girl was. Like a flame herself. Crimson, I suppose, the deepest red. No, call it cadmium red. Like a bottlebrush flower or the flowering peas that grow in the desert.

And quite a dancer she was. The man was urging her on, slowing her up, making her race, laughing at her, soothing her. Bringing the best out of her. In that place of all places. On that part of the hill that had been … *consumed.*

They were playing music too, pretty loud. I didn't recognise it, maybe it was their own concoction. One track was drumming. But there was also something else. Sad and mysterious. A silvery sort of music.

We saw the dancer stop for a drink and start again. Only now she was naked, peeling off the swimsuit and throwing it into the Shogun. Then she walked out into the untouched ash. That ash like a snowfield.

I tell you, the girl was naked in the firedust and dancing like I've never seen anyone dance. And the man was filming everything, every movement she made, every breath. And then she tumbled. And lay still.

That's the last thing we saw, the girl falling to earth. A cloud covered her, a veil of dust and grit.

She lay there, smeared with ashes like mud and mortar, mixed with her own sweat. Grey and spent. And only then did the music stop.

Yes, when that music stopped there was silence. But the man carried on filming.

TWENTY-TWO

I

Parry stared at the street. The mist hung in the air. Icy smoke. Bone-coloured blossom. The foghorn moaned down the coast.

Fret, he said to himself. Warmer air, colder sea. That had always been the cause of such weather in the old days.

Like cuttle, he thought. With a yellow tinge. And an acid taste to such mist. But the colour of an old woman's jewellery. An old woman's saltwater pearls. Or owls' eggs. The pride of the collection. Dirty behind glass.

II

Last night a spasm of hail. He'd watched it in the gutters, smoking as it vanished. A creature that became a negative of itself. Now nothing moved. No traffic sound. No traffic.

Parry looked up at the first floor over the shop. The finial beside the aerial was still there. But bleached to matchwood. It was the last one to survive on that part of the street.

Home, he thought. And shrugged. Or maybe it was a shiver. Bedsit. *Bed-sitter images*. With the grey lace curtain, the cactus on the sill.

Last night he had stared out of that window. At the mist that writhed in the lamp light. Not far away the sea had lain slumped yet invisible.

A man might die in a room like that, Parry thought. And he remembered back to his teenage years in the resort. A room not unlike the room he now called home, a summer room when sea frets also intruded. When mists gripped the town and hid, he always thought, the people from themselves.

But there were better times. Times when the swifts arrived. Or came back. To Amazon Street. Now, unexpectedly, he was thinking of swifts.

Out of the attic window of his boyhood, through its aquarium gloom, he had watched the swifts arriving in May. Swifts screaming between the houses. Over the roofs and the reefs of air, seaward and westward. Swifts over the water, that water the colour of June grasses, the sea moving as the grasses moved on the dunes. The swifts arriving from Africa.

Yes, swifts. Sleepless swifts back out over the ocean. Black swifts arriving and immediately taking back the street, the shore, the sky with their screams. Taking back the swiftless world. Swifts reclaiming the light through the cobwebbed pane. As if they had never been away. Had never been missed.

But Parry had missed the swifts. Their stoops, their steepling climbs. Their absence an ache. Swifts that might never come again, even after the million miles each swift flew. Swifts gone from the rafter. The creosoted beam.

And what might unreturning swifts signify? Grief, he thought. A grievous shade to the world. A deeper shadow.

An absence of swifts meant a code had vanished. The prehistoric code of wings and wingbeats. And if the swifts failed he failed. Or so he thought.

Yes, that was something else to worry about. Some sign or signal. To bring him down to earth.

And he remembered coming off the beach with Sev. They

were walking down Amazon Street on a blistering afternoon. Sev's brown skin was peeling, so it appeared silver. Yes, Sev was silver that afternoon, Sev in his Californian shorts, his bleached daps. Parry could only squint at his friend on that hottest day of the year.

Then Sev had turned away and ducked down.

What's that? asked Parry.

Dunno.

Sev was bending over the gutter. His face lay against the kerb as he inspected what he had found.

It's dead.

What's dead?

Must have died seconds ago.

What's dead?

Hardly a minute.

What's dead?

Maybe a car.

What's dead?

That red mini that sped past us.

What is dead? demanded Parry.

Sev stood up, both hands cupped before him. Parry could only turn his face from the glare. The spectral boy was outlined in black.

Swift.

Swift?

Dead swift. Still warm.

That car killed a swift?

Still warm.

Parry turned his face away once again.

Fuck. What kills a swift?

Car might.

Fuck.

Or…?

Yeah?

You know.

Yeah.

Smooth it. Go on.

Parry bent towards Sev's proffered hands.

Yes. It's warm.

Sev's right forefinger was under the swift's chin. It was as if he was bringing water out of the gutter. And offering it to Parry.

Then Severin took both wing tips and was spreading the bird. A dark crescent, the swift. Chocolate brown when Parry looked closely. Not black at all.

Didn't know they had white throats.

Evening glove, said Sev.

You what?

It's like one of my mother's evening gloves.

What are evening gloves?

For women to wear in the evenings. Dances.

My mother doesn't go out in the evening. 'Cept the allotment.

Come on.

What?

We'll bury it.

Bury the swift?

Yeah. Or we can let the ants carry it away.

III

Parry might have dreamed. But no, it was a memory. So vivid it could have been a day this week.

Everybody had broken up from college. They had agreed to walk to The Horns. Then keep walking.

Maybe a kind of farewell, Parry now thought. They were

going their own ways. Careers were beckoning and Sev was already long gone. He had never heard from Sev again.

There were Vine and Sian, Gil, Fflint, Dai Pretty and Branwen. And someone else, someone on the edge of things. But Lizzy, of course. She'd certainly been there. He counted Lizzy first.

They'd wandered as far as The Tramlines, looking at the seams of quartz that coloured that part of the coast. The Caib Caves, as it was known. Those caves and gutters submerged at high and middle tides.

The idea was to camp out. Some had brought sleeping bags. It was a scorching day that became a warm evening. Parry remembered the tide going out from around midnight. The air was alive with the reek of salt and weed.

The Tramlines marked the boundary between limestone and sandstone. The new rock to the west was not grey but pink. The beach pavements, cave walls and drifts of pebbles from then onwards were the same pink.

Gil had been enthusing about Roxy Music. This subject exasperated Parry. As ever, they'd built a driftwood fire, and were roasting potatoes in silver paper, coaxing one another to sample the flagons, red wine and two bottles of scotch.

For the camp they'd chosen an area of sand and flowering sea holly above a red sandstone pavement.

Diamonds, said Lizzy. These look like diamonds.

She was passing pieces of quartz from hand to hand.

Onyx, Vine had said. That's what I think these are.

To Parry the quartz did indeed resemble diamonds. He watched the firelight gleam on the metal ring between the cups of Lizzy's bikini. Then looked away.

Fools' gold, he laughed.

No, people collect these stones, Lizzy had insisted. And make jewellery. So, they might be onyx, yes. That's a precious stone, isn't it? It sounds precious enough. Yes, *onn-yxx*. In fact there used to be a girl in school whose parents started a business making jewellery. Don't know how, but they made money. And it's all here, lying around. Waiting for us. All free.

Parry tipped the whisky to his teeth. The bottle glinted in the fire which both he and Dai Pretty had wanted to light. Parry had won so Dai would have the last task of pissing it out.

Parry had pressed his cheek into the sand around the driftwood. Some were white as ivory, some hollow as flutes, those sticks from the sea's forest, laid low along the shore.

In the 3am. darkness the embers were a blue-white nest. Around the gang the sandstone was redder than chilli oil.

No one had to suggest skinnydipping. That holiday it had become their usual practice. They knew the waves were warm. The girls agreed it was dark enough. Gradually, everyone had stripped off.

IV

When he awoke Parry found himself in a crimson world. The sun was coming up in a sky the colour of the sandstone beach. A flock of turnstones was going past, low and silent. There were ingots in the driftwood ash.

Someone was nearby.

Oh God, breathed Lizzy. I'm so incredibly … *stiff.* Whose idea was it to sleep on the beach? The tide could have come in.

Still well out, said Parry. Another hour. But yes, I think I slept an hour at most. How's your hangover.

He watched Lizzy unzip her sleeping bag and start putting Dai's coat over her denim shirt. Dai Pretty was the best swimmer and had been encouraging the girls to try further out.

Parry looked round and found there was nobody else.

Maybe they slept in that biggest cave, Lizzy said. Or are they back in the water?

The pair stood together on the sandstone pavement. Brighter now that bloody reef. The rockpools here were pink with coralweed.

Can't ever remember a dawn like this before, she smiled, raising her arms to the orange sky. What's that word in *Macbeth*?

The pair moved across the sandstone to the mouth of the cave. Parry knew the others couldn't be there, the space was too small. But Lizzy seemed intent on looking.

Hey, she sang out. You lot. Hey Sian! Wake up.

You see, we're at a boundary here, said Parry. It's where different types of rocks meet.

Sian! called Lizzy again.

They'll be up by the sea holly, said Parry looking away. I know where they're…

Then Lizzy was kissing his mouth. Putting her tongue between his teeth. Hard and sour her tongue. Her tongue that tasted of salt and wine and whisky. Determined, that sudden tongue. Practised.

Parry gasped at the girl's bitter breath. Behind Lizzy's tilted head he saw the sun brighten on the quartz walls of the cave. He glimpsed a purple he had never seen before, a yellow he'd heard others describe.

In the cave was a slab of sandstone, seamed with quartz. Three hours earlier the gang had been standing round this rock in candlelight. There was a cloth still draped over the stone and an assortment of bottles and wrappings. Remnants of the feast.

Lizzy and Sian had sat on smaller stones. In a space at the rear of the cave Fflint and Gil had attempted a version of 'Dipsomaniac Blues'.

As Lizzy kissed him he wondered why, in all the times he had explored Caib Caves, he hadn't noticed the coloured quartz.

But it was Lizzy who slowly released him and breathed the name of where they stood.

Now I know, she smiled into his eyes. Now I know why they call this the cave of lights.

Three hours previously, although it felt like weeks, they had taken burning driftwood torches into the caves and looked at the quartz in the firelight.

Sian had brought a box of tea candles. They'd lit them all together, toasting the night, the girls starting to shiver, Fflint and Gil and Dai Pretty still dripping from the swim. Dai brandished a driftwood staff, bleached white, he had discovered. He had been drawing something in the sand.

Do you know, whispered Lizzy, how long I've been wanting to do that?

And Fflint's coat was at her feet, and somehow the shirt also. And there were her breasts, blue-white and round as the ammonites at The Horns. Lizzy's nipples were cold and sharp. Lke the quartz she had pressed into his palms.

The sun was shining now into Parry's eyes. For one minute at most its beam would travel directly into the cave. But already the colours around them were fading.

In a crevice above Lizzy's head he saw a candle stub in a circle of white wax. The same colour as the quartz outside on The Tramlines. The seams where he and Sev had chased after one another. Had invented games.

Look, Diz, he muttered. You see…

How long he had stared at her limestone breasts, he never knew. There were salty curls at her neck. Fronds of weed, those dead man's ropes.

But the sun must have moved. Or a cloud appeared.

Very carefully Lizzy stepped away. She stooped and pulled the shirt back between them.

Yes, she breathed. I see. You know, I'd have… I'd have…

Then there was shouting outside and Fflint's deep voice. Dai and Sian too were calling.

The quartz had been yellow as turmeric, a web of gold. Now it was indistinguishable from the cave wall. As he listened he overheard the pools settling. The limestone breathing. Parry felt a subterranean chill.

TWENTY-THREE

I

Leads, said Parry to himself. Leads and wires. Leads and wires and … *connections*. Makes no sense to me.

He looked around. No one was listening. Parry had watched Gil and Fflint set their equipment up on the Paradise stage. There seemed a ludicrous amount. It had taken the three of them an hour to bring it in from Gil's van.

Could have been worse, said Gil genially. Could have been drums.

Hope we don't regret that, said Fflint. If that computer goes awry, drums might have been the answer.

Trust me, laughed Gil, placing one of his Apples on a table. Drums are never the answer. And remember, we're recording this. It'll be on the site. After it's cleaned up, of course.

Not the raw tape then? asked Parry.

Not when you can do what I can do. And we want it to sound its best, don't we? What about *Seamist: Live at The Paradise Club* as a title?

Stinks, said Fflint. And who the hell's heard of The Paradise, these days?

Mystery's good, said Gil. And Paradise is better than whatever it's called now. Look, if Nia wants this place to work, that's the first thing to go.

Parry had changed the CD they were playing. But the Kerala raga he had put on had drawn protests. Gil commanded them to listen to his choice.

Who's this then? he asked. Sound familiar?

Jesus, it's us, said Fflint.

Nia had appeared then, with Mina, who was clutching an early drink. Everyone had drifted over to the bar. Parry was ensuring the ragged stage curtain was as neat as possible.

It was a green velvet, possibly moth-eaten. Parry had stretched both arms out to secure it behind one of the amps. He was standing in the far corner of the club. The only man on stage.

But there must have been someone else. Someone behind him. Maybe Mina, playing about? Mina after her second, no third drink of the evening. Or Fflint, come to help with the curtain, with the amp? Maybe Gil, meticulous Gil, or Nia, wanting...

Yet surely no one would have held his arm so tightly? As if they wanted to cause him pain. For there was sudden agony in this right shoulder. Quickly the grip moved down his arm. By the time it reached his wrist it was an icy tourniquet. Taut as a reef-knot. It was as if his arm was encased in a gauntlet.

Parry looked around. Everything seemed as it was. There was Mina, laughing with Gil at the counter. There was Fflint with a camera, making a shot. And there was Nia, nervous Nia, with her own wineglass, introducing one or two of the Elvises. Who seemed to be arriving. The gig coincided with an Elvis Presley festival.

Everything was clear. Startlingly clear. Now the pain was incredible. Yet it concentrated Parry's vision. There was Glan, zipping his flies as he slouched out of the men's room. Glan who had not helped set up the equipment. Glan in Parry's pink shirt. Glan already drinking the wine Parry had organised at the counter.

And there was Serene in her purple blouse and purple tights. Despite the weather, her belly was bare. Her fingers lingered on the purple tattoo.

Yes, Parry noticed, there was someone else at the bar. He had noted them at once. Because now he saw everything. He remembered it all.

This someone was wearing black, was a little removed. Parry could even see a crust of dew on the figure's shoulders.

This someone, like everyone else in the room, had come in from the gutters of the town. This someone had come in from the fog in Senhora Street. From the fret in Amazon Street. This someone had come from the salt and the stink of The Ghetto. From the tunnels beneath the rattling Ziggurat. They had come from the Caib Caves and from the Tramlines, from The Horns and from the slipway, from The Chasm and the hollow dunes.

Parry was going to call out. He felt he had to protest against the pain. But he knew what was gripping him. At the bar the figure in black, might, Parry thought, have been female.

II

I've been meaning to ask, said Mina. How did you find that little town?

Goolwa's not so remote, said Parry eventually. But as I say, distances are different. Some people love the *absence*. Over there.

Over here it can be hard to breathe. In Oz, at least there's oxygen.

I was exploring the peninsula around Adelaide. Looking at the beaches, the tiny towns. Fetched up in Goolwa, parked in the high street behind the motel, went in for a spot of lunch. The meal lasted four hours. No, all night, because I stayed. Room 33 as I remember. It's following me round, that number.

'Dipsomaniac's Blues' had now lasted for over thirty minutes. The crowd had thinned. Parry and Mina had moved from the front of the bar to one of the empty tables.

Gil was repeating a chorus, hunched over two different keyboards. Parry seemed to be mouthing lyrics, with Gil immersed in improvisation. Nia passed their table carrying a bottle and topped up Mina's glass. Although no one could hear him, Parry continued to talk.

The Dutch couple who kept the motel seemed friendly. If a little misplaced. We started chatting about roots. And how peculiar Australians were. Usual thing. Eventually, they told me about the empty shop. Next door.

Just pop in, said Toon. If only for a look. It's a funny little place. They kept the keys, you see. It had been untenanted for twelve months, I think.

Strange curved shop window, the glass with a green, rainwater tinge. And double frontage, so it looked bigger. On one side was a glass dome in the roof. Bottle glass with bubbles like a spirit-level. Yes, blisters of glass.

The front room was the biggest. Behind that were three smaller, one of which became my bedroom. The others used for storage. Our bathroom was tiny, with the toilet outside.

No, not your traditional dunny. There was water piped over. A proper system. But I grew used to swilling in the sink, or going over to the motel for a soak.

One thing led to another. The wine and the Dutchies' weed, and the hospitality of that town by the Murray made its mark.

So I never forgot Goolwa. Even when school was overwhelming. As schools usually are. In my fifth or sixth year, I checked up on it. Rang the motel.

Spoke to Toon through what must have been a cloud of dopesmoke.

No, no one there, he laughed. People come, people go.

Everyone seems to disappear. Look, you could do worse. Could do worse.

And it was Toon who did most of the work to begin with. After all, he took care of all the motel jobs. More than handy.

I paid him some money, to show I was genuine. So he sorted out a few repairs. Carpentry and plumbing, the necessary electrics. He rewired the water heater I used till the end.

No, the shop wasn't in bad condition. But it needed to be loved. And yes, it was Toon who found Lulu. Soon she was painting, washing the windows, tidying. In return for free accommodation.

Lulu had been hanging around the motel too, you see. But don't we all hang around? Somewhere? Yes, everybody seemed to know Lulu.

So I started going over when I could. Of course, there were weeks when it was impossible. But I began to find I was thinking about *Hey Bulldog*. Wondering if I could make something happen. As I'm thinking about *Badfinger*, now. And Glan.

And the girl, added Mina. Don't forget Serenissima.

She stood up to go to the Ladies'.

Parry continued talking to whoever might hear him.

I cleaned everything, he nodded. And everywhere. Took a brush to that outhouse and swept away years of spiders' webs. Some big buggers, you can imagine. One of them bit me. Ever seen spiders' teeth marks? Little punctures. And yes, that bite hurt. Don't think it was poisonous.

There were wasp-husks hung up in cocoons. I gritted my teeth and brushed them away. Yeah, cleared away those ghosts. Grey as Caib coral.

Someone, years earlier, had painted the privvy yellow. So when the plaster fell, it looked like gold, caught in those webs. The original paint had turned to golden powder.

So I cleaned all that myself while Toon did the skilled jobs. The toilet door had been broken and people had shat wherever they chose. I unblocked it with rods from the motel.

Must have wanted it, mustn't I? Must have loved it. Like I'm doing now, with 33, Caib Street. But *Badfinger* is in better condition. I don't need a Toon.

Even so, I've painted it myself, the downstairs toilet at *Badfinger*. Can you guess the colour? Have you been in there? Yes, it's aubergine. Really is. Gorgeous aubergine. Did it for Glan. And Serene, of course. That purple pair.

Look at Glan now. He's great, isn't he? Don't you think? Pity we can't hear him. Bloody Fflint's been repeating the same chord for twenty minutes. His fingers must be raw.

But Glan looks good, I think. And what about that shirt? Fits him perfectly. Never thought he'd wear it. Never thought.

III

Nia and Mina stood together upstairs in the Paradise, looking east. Below them were the lights of The Caib, masked in mist. Beyond the funfair was the black silhouette of the dunes.

Mina remembered the posters around the bar. Printed poems and songs Nia had provided. Exhortations to use the language.

Did people speak to you? That special night? Did they use … *it*?

A few, smiled Nia. Oh yes. They dredged words out of their memories. Words they hadn't used for years. Words they never used. Words they were afraid to use. Embarrassed to use. Yes, a few got their orders in. And I paid up.

Mina looked at the girl.

You've the passion, I'll say. Haven't you?

You have to feel strongly about something. My mum showed me that. And my dad. He's coming back, you know?

From where?

Been away, hasn't he. But he'll be back. Soon.

Even when she rubbed the window, Mina could see nothing clearly. The dunes were a missing space in the world.

Couldn't have picked a worse time, could you?

You mean with…

I mean with the kids. The boys. The girls who…

Strung themselves up? said Nia. Those fools. Those cowards. I was in school with two of them.

Someone came in the shop the other day, said Mina. Had all their names in a rhyme. I couldn't believe it. Like it was a song. Kyle. Keeley. Names starting with K…

Maybe it's something else, said Nia. As if there's a taint in the air. Around us. Something that shouldn't be here. Or maybe, there's something missing. Missing from The Caib. Something we lack.

The room where they stood seemed full of the fog.

Will you stay? asked Mina, hunching her shoulders.

Will you?

I have to, said Mina. I'm that age. But if I was you, oh boy. If I was you, I'd be making my plans…

Maybe I am.

Oh?

I want to travel. Course. But look, look out there. It's why I brought you up here.

Can't see anything.

The dunes. That black space. That emptiness.

Scary, isn't it? agreed Mina.

No, said Nia. Look harder.

Like I said, I can't … seem to work out where we are… Or what we're looking at. But yes, if I look… There's a darker place in the night.

Yes, it's pitch over there, said Nia. You know the very top? Where the stones smell of sulphur? And there is all that coral? The colour of dead grass?

Stayed well away, love. My mum didn't allow it. Over there's where that girl was found, they say. That prehistoric girl. No, I never dared.

Well, under there, said Nia, under that black space, under that dark hill, are caves. Caves and springs. A whole cave system that might go on for miles. I mean it. For miles.

She smiled again to herself, thinking of hot sand and moon-coloured coral dust. The sulphur-smelling summits of the dunes.

News to me, said Mina.

And I've been thinking about the fact that nobody's ever explored those caves.

Yes, it's easier now there's so little streetlight, said Mina. But I can't remember what's there in the day. Let alone now.

There might be hidden entrances up there, said Nia quietly. Hidden in the limestone. But the springs are fed from sources miles away. Maybe fifty miles.

You wouldn't get me down any caves, said Mina. And seemed to shiver.

I went caving in Uni, said Nia. There was a good group of us. Started to get the feel of it. Then, well I left, didn't I?

Because of Gil?

And all this time, yes it's taken me all this time to come to … terms with it.

With Gil? repeated Mina.

I don't know. With what I was thinking. If I was thinking anything. But it's taken me … years, if I'm honest.

Well, face it, said Mina. Older man, younger girl. Classic situation.

Sounds like you…

Understand…? Hey, you have a habit of underestimating me, young lady.

Look, sorry, said Nia. But maybe I was numb. Dropped out of college and ended up. Here. Dropped out of caving, of the arts group, everything.

But yes, it might work, she added. This place. I really think it might. But what about you?

It's no secret now the Basement is closing. So no job. And I'm the wrong age for a pension. Really lousy luck. But maybe I can hold on to the flat.

IV

You sure you're all right? asked Mina.

Fine. You keep asking. Why?

You know why.

I'm alright.

You're looking grey. Not yourself.

Like the fog, said Parry. The fog's inside the club now.

Have you noticed? Yeah, fog in paradise. Who'd have thought it?

I mean grey in the face, said Mina. No, not yourself.

My latest incarnation. But grey? Blame Gil's smoke machine. Thank God it packed up. But it made people cough and it gets me like this every time. What's that bloody smoke made from? Smells like brake linings.

Well, if you're sure? said Mina. Looks like Serene's taken Glan home. What was he on, I wonder?

Pretty obvious, I'd have thought, said Parry. Where's Nia?

Talking to Gil, next door. About what happened. Or didn't. And Fflinty?

Gone home to Mum, laughed Mina.

That's rock and roll, kid. Weren't great, were we? Or were we?

You want the truth?

Never.

I've heard worse, said Mina. But that long number could have been cut. Same thing over and over...

...and over. And over? I think Gil wanted to create a trance-like state.

At the Paradise? asked Mina. It's waking us up you want to work on, lover. Not putting us to sleep. Short and sharp, is what was needed.

Well Gil...

Had his back to the audience, most of the night. Laughing with you. All those little private jokes. Very in-crowd. Very exclusive.

So our driftwood soul could have been better?

You what? That's the story of your life. But does driftwood come back to where it started?

What was Serene like?

Good dancer. More confident than I thought she'd be. That's who people were watching. And you know why.

Yeah, Serene's great, said Parry.

V

He and Mina walked out of the club. They stood beside a gutter and overflow pipe. There was a beard of mould beneath the spout, the air filled with a mesh of rain.

Then they turned left. On the corner of Cato Street, the man paused and looked around. The Paradise audience had disappeared and the town was deserted.

Listen, Parry said.

302

To what?

That's high tide you can hear. Black waves to the top of the slipway. And I can describe those waves exactly. I've watched that tide so many times.

You need to be indoors, said Mina.

Neon on the black waves, smiled Parry. That's what I can see. A desperate message, I used to think. But maybe…

Don't think I haven't watched it too, said Mina, hunching her shoulders. Scribbled in red. Maybe in green… And upside down. Sometimes I've thought it was language melting. You know, melting in the sea. Or maybe the sea was dissolving the words. Like acid, those waves. A kind of acid bath.

They were standing under one of the few working streetlights. Mina's hair was a web in the fret. When she looked at Parry, he seemed drenched in light. The rain on his face was like wire. There were seed-pearls in his hair.

But people came, he insisted. Didn't they? Forty's good. Isn't it? Forty?

Yeah. Forty's good. Ish. But more like thirty. Including us.

No, I counted. It's good, isn't it? Forty?

Forty's wonderful. In this filthy fog. And your little talk was spot on.

Parry shivered and shook himself, rubbing his arm, flexing his palm.

Listen, he said quietly. To that black tide. After all these years, it's still difficult to know when the tide's coming in. Or when it's going out.

Suppose so, said Mina.

And I suppose I've always looked for that one moment when the tide's … *perfect*. You know? When everything's balanced.

He rubbed his arm again.

Come on, he said. I'll have to deal with the human wreckage

303

of Glan now. Looked good, though. Didn't he? Dusky pink, eh?

He'll sleep the clock round, said Mina. But I thought you were going to wear that shirt.

The woman glanced up Amazon Street. Yeah, he looked okay, she agreed. But the little shit can't sing. And the little shit can't play…

But maybe he's in the right place at the right time, insisted Parry.

Right place? Mina held up her arms and opened her hands. Right time? Hey, look around, lover. Look around.

VI

There was no one left. Yet Nia decided to take the steps back to the room where she and Mina had stood together. In the far corner another flight of stairs led upward. She decided to try these.

Nia climbed carefully. The single bulb in the top landing was working, but was very weak, so she had borrowed Gil's torch. The girl could feel plaster crunching under her feet on the wooden boards.

As far as she could make out, there was one dark room, with three other doors leading off. She was surprised there was so much space. Nia had been here only once before. That was her first exploration, after being made what…? Manager? Dogsbody?

She remembered one of the old men on the committee saying, 'oh yes, we'd be so very grateful, so very grateful… As you know, there's not much call now…'

Was it duty? she wondered, listening to her steps disturb the dust. Her shoes scratched as if she was walking through sand.

And yes, there was sand, even here, on the third floor under the roof. Sand in veils of grey grit. Sand clogging the webs. In one corner was a radio with scattered CD cases.

Under the window was a pile of clothes. She identified a blanket, a leather jacket, a yellow tee shirt. Then stepped closer and saw a sleeping bag.

Nia was sure it had not been there when she had first explored. There was also a wine bottle and two glasses. The heel of a loaf. She counted seven candle stubs.

It was damp in the room and she felt a draught from the window. Stepping closer to the glass she found an attempt had been made to repair a missing pane. A piece of cardboard was inserted into the frame.

Nia tried to remember overhearing attic sounds. Yes, the roof groaned in high winds. But she had imagined it was the building settling itself. The girl wondered if she had ever heard the radio in that room. A room such as where the boys were found. Bodies not discovered for months. Footprints of rats in the dust. Words on a white wall. Unread.

Kids, she thought.

Just kids.

ACKNOWLEDGEMENTS

The author acknowledges and is grateful for the award of a Literature Wales/Llenyddiaeth Cymru bursary which allowed him to work on this volume.

ABOUT THE AUTHOR

Robert Minhinnick published his first novel, *Sea Holly* with Seren in 2007. He has also published a collection of short stories, *The Keys of Babylon* (2011), and three collections of essays, two of which have been Wales Book of the Year. The latest of these collections is *Island of Lightning* (2013). His *Selected Poems* appeared from Carcanet in 2012, containing his two Forward prizes for 'best individual poem'. From 1997 to 2008 he was editor of the international magazine, *Poetry Wales*. Robert Minhinnick is an advisor to the charity Sustainable Wales, and was co-founder of Friends of the Earth Cymru.

Well chosen words

Seren is an independent publisher with a wide-ranging list which includes poetry, fiction, biography, art, translation, criticism and history. Many of our books and authors have been on longlists and shortlists for – or won – major literary prizes, among them the Costa Award, the Jerwood Fiction Uncovered Prize, the Man Booker, the Desmond Elliott Prize, The Writers' Guild Award, Forward Prize, and TS Eliot Prize.

At the heart of our list is a good story told well or an idea or history presented interestingly or provocatively. We're international in authorship and readership though our roots are here in Wales (Seren means Star in Welsh), where we prove that writers from a small country with an intricate culture have a worldwide relevance.

Our aim is to publish work of the highest literary and artistic merit that also succeeds commercially in a competitive, fast changing environment. You can help us achieve this goal by reading more of our books – available from all good bookshops and increasingly as e-books. You can also buy them at 20% discount from our website, and get monthly updates about forthcoming titles, readings, launches and other news about Seren and the authors we publish.

www.serenbooks.com